P9-DCG-859

BY MADELEINE ROUX

Allison Hewitt Is Trapped

Sadie Walker Is Stranded

Salvaged

THE HOUSE OF FURIES

House of Furies

Court of Shadows

Tomb of Ancients

ASYLUM

Asylum

The Scarlets

Sanctum

The Bone Artists

Catacomb

The Warden

Escape from Asylum

WORLD OF WARCRAFT

SHADOWS RISING

SHADOWS RISING

MADELEINE ROUX

NEW YORK

Published in the United States by Del Rey, an imprint of Random House, a division of Penguin Random House LLC, New York.

LIBRARY OF CONGRESS CATALOGING-IN-PUBLICATION DATA
Names: Roux, Madeleine, author.
Title: World of Warcraft: Shadows rising / Madeleine Roux.
Other titles: Shadows rising
Description: New York: Del Rey Books 2020.
Identifiers: LCCN 2020008859 (print) | LCCN 2020008860 (ebook) | ISBN 9780399594120 (hardcover) | ISBN 9780399594137 (ebook)
Subjects: LCSH: World of Warcraft (Game)—Fiction. | Imaginary wars and battles—Fiction. | GSAFD: Fantasy fiction.
Classification: LCC PS3618.O87235 W67 2020 (print) | LCC PS3618.O87235 (ebook) | DDC 813/.54—dc23
LC record available at https://lccn.loc.gov/2020008859
LC ebook record available at https://lccn.loc.gov/2020008860

Printed in the United States of America on acid-free paper

randomhousebooks.com

246897531

First Edition

Book design by Jo Anne Metsch

For my brothers, who built my first computer,
introducing me to the wonder of videogames.
And for all the devs, writers, artists, and
players who love Azeroth—
this one is for you.

NAZMIR
VOL'DUN
ZULDAZAR
ZANDALAR

GARDEN OF THE LOA
ATAL'DAZAR
XIBALA

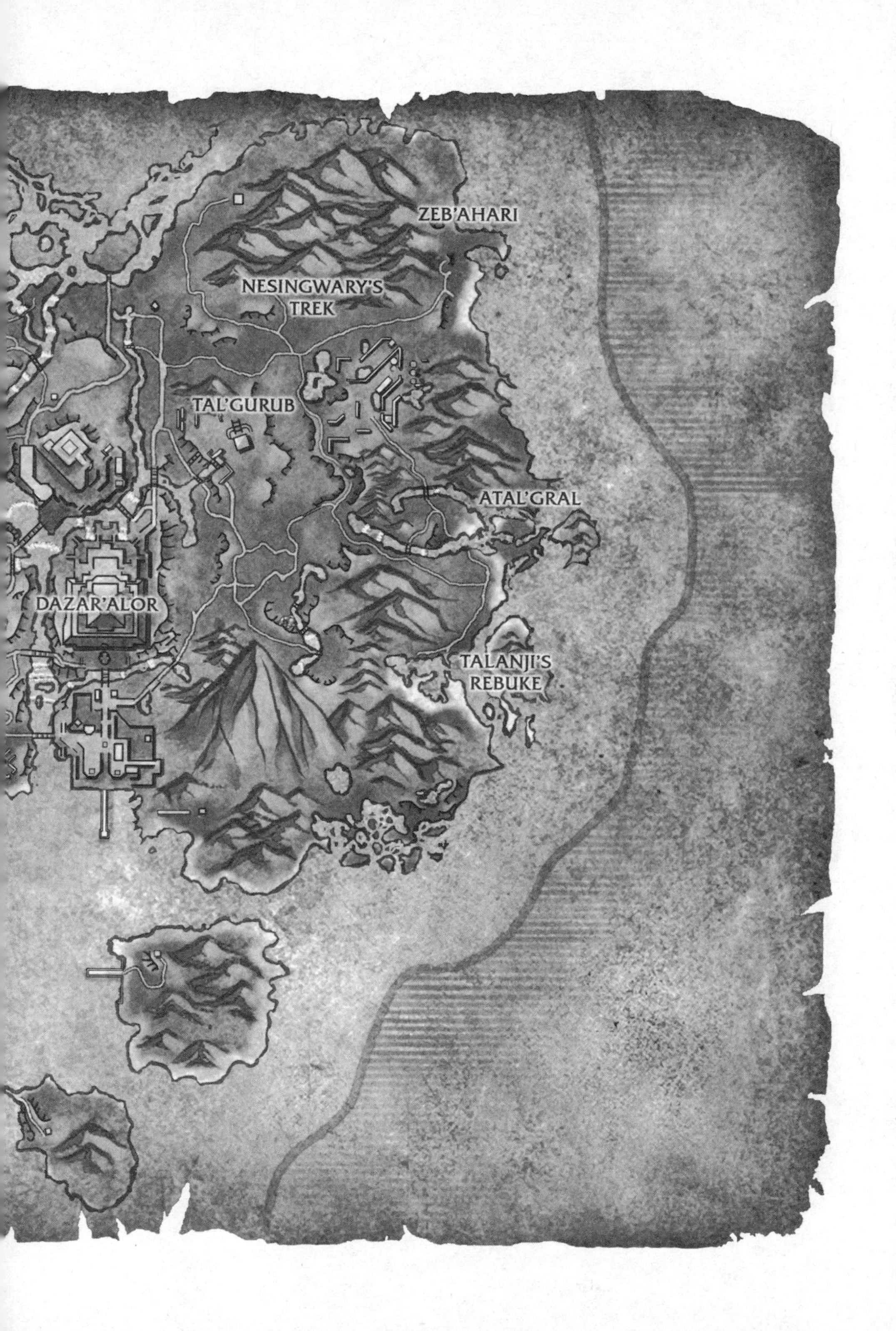
ZEB'AHARI
NESINGWARY'S TREK
TAL'GURUB
ATAL'GRAL
DAZAR'ALOR
TALANJI'S REBUKE

WORLD OF WARCRAFT

SHADOWS RISING

PROLOGUE

Westfall

Anduin Wrynn rode as if a thousand screaming servants of the Void followed close at his back, thunder booming above in the sky and crashing below as his horse's hooves beat the ground hard, carrying him across the wounded plains of Westfall. No one but his loyal friend and spymaster chased him, but it didn't matter. Darkness nipped at his heels, and he would do whatever he could to outrun it.

At least for the moment. At least for *one* moment.

"Sire! Sire! Damn you, my horse is going to throw a shoe!" Mathias Shaw's voice managed to rise above the rumbling overhead and the din of the horses.

Anduin ignored him, clucking his tongue, spurring Reverence faster. Faster, faster, faster. He couldn't slow down, not for anything.

In the distance, a tower of debris and energy rose like a crystalline spike from the low hills of the farmlands. He couldn't take his eyes away from it as the thickening clouds above rolled closer, casting a shadow over the land. He remembered thinking it impossible that Westfall should change so drastically, but the Cataclysm had raged, heedless of a young man's nostalgia. And yet it was as if his own childhood, his own deeply held memories, had been rearranged. He was but a boy then, untested; now he felt honed as a blade. That untested boy had thought certain things remained constant, but now he knew such beliefs to be childish. Nothing was permanent. Any city could crumble, but foes could also become allies, even friends. There was no more wisdom in cynicism than in optimism.

"Sire!"

He relented at last, pulling gently on Reverence's reins, the magnificent white horse slowing to a canter, allowing the spymaster to gain ground and trot up to his side.

"My apologies." Anduin sighed, tossing back the hair that had fallen into his eyes. "That must have been a taxing ride for your old bones."

"You didn't tell me this was a race," Shaw grunted. Despite Anduin's teasing, the older man, weathered but still strong and cunning, wasn't even out of breath. "With fair warning I would leave you crying in the dust. Your majesty."

"Well." Anduin reined his horse around to face the wall of forest behind them, across the river in Elwynn. "We shall have to put that to the test."

"Maybe, but first you're going to tell me why you're riding like a madman today. The last thing we need is you getting thrown and snapping your royal neck."

Shaw had a rough way about him, and his voice was equally gruff, as if he gargled with sawdust each morning. But that harsh, forward manner was a comfort to Anduin. While most at court bowed and scraped around in the king's presence, Shaw always gave it to him straight.

The clouds overhead bunched and threatened to unleash a

downpour, but Anduin ignored the coming rain, jumping down from the saddle with the ease of a practiced rider. Reverence seemed agitated, tossing his great white mane and gnashing his teeth. The king made his way around to the horse's head, taking a few slivers of apple from his pocket and offering it to the beast. Ah. His halter had gone crooked. He let the horse lean its warm, soft nose into his shoulder while he fixed the bit and touched his forehead to the spot between Reverence's eyes.

"You know, when I was very young and learning to ride, my father took me to the stables and gave me my first pony. Dappled. Gentle. Thirteen hands. I asked my father why horses were measured in hands." Anduin smiled wanly at the distant memory. "He only grinned at me and said he didn't know, then he barked at the groom, asking if he knew. Nobody did. I think the groom probably soiled himself he was so embarrassed; the poor lad was hardly older than I was. Marvin was his name, I think."

Shaw was still in the saddle, his expression suddenly distant. "I didn't know him."

But Anduin knew better, knew Shaw was holding something back. He almost certainly had known Marvin, and Marvin had probably died somehow. In one war or another, by an orcish axe or a poisoned Forsaken blade. Maybe his house had collapsed in the Cataclysm and the ground had swallowed him whole.

Anduin pushed the bitter thought aside. "I was shocked. My father, the king of Stormwind, had just admitted his own ignorance in front of a servant. I told him as much, and do you know what he said?"

Shaw shook his head no.

"He said: Only the fool thinks himself an expert in everything. The wise man admits his limitations and endeavors to know more."

They were both silent for a moment, listening to the storm roll its way across the Dagger Hills, moving north toward them.

"He wasn't an easy king to serve, but there was satisfaction in the challenge. The same can't be said for all rulers."

At that, Anduin winced. "Ouch."

"Oh, there's satisfaction in service to your crown, too, it's just . . . a bit *more* of a challenge," Shaw replied with just a hint of a smile, and that was the most the enigmatic spymaster ever gave. "Case in point—you're avoiding my question."

"No, Shaw, I was answering it." Anduin held Reverence's reins loosely with his left hand, pointing to the forest with his right, and beyond that, the spires of Stormwind City rising in the misty distance. "I'm acknowledging my limitations. Today was . . . Today was . . ."

Anduin groped uselessly for the word. Difficult? That didn't cover it. Disheartening? Vexing?

Crushing.

Tyrande and Malfurion had fled to Nordrassil, and all of his missives went unread. A messenger had returned that morning with his letter to them unopened. The man looked shaken, more so when Anduin told him firmly to leave, return to Nordrassil, and try again. No matter how much Anduin attempted to console himself that the rift between humans and night elves could be bridged, its mere existence dismayed him. They ought to be united, solid, though he could not begrudge them their anger. Had Stormwind burned to the ground under his rule, he wasn't sure forgiveness would come easily or ever. A plume of smoke shot up just west of Saldean's farm. An accompanying boom might have been mistaken for thunder were it not for the distinctive sound of splintering wood and a man's scream that followed.

"What was that?" Anduin murmured. He charged off toward the commotion and the smoke, with Shaw grumbling behind him.

"Caution," the old spy said. "It could be an ambush."

"These are my people, my lands."

"And your enemies would use that against you."

But Anduin had heard anguish in the cry from the barn, and he couldn't stand by helplessly while one of his subjects suffered. They reached an open field, the hay gathered and formed into rounds as high as a man. Chickens scattered at their approach, and Anduin and Shaw used a gap in a broken fence to enter the field, leaving their horses with their reins looped around the jagged posts.

"Could it have been an explosion? I hope nobody is injured . . ." Anduin quickened his pace, raised voices growing clearer and more numerous as he and Shaw were enveloped by the changing wind and, with it, the choking smoke.

Anduin batted at it, squinting ahead to see what remained of the barn roof, collapsed in on itself with three men in a heated argument. One fellow, the tallest, was dressed in little but rags, his hair matted and dirty, debris from the explosion hanging in his beard. The other two men wore the simple homespun garb of farmers, patched and pricked with grass, their faces weathered from their labor.

"Jago, you miserable halfwit! I said you could shelter in my barn, not use it for your mad experiments!"

Closer and with the smoke dissipating, Anduin could tell that the two farmers were related, one father and one son, the latter his parent in miniature, with even the same ruddy beard, just with less gray shot through it. The older farmer lunged at Jago, fists balled and at the ready.

He stopped at the unmistakable sound of steel being unsheathed. Spinning, he was met not with a blade itself, but simply Mathias Shaw's stony face. The sword never came free of its scabbard; the suggestion that it might was enough to give the farmer pause.

"Gentlemen," Anduin said softly, putting up his hands. "Is there a problem here?"

"He's no gentleman!" the farmer bellowed. "He's a lousy drunk, using my barn to brew his bedeviled moonshine. Look at my roof! How am I to afford the repairs?" It took him a moment to realize whom he was addressing, but he only made the most meager attempt to bow his head with respect. His son, by contrast, went white as a sheet.

"I would have his side of the story, too," Anduin replied. He turned toward Jago, whose only response was to spit loudly and wetly on the ground at the king's feet. Just that much made the man nearly topple over, and his hiccup could have been heard all the way back in Stormwind Keep. The smell of burned wood and burned moonshine wasn't enough to cover up the telltale sour ale stench on his breath.

"There," Jago slurred, pointing at his own drying spittle. "That's all m'side a'the story is worth. That's all I've left in the world. Me bones, me blood, me bile. Nothing . . . I've nothing." His eyes flared wide for an instant, his face turning red through the soot coating his face. "*Nothing*."

He sprang at Anduin clumsily, but even so, Shaw was there to intercept him. Like a flash, the spymaster leaped in front of the king, keeping his weapon half sheathed, his hand clamping down on the drunkard's shoulder.

"I wouldn't," Shaw growled.

"Do it, use that sword of yours," Jago sputtered. Over Shaw's shoulder, Anduin met the man's tear-swollen, bloodshot eyes. The more he looked at him, the more he seemed somewhat familiar. "I was there! I was there when the Forsaken queen turned on her own!"

Anduin froze, watching as Jago's legs turned liquid beneath him and he slumped down to the ground, the blackened motes on the air settling around him like a blackened snow.

"Arathi . . . I went. I was there. My Wilmer. He was there'n . . . He was changed. One of them, all rotten and strange but still Wilmer. Still . . . still the best man I ever knew and loved." Jago's rage took him again, and he snarled, jabbing a finger up at Anduin. "You could've stopped her. You could've saved them . . ."

Shaw carefully lowered Jago's hand. "That is not how you address your king."

"My king? My king?" Jago laughed, high-pitched and half-mad. "Not my king. The king of fools, maybe."

Anduin forced his voice to be steady and moved the spymaster aside. "It's all right, Shaw." Then he knelt, disguising the quivering he felt in his knees. The shame he still felt about that day, about that failure . . . He had gone to the Arathi Highlands in good faith, to try to mend the rift between those who had become Forsaken, undead, and the human family members they had left behind. The talks had gone well until they hadn't. The queen of the Forsaken, Sylvanas Windrunner, now the most hunted person on Azeroth, had killed her own people, executing any of her kind who chose to reunite and stay with their human loved ones.

"I'm sorry, Jago," Anduin said. "I'm—"

Jago pushed him aside, hard, then managed to climb to his feet and run a few paces out into the field. Swiftly, Shaw turned to apprehend him, but there was no need. Jago fell facedown in the dirt, arms splayed out to his sides, and he had managed to fall inches from the pointed leather boot of Alleria Windrunner. Anduin had not heard her approach, and no horse waited beside her, but the ranger had more creative ways of traveling anyway.

She nudged the fallen man with her boot and shrugged. "Still breathing."

"That's a relief," the farmer muttered dryly.

Anduin rose and walked resolutely toward Alleria while the farmer detained Shaw, complaining about his ruined roof. "Just how am I to pay for this? Jago doesn't have a copper to his name."

"Speak with Captain Danuvin," Shaw was telling him coolly. "He can lend you some of the garrison boys to see to the damage."

"Sure," the farmer grunted. "I'll bet he will . . ."

Anduin stopped a hair's width from Jago's feet, staring at Alleria over the man's toppled body.

"You're early," he said, breathless. He didn't intend to ignore the issue at hand—Jago mattered, of course, every subject in his kingdom mattered, but Alleria's appearance had everything to do with Jago's pain. Alleria had been sent on the most urgent of missions—to find Sylvanas Windrunner—but the king had not expected her so soon. Wilmer was just one of Sylvanas's innumerable crimes, and the murderess responsible for his death was to be found and brought to justice. Anduin took Alleria by the arm, leading her away from the field and back toward their restless horses.

"Is early a good sign?" he pressed.

Alleria Windrunner's delicate, pale face was half hidden by her hood, but even so, Anduin read only disappointment in the taut line of her lips. She kept her eyes down on the ground as they walked, her body tellingly rigid.

"No," Alleria whispered. Just that one word and her voice cracked with emotion. She looked tired, drawn, dark smudges making her void-touched eyes all the brighter. "No, my king, I have no good news for you this day."

They had reached the fences. Anduin grasped one of the crossbeams and squeezed, the old, battered wood creaking. He wanted to break it. He wanted it to snap. A surge of anger made him close his eyes, as if he were afraid of what Alleria might see there.

"My sister is not some slovenly boar bumbling across the open plains," Alleria continued, drawing back from him and crossing her arms over the green-and-gold cuirass beneath her cloak. "She is cunning and using all of her dark power to conceal herself."

"And you are the finest hunter I know," Anduin said through clenched teeth. "And not one I expected to fail. You know her best, Alleria. You were our greatest hope."

Shaw joined them silently, his gaze trained on the void elf. For a moment, none of them spoke, the storm speeding toward the grasslands whipping the winds into a frenzy. A small herd of gore-tusks screeched in alarm and galloped away from the fields. A gryphon soared overhead, destined for Sentinel Hill. The wood still creaking in Anduin's grasp shuddered in his palm, and still he wanted it to snap.

It would feel cathartic to break something.

They had overcome the Legion, the terror of Sargeras raining fire and doom upon their world. Yet they had persevered. How many had fallen to that same Legion? How many minds had been corrupted and shredded into ribbons of madness by N'Zoth? Yet even an Old God fell to their strength. But one woman . . . *one woman* evaded justice. It seemed such a small thing, to find her, and yet it was proving a costly—perhaps impossible—task.

"We will keep trying," Alleria said with mollifying confidence. "She cannot hide forever, soon enough she will have to show her-self, and when she does, she will have the full might of her ene-mies bearing down upon her."

Anduin opened his eyes slowly, turning his head toward the blonde elf, and as their eyes met he felt a jolt, an unpleasant whis-per from the dark recesses of his memory. Once Alleria had sug-gested to him that Sylvanas face N'Zoth. She and her sister Vereesa had been convinced it was the wisest course of action. To Anduin the request seemed absurd; it still did. Blood was blood, of course, and they had every right to believe in their sister's prow-ess. Why not let their most pressing threat fight yet another press-ing threat? But Anduin had refused. Her power was not in question, but now . . .

He thought perhaps Shaw had said his name, but he felt lost in the dark power of that memory. Why had Alleria asked such a thing of him? How could she be so blind as to extend a chance, any chance, to someone as treacherous as Sylvanas Windrunner? And now she had failed in her one explicit task, to track her sister and help him bring her to justice.

Maybe she was hiding something. Maybe the cold glow of her eyes concealed more than just the boundless mysteries of the Void. How could he be certain of Alleria's loyalty? Was it a risk, a foolish, reckless risk to keep her at his side?

A foolish, reckless risk just like trusting Sylvanas in the Arathi Highlands, when a naïve boy-king had believed the words of a snake . . . No. Alleria had proved herself many times, and she spoke true—Sylvanas was no simple quarry. The hunt would continue, and he, as king, would find a way to keep faith in their odds of victory. That was his duty. A man had to know his limits, but he could not reach that limit, not yet; too many depended on him now.

The fence beam snapped. Just another thing to fix.

Another in a long, long line of things to mend.

"Come," he said quietly, turning his back on them both. "The gale is nearly upon us. Let us return to Stormwind and decide our next approach. Sylvanas will not rest, and so neither will we."

CHAPTER ONE

Orgrimmar

Much as it surprised him, the dry heat and endless noise of Orgrimmar felt like home. Perhaps it was like returning to a wayward, peculiar family, one Thrall had not necessarily chosen, but that he had come to respect. Thrall, son of Durotan, former warchief, had expected to recoil at the familiar scents and mayhem of the Horde city, but he slipped back into its rhythm with surprising ease.

In a way, the familiarity of it frightened him. Things had changed, of course; the Horde itself had changed. It had to. No longer could a single warchief rule them all. No, like a strange family, the Horde had grown, suffered, expanded, retracted, and finally, he thought, they were beginning to find their feet not as different nations united by a single voice, but as a chorus of strong voices raised as one.

Wolves grew stronger as a pack, in numbers, and there in Grommash Hold, among the Horde Council, he saw many fine wolves at his side.

Do not fear this, he thought, gazing around at those assembled. *You lead no one. You simply sit among equals.*

His pride did not chafe at the thought; in fact, he welcomed it.

Thrall placed his hands on his knees, leaning forward as the two young tauren braves giving report in the center of the rotunda finished recalling their tale. They had sighted two dark ranger spies on a ridge in the Northern Barrens, and after alerting a senior patrol in the area, the rangers were tracked and captured. The spies had swallowed some foul concoction and died before they could be questioned, but still, they would no longer be allowed to be the Dark Lady's eyes in Durotar.

A smattering of applause went around the room, and the two braves stood tall, puffing out their furred chests and holding their spears straight. Thrall couldn't stop himself from wondering how long they would live, what cold, bleak place far from here would be their end, what families they would leave behind as they gave themselves over as grist to the mill of war.

No. *No*. They were putting a stop to all of that. That was the purpose of the council, to eschew the bloody whims of one in favor of more tempered policies. And while many still flinched at the mere mention of the armistice, Thrall thought it a reprieve the Horde sorely needed.

"Well done!" Lor'themar Theron called to the two braves. The leader of the blood elves with his long, pale hair, scarred and dead left eye, and painstakingly groomed beard raised a chalice. "Bravely done. A toast to these fine soldiers of the Horde. *Lok-tar!*"

"*Lok-tar!*"

Thrall raised his own cup, but his eyes fell on an empty seat beside the crimson-clad leader of the blood elves. Other pairs of eyes and Lor'themar's good one had wandered to that spot throughout the afternoon. It seemed almost too ironic—here they were, a council in response to Sylvanas Windrunner's controversial leadership and self-exile, and nobody sat in her place to speak for the Forsaken.

Even the new queen of Zandalar, Talanji, had come from her far-off nation to meet with the council. She sat almost exactly across from Thrall in the circle of chairs making up the council in the hold, and she had said little so far, something, he knew, that was uncharacteristic of the brash young queen.

Beside her, nearest to the entrance, sat the also newly risen trade prince of the Bilgewater Cartel, and while Gazlowe might have been diminutive in size, he had made his larger-than-life presence known throughout the day's reports, discussions, and disagreements.

The goblin had just poured himself more ale when two figures burst through the open archway, startling the tauren braves and Gazlowe, who slopped half of his drink down his shirt. He grumbled and swore, his single tuft of brown hair wobbling back and forth as he wiped furiously at the stain.

Their conspicuously missing council member had at last appeared. A slight, blue-eyed undead woman ran breathlessly into the hold, her gaze flicking in every direction, her posture suggesting she was not at all sorry for their tardiness. Behind her, a ghostly pale woman, also undead, stood with far more poise. They could not have been any more different, the two ladies, one ravaged by her affliction to the bones, the other smooth and unblemished, glowing from within with an arresting light.

Lilian Voss, interim leader of the Forsaken, and Calia Menethil had arrived, stealing the attention of every breathing creature in the hold, and leaving the two reporting braves to shift awkwardly in the sudden silence. Calia seemed to be watching Lilian's every move, as if she might be tested on it later. Finally, Baine Bloodhoof gestured for them to step away, and the two tauren shuffled toward him, kneeling on the floor behind their high chieftain.

Nobody spoke, and nobody seemed to know what to say, least of all the new arrivals. Lilian Voss adjusted the worn pack on her shoulder, her boots, grieves, and cloak spattered in fresh mud.

To Thrall's right, the white-haired and white-tattooed First Arcanist Thalyssra coughed delicately into her fist.

I am not their leader. The silence stretched painfully on. Thrall stood and opened his arms wide to the newcomers, conjuring a warm smile.

"Your absence was keenly felt," Thrall boomed. "The Horde is not the Horde without the Forsaken."

Lilian nodded, biting down so hard on her lower lip that Thrall worried she would break the skin. Her companion, the luminous Calia Menethil in priestly garb, glided forward, inclining her silver head toward him. "Graciously said."

"Join us, please." Thrall returned to his seat and indicated the open set of high-backed chairs reserved for their party.

"You will find Orgrimmar's finest foods and all the wine or mead you can . . . er . . . I mean, we are at your disposal," the vulpera Kiro said, paws washing over one another after the mistake. They were new to the Horde, after all. More softly, he added, "Please take a seat."

The gaffe broke the tension, and Gazlowe got a good chuckle out of the tawny vulpera's misstep. The undead had no need of food or drink, and Thrall was glad to find their new Forsaken leadership did not take offense. Instead, they were welcomed by the immense and feather bedecked Baine Bloodhoof and Lor'themar, sitting on either side of the empty chairs.

"May we ask what detained you?" Lor'themar inquired as the ladies were seated.

"Our people can't stay in Orgrimmar forever," Lilian replied, at last finding her tongue. Once she had sat down and unburdened herself of her pack, she appeared more at ease. Her blue eyes flashed brighter as she straightened her back and removed her leather cloak. "It's too hot. We prefer the shadows and the damp. Perhaps in time the ruins of Lordaeron can be reclaimed and our home there restored. Things are a little less heated with the armistice, but that doesn't mean Alliance ships are happy to see our flags at sea."

Across from them, sharpening a knife beside the trade prince, the Darkspear troll Rokhan hissed and leaped to his feet. His tusks gleamed as readily as his dagger. "They give you trouble?"

"We took the long way 'round," Lilian rasped. "Added a few days to our journey."

"Better to be careful in these tense times," Calia added softly. "Lest we cause a diplomatic incident." Then she shrugged, weary, and removed her sun-faded blue shawl, folding it neatly. "I am sure if we were intercepted, Derek Proudmoore could intervene on our—"

"The Proudmoores can do nothing for us."

Just when Thrall felt the thrum of nerves in the room dissipating, the young Zandalari queen was on her feet, icily rigid. Talanji slashed her hand through the air, her many golden piercings twinkling softly as she did, her tall, jewel-encrusted headdress casting a looming shadow that reached across the hold and flickered in the firelight.

Leather squeaked and iron jangled as the murmurs and shifting began. Behind him, Thrall heard his page, Zekhan, blow out a long breath.

"The Horde could not stop the attack on Zandalar, a failure I took in stride, believing that when we had recovered, we could take the fight to the Alliance, to the Proudmoores," Talanji continued, her voice shaking with emotion. "Peace with the Alliance means peace with the Proudmoores, with Jaina. I was foolish to believe my people would have their revenge."

Thrall squeezed the bridge of his nose. And it had all been going so smoothly. Perhaps he should have expected this. They were all so different, these assembled leaders, with conflicting ideas on what it meant to be part of the Horde, and no doubt their visions of the future varied as well. The tide of uneasy voices in the room began to crest.

Before he could offer something mollifying to the new queen, Lilian was quick to respond. "Derek is one of us now. You will have to accept that."

Talanji snarled, taking a single menacing step toward the Forsaken leader. "I have to accept *nothing*. You need me, and I had thought we had need of the Horde; now I see you will not help us seek justice for the siege of Zuldazar."

Without blinking, Lilian stood up, poking a bony finger in the troll's direction. "Zandalari justice is not the only justice that matters! The Forsaken have been cast aside, spat on, and ignored for long enough. Derek is Forsaken and the Forsaken are the Horde."

A smattering of agreeing noises traveled around the hold.

"Are the Zandalari not the Horde?" Talanji replied hotly. It was her time to hold court, apparently, and she strode to the center of the room, raising her voice above the many muted discussions that had broken out. "Where is the Horde response? Where is the support for my people? When will you acknowledge our wounds?"

"If we act rashly then we endanger the armistice," the nightborne arcanist, Thalyssra, interjected, wisely in Thrall's opinion. She sat calmly with one calf resting on her knee, her hands propped gracefully on her thigh as she observed Queen Talanji and Lilian Voss inching closer to blows.

"Our resources are stretched thin as it is," Lor'themar put in reasonably. "We must be thoughtful if we are to commit our navy to your struggles. Perhaps diplomacy is the answer here, and a delegation could be dispatched to Kul Tiras to—"

"Delegation? Diplomacy?" Rokhan thundered, shaking his

head. "*Pah.* My ancestors be weepin' to hear this cowardly talk in Grommash Hold."

At that, the Mag'har orcs clustered next to the Darkspears grabbed their weapons and slammed the pommels on the ground in agreement. One managed to raise his voice even above Rokhan's protests.

"There!" Talanji pointed to Rokhan. "At least there is still one among you who has not been left toothless by this talk of peace!"

"We all have our grievances," Baine Bloodhoof reminded her. "But those must be weighed against the interests of the Horde now. It is not easy, your highness, nobody thought it would be. In time, we can seek to right the wrongs done to the Zandalari."

"In time," she whispered, aghast.

It was then that Thrall realized he was one of the few left sitting. The room erupted into splintered arguments, fragments of those long-simmering grievances reaching him as he locked eyes first with Baine Bloodhoof and then Lor'themar. Leader or not, it seemed the unpleasant task of restoring order would fall to him. Baine had tried his best, but he required solidarity.

Thrall stood, then Baine, then Lor'themar, finally Thalyssra, each of them silent, and it took only a moment for the others to notice. One by one the voices died down until all gazes turned toward them. Before Thrall could call for quiet, Talanji stormed out of the assembly, her bodyguards scrambling to keep pace, making nervous, half-apologetic bows to Thrall as they fled after her.

"Perfect," he said with a sigh. "Meeting adjourned. We will eat and drink and come together again." If *we can come together,* he added silently.

It was a warning wrapped in silk, but it was not misheard. Sheepish eyes slid away from him as he cut a path through the leaders and their entourages, the crowd parting silently for him as he made for the door. He was not yet an old orc, but each one of those steps through the hold intensified the exhaustion settling in his bones.

What had he agreed to? He pinched his nose again, warding off the searing headache brewing at the base of his skull. Physical brawls left him feeling less bruised. The scents of prairie grass and churned earth carried on the hot afternoon sun flooded him with memories. He blinked his way into the brightness outside, shielding his eyes, remembering a moment not long ago when he stood with the same smells blowing around him, high above the scooped valley of Mulgore, perched on the cliffs of Thunderbluff. Jaina Proudmoore, Talanji's nemesis, had stood beside him, assuring him that a fragile alliance between them was worth the blood and strife it would surely cost.

"Horde. Alliance," he had said to her. "We've come to this crossroad again and again, Jaina; it always falls apart. What's different this time?"

Her hand had lain softly on his arm, and perhaps more than her words, that one simple gesture moved him. "We are."

Thrall had believed her, but now he wasn't so sure, with his head being split in two by the council's argument ringing in his ears.

A haze of dust over Orgrimmar dulled the relentless sun. Ceremonial torches outlined a smoky trail out of Grommash Hold and toward a dozen or so feasting tables laid out beneath makeshift red tents painted with the Horde emblem. Predictably, a crowd of curious onlookers waited outside the hold, filling the valley with their curious whispers and gasps of interest as the other council members filed out behind him. There was a festive spirit in the air, drums and flutes, pennants shaped like winged, horned wind riders flapping at the ends of sticks held by eager toddlers' fists. Parents had pressed their children up close to the perimeter of the tents, and some little ones had been hoisted onto shoulders.

Thrall stood for a moment with the sunshine warming his bare shoulders and smiled ruefully at one of two young orcs, each balancing on one of their father's shoulders. As he waved to them, Zekhan ambled up to his side. Lor'themar drifted by with First Arcanist Thalyssra at his side, listening, rapt, as she extoled the virtues of the fine nightborne wines she had secured for the feast.

"What is it?" Thrall asked. He could always tell when the brave young troll shaman had something on his mind. The boy was good for a lot of things, but hiding his emotions was not one of them.

"There's a messenger from the Earthen Ring here," Zekhan told him. The other council members overtook them, making their slow procession toward the feasting tents. Lor'themar took his time, basking in the adulation and interest of the crowd.

"I said it was feast time," he growled.

"You'll be wantin' to hear this."

Thrall had known during his time as warchief that "What now?" could in fact become a perpetual state of being. Turning away from the crowd, he found himself standing before a gray-faced old orc, pockmarked and bearded, with a scar slashed through his lips.

"Yukha," Thrall said. This was no mere messenger. He recognized the shaman at once. They had served together against the Legion, and anything that might drive Yukha from his post in the Maelstrom was dire indeed. "*Throm-ka*, old friend, what brings you to Orgrimmar?"

They clapped hands on each other's shoulders, and Yukha chewed his cheek for a moment before drawing a deep, sorrowful breath.

"The spirits, Thrall, they are in disarray. Where once we communed peacefully with the ancestors, we now find them angry and vengeful. They lash out. They deny us their wisdom. My friend . . . something is terribly wrong."

Yukha shifted his carved staff to the other hand nervously. It was not like the battle- and time-tested seer to fidget so.

"When?" Thrall asked in a low voice, keeping the conversation strictly between them. Zekhan sensed he was not invited to the discussion and took himself a polite distance away.

"I came with all speed," Yukha replied. "The journey is unforgiving on my body now, but I knew you would listen to me, old friend."

"Of course. You were never one to jostle your bones for less than the end of the world," Thrall teased, but they only spared the shortest, driest laugh together.

"You jest, but I have never seen such unrest in the spirit world before, and you know how many long, long winters I have seen."

Thrall nodded, his hand still resting firmly on the shaman's upper arm.

"I have heard you, Yukha. The council will know of this and I will see to it personally that your concerns are not ignored."

That drew a relieved smile across the orc's wrinkled face. "Haste, son of Durotan. Haste. The ancestors cry out, and we must listen."

CHAPTER TWO

Nazmir

Apari clasped her hands together under her chin, watching the last drop of life seep out of poor Seshi's eyes. No, not poor Seshi. *Foolish* Seshi. The old wound in Apari's leg throbbed, but she ignored it—her work was too important.

"You chose death," she told him softly. "When ya chose *her*."

"W-witch!"

His last ragged word echoed for a moment in the damp cave. It sounded as if the loa of death himself had torn the cry from the troll's throat. The troll's blue eyes flashed bright with desperation one last time and then went blank, his stare fixing on a point somewhere over Apari's shoulder. On her other shoulder, a hungry dreadtick sat hunched and eager, its sharp little mouth sucking at the air, no doubt tasting death.

"Not this one, Daz," Apari warned the tick. "One sip of his blood and you be flat as a coin, all your insides on the outside."

Retchweed. Common as clouds in the Primal Wetlands. Seshi lay dead on a large stone slab, all that remained of a column from the Zul'jan Ruins to the east. A harsh, foul smell emanated from the body already, his purplish skin shriveled up and sagging as if he were a dried fruit. Fluid dribbled steadily from the stone slab, joining the soft *drip-drop-drip* of water from cracks in the cave's ceiling. The constant drumming of the waterfall concealing the cave's mouth distorted for a moment, and then Apari heard the nearly imperceptible footfalls of her most trusted general.

"This is how it will be?" Tayo asked. She joined Apari next to the corpse and wrinkled her nose. A huge slice of bone pierced her septum, her elongated tusks capped with sharpened gold points. Mud and black paint made her long ponytail look like a tar spill. Tayo had been a loyal friend and lieutenant since Yazma's attempt at a coup. Her family had been sympathetic to the spymistress's ideas, and subsequently banished by Talanji, threatened with execution if they returned. "This is how the traitor queen will die?"

"Retchweed and riverbud root," Apari told her, holding up a small satchel of powder. "My own creation. A purge to remove the rot at the heart of our great land, sister."

Apari knew her weeds and herbs, her poultices and powders. After receiving a grievous injury to her leg, she had tried everything to relieve the pain, the swelling, and then the infected smell. Nothing worked. It seethed and reeked on until at last she had accepted that, like many scars and betrayals in her life, it would simply have to become another reminder of all that she had lost. In the jungle villages of Zuldazar, retchweed was everywhere, and healers used it as a purge whenever a child swallowed something poisonous. The right quantity helped, but when dried, powdered, and mixed with riverbud root, retchweed became lethal.

And it was not a gentle way to pass on to the Other Side.

Tayo nodded. "She deserves to suffer. Where will it be done?"

Apari turned and regarded her general. It was a far more pleasant sight than the desiccated mess on the stone slab. "Before the whole of her precious Horde. She has chosen them over her own people, now let her die among them," she sneered. "Ancestors be willin'."

"Ancestors be willin'," Tayo echoed, making a fist and touching it to her enameled harness. Two leather bandoliers crisscrossed her chest, packed with brightly feathered poison darts. "There is more. The pale rider is here; he arrived with an unliving elf. They be anxious to speak with you."

The body behind her let out a hiss of air, and Apari twisted, watching the muscles in the troll's shoulders and chest contort. Black bile flowed freely from between his cracked lips. She imagined that same thick ooze pouring out from Talanji's mouth, her bright eyes dim and hollow . . . Retchweed purged the sickness in one's body, but this went far beyond sickness, far beyond one troll's death. Talanji was a symbol of everything corrupting the Zandalari empire, her reign no more than a stain on their ancient and powerful legacy. She only wished she could be there to watch the traitor queen claw at her own throat in fruitless desperation.

"Apari . . ."

She nodded once, and Tayo returned to the entrance of the cave with its curtain of a waterfall. Daz squirmed on her shoulder, hungry. Outside, beyond the cascade of water and shadows that hid them, a herd of saurolisks grunted and shrieked at a passing threat.

"Go," Apari said quietly. "Hunt."

The tick fluttered its gray wings and scratched at her shoulder, then glided away, toward the water sheeting down from above. Apari watched Daz go, the sun glinting against the waterfall, a kaleidoscope of colors flashing so swiftly it might have been her imagination. But no, the rainbow remained etched on her vision, turning the shadows purple and blue. A good omen. Daz soared like a child's ball toward the sunlight, his soft wings just grazing the top of the man's head.

So. They had come. She shivered. Things were in motion now,

truly in motion, and Apari felt suddenly alive. It seemed like years, an age, since she had experienced such excitement.

Apari folded her hands together, the heavy rings there clacking as she limped toward their guests. The man—dark of hair and red of eye—brushed with annoyance at the tick, then pulled at the collar of his thick black coat. Tayo towered a head taller than he, of near equal height to his armored companion.

"Pale rider," Apari called out to him. "You are welcome here, but in two hours we depart. We do not stay long, and the sun never sets twice on our camps."

"A wise precaution." His bright gaze swept the cave, landing on the grisly sight behind her. He simply smirked. "We have come to discuss our . . . arrangement. Might we speak elsewhere, or is this what passes for courtesy in your swamp?"

"No," Apari replied. She inclined her head with respect but did not bow. Apari no longer bowed to anyone. "Not courtesy, but a promise."

The man arched one black brow, and the elf to his right sighed with impatience. Her pink skin, veined and mottled, was as sickly as a skyterror's webbing. She held a strange winged helmet under one arm, and Apari wondered just how she could fight smothered in so much heavy armor. But she did not wonder if the elf was dangerous—the murderous glint in her eye transcended culture and custom.

"A promise," Apari reiterated, answering the dead man's silent question. "A vow to my mother who drank the venom of Shadra, and to all of Zandalar who deserve better than a crown and gods who care not for them." She pulled a green stalk of retchweed from her pocket and held it up, twisting it in the light. "Shadra is gone. Yazma is gone, too, but poison lingers. Poison in my heart," she murmured, "and soon, poison in the traitor queen's veins."

Zekhan had not avoided the unforgiving boot of war by staying still. No, he had learned to make himself useful, to stay useful, and to know when that usefulness had come to its end. He had not landed on Varok Saurfang's side on the battlements of Lordaeron by twiddling his thumbs or taking a nap. And so he did not stand still while his commander descended into a quiet, intense exchange with the Earthen Ring shaman.

He casually fell into step behind the tall and well-armed leader of the Darkspear trolls, Rokhan, using his shadow as a concealment of sorts, ignoring the screams and cheers of the crowd as the assembled council members and their assorted bodyguards, advisers, and hangers-on retreated to the tempting shade of the feast tents. Zekhan wasn't foolish enough to think those celebratory cheers were for him. No, he was in a shadow and *was* a shadow, first his father's, then Saurfang's and now Thrall's.

And as a shadow he crept along, looking for something interesting enough to occupy his time. "Keep ya hands busy and ya mind sharp," his father, Hekazi, had told him when Zekhan was still knee-high to a raptor. "And ya will never want for work nor amusement."

Work and amusement would have to go hand in hand that day. A drum circle with a trio of wild dancers had been set up outside the tents to welcome the esteemed guests. He watched the goblin, Gazlowe, sidle up toward the drums, doing a silly two-step and making the dancers laugh. The music, the steady, infectious rhythm of it, gradually spread to the others approaching the tent, tense shoulders moving instead to the beat, narrowed eyes widening with appreciation at the talented (and scantily dressed) dancers.

Only Talanji and her Zandalari contingent stood apart. The detached detachment. He wasn't exactly surprised. While the Horde Council had welcomed her and her folk warmly, her response had so far been nothing but chilly. Zekhan had kept a close eye on her, intrigued and, admittedly, a little besotted with the beautiful queen. She had the most delicate tusks and arresting blue eyes . . .

She also, quite clearly, had a temper.

Talanji paced back and forth on the far southern end of the feast tables, a turquoise-skinned, yellow-haired young troll girl fanning the queen with a massive palm frond. Annoyed with the little puffs of wind, Talanji batted at the girl, shooing her away. Zekhan frowned. Had there not been more bodyguards with Talanji when they arrived? Or had one of her handmaidens gone missing? Orgrimmar was not the most confusing city to navigate in the world, but perhaps one of the Zandalari had gotten lost on their way to the meeting that afternoon.

Maybe, he thought. Maybe. He sidled closer, sensing an opportunity. The Horde needed every advantage it could get, and that meant securing Talanji's allegiance anew: an ally willing to join them in war or peace, one willing to provide troops. One willing to join the council. So far she didn't seem very impressed.

"Might I be of service, ya majesty?"

Zekhan gave a low bow and brought out his most dazzling smile. The girl fanning the queen made a tiny sound of alarm. The queen herself stared at him—through him—then rolled her eyes.

"And how could you possibly be of service?" Her keen eyes no doubt took in his humble garments and dirt under his fingernails. Meanwhile, she and her servants glittered like firebugs at dusk.

"Ya entourage be lookin' a little light. If ya need an errand run or a fresh cup of wine—"

Talanji tilted her head to the side, her earrings jangling softly as she interrupted him. "You are spying on me now?"

Not the response he was hoping for. Zekhan backed away, already bracing for the lecture Thrall would give him for bothering the queen. He threw up his arms as if in surrender, a cold shiver overcoming him, like someone had traced the tip of a knife down his spine. And then he fell backward, steady one minute and flailing the next, his elbow smashing into something hard and then wet. A goblet. Talanji's missing servant had returned, and Zekhan had crashed right into him.

The cup and its contents fell to the ground, splashing wine all over Zekhan's feet and the hem of Talanji's gown.

"Mind yaself!" the servant carrying the tray and goblet shouted, scrambling to scoop up the fallen goblet. He was older than Talanji, the servant, with scars crisscrossing his nose and a visible sheen of sweat over his brow. "Clumsy oaf! That was the queen's wine!"

"Just a mistake," Talanji said, calmly lifting her skirt to inspect the damage. "He meant no harm . . ."

But Zekhan stopped listening to the queen, staring at the stain on the fine white silk of her dress. First Arcanist Thalyssra's silken voice was suddenly in his head . . .

I cannot wait for you to sample our arcfruit sangree, Lor'themar. We have generously arranged enough for all of Orgrimmar to enjoy.

The ugly splotch on the queen's hem was purplish blue and turning black. What's more, the puddle left behind on the dirt smelled distinctly of *death*.

"Another cup for ya majesty, I will return," the servant was saying, bowing to Talanji as he shuffled away.

"No." Zekhan knelt and swept his fingers through the spill on the ground, then sniffed. Whatever it was, it wasn't wine. An herbal tea, maybe, or something worse. "What you be servin' her?"

"W-wine," the servant stammered, but the sweat on the troll's brow poured heavy down his temples. "Just wine."

Standing, Zekhan had barely enough time to wedge himself between Talanji and the scarred servant, who yanked a dagger from under his tunic and lunged toward the queen. The commotion had aroused the interest of the entire council, and now Zekhan felt the feasting tents explode into chaos around him. The drums went abruptly silent followed by hushed whispers from the crowd outside.

"Back!" Zekhan thundered at Talanji. "Behind me!"

A throwing axe flew straight over Zekhan's shoulder, close enough to give him a haircut. He shook it off, hurling a fork of lightning right after the axe—the bolt slammed the servant into a tentpole before he slumped to the ground, the throwing axe buried in the ground beside him, a narrow miss. Thrall's heavy tread came next, and then his intimidating shadow as he raced by them and toward the assassin. That explained the axe.

"Hold him!" someone was shouting.

"Protect the queen!"

Zekhan came to his senses and stumbled after Thrall, who reached the assailant a moment too late. The dagger was still in the troll's hand and swiftly put to use, jammed into his own stomach and yanked upward.

"Speak." Thrall had the troll by his neck, but the dagger had done its gruesome work. "Who sent you? *Who sent you?*"

The old scarred troll had just enough left in him to whisper a final threat, "She . . . will know our . . . b-bite." Then his head went loose on his neck, a trickle of blood seeping from between withered lips.

No sooner had the troll spoken his last than Talanji was upon them, pushing Thrall and Zekhan aside and kneeling in the blood-soaked earth beside the assassin. "He is Zandalari. One of my own . . . But how?"

"All of your people must be held and questioned," Thrall replied sternly. "There is never just one assassin."

"Question your own people!" Talanji fumed, leaping to her feet, her hands and gown covered in blood. Covered in poison. "We will return home before more blood can be spilled."

Thrall sighed and shifted, standing in her way. "I assure you—"

"You can assure me nothing—not ships, not soldiers, not my own personal safety." She straightened her head, and at her height, she could easily look Thrall in the eye. Zekhan cowered, the tension around them thicker than tar. "You do not need me here. Zandalar, my home, will always need me, so that is where I will be."

All eyes followed the Zandalari queen as she gathered her small entourage and marched out of the tents, head held high and proud. All eyes, Zekhan noted, except for those belonging to Thrall. It had all happened in the space of a blink, the assassin, the axe, the queen's outrage . . . He couldn't help but fixate on the moment when his arm knocked the cup out of the assassin's hand. He felt certain his feet had been firmly planted on the ground, that something or someone had shoved him back into the Zandalari.

The council members came one by one, drawn by the commotion, the Darkspear chieftain Rokhan appearing at his side, only then sheathing his daggers. Smirking, the taller troll clapped Zekhan on the back, and Zekhan was just dizzy enough from the chaos to sway a little from the force of it.

"Ya did good, boy. Those be the reflexes of Kimbul."

But I didn't do it.

The lightning he could take credit for, but the cup? The cup . . . He frowned, gazing around at the faces of relieved council members. Only Thrall, visible at the back of the crowd, shared his concern, his brow furrowed, his eyes dark and distant. Now all the mightiest the Horde had to offer gathered around him, echoing Rokhan's sentiments. Already he heard someone say the word "hero," and Zekhan shook his head. No, no, he wasn't a hero at all, just a boy from the jungles, from a village that would fit inside the gates of Orgrimmar a hundred times over; he only wanted to make himself useful, not win some kind of accolade.

Zekhan found Thrall's face among the throng again, but his

expression went unchanged. The single black smudge in the otherwise cloudless sky, the distant warning presaging rain. Only a few would notice it, only a few would take heed, but when the great leader worried, the wise warrior beneath him worried, too.

The Darkspear chieftain placed a hand on his shoulder, but Zekhan didn't smile; he trembled instead.

CHAPTER THREE

Dazar'alor

A hot, dry wind reached Talanji from the north as if Vol'dun itself sighed toward her. She stood atop the Great Seal and inhaled as the breeze came, hoping to absorb the very essence of her home back into her body. This was where she belonged. The jungle. The vast, golden city of her ancestors. Standing there was like standing at the edge of the world, nothing but verdant possibility and life stretching in every direction. On a clear night such as this one, she could see all the way to the tops of the mountains to the west, even above the Temple of the Prophet, to the peaks draped in emerald velvet.

Home. Zikii removed Talanji's heavy ceremonial bracelets and rings one by one, collecting them in a box lined in fabric as soft-looking as those green, green mountains. With each removed piece, Talanji felt lighter, but also . . . strange. Vulnerable. For a moment she tore her eyes away from the jungle and instead watched Zikii work with deft little hands. Those serving the royalty of Zandalar were trained to be all but invisible, to move on silent feet, to dress the royal body while barely being perceived. But she perceived the young troll then, her simple plaits of dark blue and sweet young face, unpierced, unscarred, untouched by time and suffering.

Had Talanji ever been that innocent? Had she ever looked so serene?

When Zikii finished, Talanji saw her close the box, set it down, and then unclasp the jade- and jewel-encrusted surcoat the queen had worn to the gathering in Orgrimmar. She then waited, patiently, for Talanji to pull the white satin shift over her head.

"Go," Talanji told her. "I must be alone now."

"My queen, your gown is stained—"

"Later. You are dismissed, Zikii."

She didn't have to raise her voice. The young troll nodded and collected the queen's raiment, then disappeared into the throne room, through the hidden servant's passage.

Talanji turned her back on the jungles and mountains and retreated toward her throne. Sometimes when she only glanced in its direction, she could still see the outline of her father, Rastakhan, seated there, his skin brightened by the ever-burning torches at his sides, his brooding eyes peering out beneath the weighty plumed crown on his head.

But Rastakhan was gone. Dead. *Murdered.*

Her hands turned immediately into fists as she approached the throne. When she was a child, Rastakhan sometimes let her sit on the massive chair, its sunlike spikes soaring high above her head. His warmth lingered on the cushions, as if he were actually *part* of the throne.

She cringed then shivered, the hot Vol'dun wind turning cold as daylight slipped away. They had departed Orgrimmar before anyone could convince her to stay, and while Talanji was grateful to be home, she couldn't escape the feeling that leaving the summit so soon was a mistake. Maybe if she had remained and pressed her case, the Horde Council would grant her reparations for Zandalar's people. That was all she could expect from the Horde, for their precious armistice meant too much to them, and justice for Rastakhan's murder would have to be found a different way.

Instead, she had left Orgrimmar with nothing.

No, not nothing, with fear in her heart and a black stain on her dress. Had that red-haired troll not blundered into the assassin and spilled the poisoned cup, she might be dead on the sands of Durotar, flies buzzing about her lips.

"Bwonsamdi," she whispered, speaking the name of the loa of death. Her father, with his dying breath, had passed his cursed pact with the loa onto his daughter, and now Talanji carried not only their bloodline but their bane.

A gray, curling fog drifted over her feet, colder than the changing night winds. That same mist filled the throne room until at last she heard a familiar sound. Bwonsamdi had come, heralded by the strangled sigh of their realm, less a fanfare and more a dirge.

The loa of graves hovered above the Zandalari throne, coils of blue smoke unfurling around him. A bony, skull-shaped growth covered most of his face, though his permanently smug smile remained unfettered. White tattoos glowed across his chest, wild black hair piled on his head, spiky and stiff as a fern.

"Oh," Bwonsamdi chuckled. "Oh, oh, oh, *oh*. The queen is in distress. Why not unload ya problems on ya old friend Bwonsamdi?"

Talanji crossed her arms. "I'm not in the mood, ya old windbag. One of my own people tried to poison me, and he tried it in front of the Horde Council. In broad daylight! My enemies are getting bold."

"Ha! I nearly had ya soul then! So is that why you summoned me?" He floated closer, and Talanji could see him batting his lashes like a fool behind his skull-like brow. "Thoughts of death made ya think of ya best friend on the other side? How flatterin', ya majesty."

"No, no, Bwonsamdi, it's nothing like that," Talanji insisted, turning away with a grunt. "I want to speak to my father. You are the keeper of souls, the lord of death, surely you must know where his soul resides. Can you not arrange an audience?"

The loa laughed uproariously, and the palace shook beneath her feet, rattled as if by thunder. He appeared above her, contorted, his face upside down as he came almost nose to nose with her. "What am I? Some servant to do whatever ya bid? Think I keep ya fa'da in my back pocket? The spirit of a king is no trifle, girl."

"*Everything* is a trifle to you," Talanji bit back, refusing to shrink. "Everything is a game."

Bwonsamdi's smile faded. He sniffed loudly at her, snuffling like a hog. "You reek of death. It came close to ya, didn't it? Real close. Maybe you be wantin' to ask your fa'da what it's like on the Other Side."

Talanji waved him off, marching forward and through the loa, who popped out of sight. She returned to the balcony, where the whole of her city and the jungles beyond waited. Hundreds of torches glittered as night approached, bright and curious, like a field of eyes staring up at her. *Needing* her. "No. I will find that out on my own terms, and no time soon. I ask as a queen who needs the council of her elder, nothing more, Great Spirit. Bring me the king; bring me his spirit so that I might know his wisdom."

"I can do no such thing, girl."

Bwonsamdi reappeared at her side, reclining casually against one of the large golden pillars crowned with a cauldron of fire.

"You don't control me," he reminded her. "And I don't control you."

"Not according to my enemies," Talanji muttered. She hugged herself tighter. "Half of Zandalar thinks I answer to you. If they keep thinkin' that way I will never keep control. *Pah.* No wonder that assassin came for me today—I have my father's blood, his crown, his loa, and now his rebels. If I can't be rid of them my reign is as good as over."

"'Tis now all doomin' and gloomin'," Bwonsamdi said, gesturing to the large stain on her hem. "Who do ya think protected you today? You might show a little gratitude to your savior."

Talanji snorted, shooting him a sideways glance. "You cannot take credit for one troll's clumsiness."

Bwonsamdi grinned, a twinkle in his eyes behind the mask-like bone around his orbits. "I gave him a little shove. Just a *teensy* one. But no action taken by the powerful is ever little, ya see? And now ya be learnin' what it really means to be powerful. Everyone always wanting something from ya, always asking, just like ya be askin' me now. That assassin wanted ya death but I wouldn't give it to him, and I won't give you ya fa'da neither. Unless . . ."

Bwonsamdi held on to the word until it sounded like the warning hiss of a snake.

"Unless what?" Talanji snapped.

"Unless you be wantin' to make a deal? It seems fair, no? I save your life, you make a deal with your friend Bwonsamdi . . ."

Talanji scoffed, pacing to the very edge of the terrace while the loa's eyes burned into the back of her skull. To be bound to him was a curse, and she would thank him for nothing. "And will you be there to give a little shove the next time? And the time after that?" She sighed. "There is unrest in my city and the Horde will do nothing to stop it. They will not send me ships or troops, they will do nothing. The fate of Zandalar is in my hands, but how can I bring prosperity and peace to people who do not trust me? My father would know what to do. He *always* knew what to do. Or perhaps his loa, Rezan, would have known even better."

Silence. The torches spat and flared, the watch changed below, and the clank of armor and footsteps rose up to meet them. The city, to her, seemed ominously quiet. Just like her loa. She expected a jab, a joke, some taunt meant to twist the knife of her doubts, but he simply stared at her.

Either she was mad, or there was a flicker missing from his eyes then. He seemed . . . dimmer. *Sad.*

"What?" she prodded. "Nothing to say? Not a single sly word? That is not like you, Bwonsamdi."

The loa finally shook his head, and the mist that gathered at his feet grew thicker, obscuring him until only his strange blue-flame eyes remained visible. "Our bond is strong, little queen, but that does not make me your servant. I will not summon your fa'da's spirit. I'm afraid you're on your own tonight."

CHAPTER FOUR

Nazmir

There was no shame in retreat: Sylvanas had taught him that. Retreat prevented outright failure, which Sylvanas had also made clear, along with her utter contempt for the concept. Nathanos Blightcaller spurred the winged lizard faster, digging his heels into its leathery sides and ignoring its pained shrieks. The Zandalari rebels who had gifted him the thing called it a pterrordax, but that mattered little. He only cared if it could fly fast enough to lose the patrol that had spotted them in Nazmir. The thing flew fast and reckless, and he closed a hand over his coat pocket again, making certain the vial was still there, that it hadn't tumbled out into the jungle canopy. Ah. There it was. He buttoned his pocket tighter just to be safe.

Retreat. A familiar concept. It didn't irk him, but he was annoyed that the rebel leader, Apari, had been sloppy enough to miss the Zandalari patrol approaching their position.

"Use only their own arrows!" he shouted, the wind carrying his voice to the dark rangers flying in a V pattern behind him. Their aim proved true, and he watched the rain of brightly colored arrows descend with cruel precision, striking first one mounted Zandalari and then another. Eight of the patrol remained, growing wise and ducking off the path, riding under the dense tree cover.

"We cannot allow them to reach the *Banshee's Wail*!" Sira called. She had sprung ahead, but carefully reined in her beast, its wings slapping the air rhythmically as she waited for Nathanos to catch up. "Allying with these rebels was a mistake."

Nathanos kept his head low, avoiding the sight lines of the ground patrol racing after them.

"Go sharply south; the mountains are impassable on foot."

The rangers escorting them east to the sea broke formation, diving down at breakneck speed toward the canopy. They wore the coarse, torn rags of jungle villagers, but even so, if any of the Zandalari patrol came near they would surely see that these were not trolls fleeing toward the South Seas.

"Blast," Nathanos cursed, pulling his nondescript brown hood higher over his head. A beast much like the one he rode burst from the canopy, a spray of leaves fluttering in its path as it careened toward Lelyias, the dark ranger to his right. The cursed Zandalari must have been druids, springing into a creature's form more fit for their pursuit.

"Bring it down!" Nathanos bellowed. He pulled his own bow from his back and twisted in the saddle, risking recognition or, worse, an interminable tumble down to the rocky hills below.

Lelyias joined him in peppering the green, winged creature with arrows. Her hand blurred from the speed of her pull and fire, and at last two shots struck the Zandalari in the wings. It let out a piercing cry, then fell, its body shimmering strangely before reverting to its troll form, arrows prickling its shoulder.

He lost sight of Lelyias and the others, pouring his attention into reaching the beach with all haste.

"It's no use!" Sira spat. "They're going to discover us!"

"Never," Nathanos assured her. "The queen's will must be done. Fly ahead. Alert the crew, bring her around and into the bay, have archers at the ready."

"Take the ship to shore!? Are you mad?"

"Just do as I say!"

Even under her hood and through the narrow slits in her helmet, Nathanos detected a flicker of resentment. Sira Moonwarden never enjoyed taking his barked orders. She never enjoyed anything, as far as he noticed. Sira did little but balk and glare at him, her willingness to follow orders contingent on a high enough body count to keep her satisfied. She raged, at everything, at him, at her goddess, Elune, at a world that had left her in isolating darkness. He knew the feeling, but had chosen to embrace it and grow stronger. What she had grown in, he could not say. But from what he had observed, she had her anger, and nothing else. He often found himself wondering if she was truly loyal to Sylvanas, or if her loyalty was simply to killing itself, and its way of distracting the mind, granting a heady if fleeting catharsis.

After giving him one last glare, Sira did as he commanded, leaving him behind and sailing down in a remarkable spiral, becoming little more than a speck against the blue canvas of the sea, and farther on, the ship anchored far offshore.

Nathanos searched among the trees for the rangers, but both they and their assailants were running out of jungle. Fighting in the open could be a mistake. If any of the Zandalari escaped, their plans would be in jeopardy, but this was their land, and they knew how to defend it. He doubted that they could best the dark rangers stationed on deck in a fair conflict. He pressed two fingers to his lips and gave three sharp whistles. The dark rangers gathered to him, re-forming and leaving behind the skirmish in the trees.

"We take them out in the open." Nathanos gestured to the beach below. "No survivors."

It proved a quick if messy solution. The Zandalari, perhaps too committed and proud now to give up, did exactly as Nathanos expected. They raced out of their hiding places in the jungle, their raptor mounts eating up the sand quickly as they followed Nathanos and his escorts, taking the bait. Nathanos ducked down again, avoiding the occasional arrow that managed to zing near him.

The Zuldazar jungle gave way to a sloped sandy hill spotted with jagged rocks, a long stretch of open beach dividing the hills from the foamy shore. Hungry birds circled, expectant of a big meal, and Nathanos so hated to disappoint.

"Slow down," he called to the riders, whistling again. "Draw them out."

He watched the *Banshee's Wail*, sails replaced with simple merchant's colors, careen toward them, the long bowsprit bobbing gamely as the waves hit the boat with full force. Captain Deliria Dawes brought her around beautifully, the broad side of the purple-chased hull now near enough for the naked eye to see a dozen dark rangers perched on the railing, bows at the ready.

"Land," he gave the order. "Fearless, now, let them think they have a chance."

The three dark rangers with him obeyed at once, and together they hit the sand, then spun around to face the seven riders bearing down on them, blood up, curved swords raised, their eyes aglow with the promise of battle.

It was a promise that would never be fulfilled. They fell before coming in striking distance of Nathanos and the others. The trolls had taken the bait, and it doomed them. A storm of arrows arced over him and the other dark rangers, fired from the ship, landing in a deadly and precise cluster. He watched the trolls smash into the ground one by one, then dispatched Lelyias to the *Banshee's Wail*.

"Tell Moonwarden of our victory here, and have the ship made ready to sail. We cannot anchor here again for a time," he explained.

Lelyias gave a sharp nod and kicked at her beast, soaring into the air and sprinkling them with a fine arc of sand.

"Strip the bodies, recover the weapons, and put them into the sea. Make sure they are not found." He prepared to follow Lelyias, trusting the rangers to carry out his orders. "Remember, rangers: We were never here. Fly north to find us when you are finished."

On deck, Sira commanded things tidily, as he imagined she always did when he was absent. The skyterrors were seen to, fed, watered, and kept below deck for further inland incursions.

"Adequate sailing as always, now take us out," he told Captain Deliria as he found his way quickly to the spacious great cabin at the stern. The captain snapped him a sharp salute, her long, black hair whipped wildly by the sea winds. She stood taller than many of the other rangers, with strong features and delicately arched brows. So far, serving with her onboard had proved a tolerable experience.

"That was close," Sira hissed, removing her helmet and shaking out her hair as she followed him through the ship's narrow corridors. "Much too close. I am beginning to think this Apari is not reliable. This might have been a trap."

"I do not think so," Nathanos replied calmly. He shook the sand from his cloak and then plucked it off. It would take hours to get all the grit out of his coat and boots. "I looked in her eyes, and the hatred I saw there is real. She wants to be rid of Talanji and the Horde as much as we do, and we cannot succeed here without her help."

He opened the door to the cabin smoothly, but Sira appeared ready to kick it down. The dark warden stalked to the bright, mullioned windows and glared out at the waves.

"We do not need a bunch of unorganized, desperate rebels."

Sira slammed her helmet down on the banquet table, shaking the candelabra. "One squadron of dark rangers is worth two hundred farmers with pitchforks." She snatched off her gloves, examining her fingernails. "And I alone am worth twice that."

"Your enthusiasm is appreciated, Sira, and noted. However, our task here does not just require precision but utmost secrecy. Do you remember what I told you when we came aboard in Dragonblight?"

She chewed over the question for a moment, then slumped into a chair. "We were never in Zandalar."

"Correct," Nathanos replied. He joined Sira at the long table, moving aside two chairs and taking a rolled parchment from a stack of them bundled at the center. Unrolling a map of the region, he smoothed it out, carefully removing the creases from each corner. "We are not here right now. We will never be here. Their sloppiness is an asset. *Chaos* is an asset. Our new friends are the storm, and we are the single bolt of lightning that strikes."

His forefinger landed in north Nazmir, leaving a smudge of dirt across a small rectangle and its accompanying label.

THE NECROPOLIS

"I still say my talents are better used elsewhere." Sira twisted and placed her forearms on the table, stacking them. "Like at Windrunner's side, where the most killing is to be done. I have no taste for discretion, only carnage will satisfy now."

Nothing will ever satisfy, he thought, such was the nature of undeath, but he forced himself to smile. "Sira, you are greedy indeed if you consider the death of a god unsatisfying. Bwonsamdi is the last aching thorn in our queen's side, and it is our job to pluck him out—he is powerful and irritatingly loyal to the Horde. We cannot know his plans, but we can assume he will use his knowledge of death against her. Against *us*. Was it equal to an errand boy then she would have sent as much. Our queen has determined you will serve her best here, and it is not our place to ponder such decisions."

"Are you questioning my judgment?" Sira growled, her red eyes burning with hotter fire.

"No, you are here, and in being here you have not chosen an easy path but the right one. We must save this world from itself, and that might require us to swallow the bitter with the sweet. I know you crave death, Sira, but you must deliver it here." Nathanos sat back, letting the map roll itself up and snap shut. "If this was not suited to your talents, Sylvanas would not have chosen you."

Sira blew out a long, tired breath. "I will try to consider this mission as the opportunity for mayhem that it is. Still . . ."

Nathanos caught a sigh at the back of his throat—he needed Sira to accept her role in the Dark Lady's plans. He needed her focused and committed.

"Still, do you not think we should be at her side? Both the Alliance and the Horde hunt her, and if they should succeed in learning her whereabouts—"

"They will not," Nathanos interrupted sternly. "She will triumph over them both, and why?"

Sira stared at him, silent, and yet she shifted forward ever so slightly. At least she was listening.

"Because the Alliance leaders do not trust each other, they are fractured and in disarray. And the Horde? The Horde will prove even less competent. So many voices, each with their own agenda, their own secrets and needs? Impossible. They will accomplish nothing. No, we are most useful here, that is her determination and so we shall carry out her will."

After a moment, Sira gave him a wry smile. "Very well, Blightcaller. I am convinced."

"Good, see that you remain so. Bwonsamdi is a menace and

knows too much. Once he is dead and the Dark Lady's plans are in motion, there will be no more pain. We will be free of the cruelties of this world." He paused and watched the dark warden gather her helmet, standing and preparing to go. "This is an honor, Sira. The queen has so few loyal servants remaining, we who still stand must not disappoint her."

"My goddess abandoned me; Sylvanas provides the succor of flesh and blood that will suffice," she said, pausing at the door. The ship swayed, the timbers creaking softly beneath the crash of the waves. "For the moment."

And then he was alone. Nathanos stood and crossed to the curved windows that looked out onto the sea. A chill passed through him as his thoughts drifted, as ever, to his dark queen. To be so far from her was almost a physical pain, as if the tether that bound them grew taut and frayed with distance. Every moment plucked at that string, straining it further.

Nathanos closed his eyes, imagining the snow blowing in unforgiving white-and-silver drifts, a pair of bright crimson eyes piercing the storm.

"I will not fail you," he whispered.

A sharp knock came at the door, and he frowned, chiding himself for his sentimentality. Only the mission mattered, only the queen's vision.

"Enter."

The candles hanging in the great cabin illuminated the soft, pale face of Visrynn as she bowed and then pulled back her hood. She was a kaldorei dark ranger, the leaves tattooed on her face as crimson as her piercing eyes.

"Ah. There you are. Were you spotted?" Nathanos had long awaited word from the ranger, and seeing her safely returned put him more at ease.

"I believe I traversed the highlands unseen," Visrynn replied smoothly.

"You *believe*?" he scoffed, that ease tarnished. Examining her more closely, he noted a tattered and bloodied bandage around her left wrist. "Your belief is not satisfactory. There can be no mistakes, Visrynn. How exactly were you injured?"

"I ran afoul of some beasts in the highlands, nothing serious. I beseech you, Ranger Lord, there are more pressing matters. Lelyias tells me word has come from the rebels."

"And?"

"Apari's plan has failed. Our spies report Queen Talanji has returned to the palace this night, though some report a large stain on her gown. She may have been injured in the assassination attempt."

Nathanos refused to show his disappointment, though a single twitch in his jaw could not be stopped. For a moment, he considered the most effective approach. They were already conspiring with rebels; why not fan those flames hotter with the right misinformation. "Then come dawn we have much to do. Gather the rangers, Visrynn, and contact our eyes in the city. Have them spread rumors that the Horde has lost faith in the queen. Perhaps they are even seeking to usurp the kingdom for themselves."

"But—"

"We are not here to spread a campaign of truth," he snapped, whirling to face her. His fist fell with a deafening thump on the table. "We are here to create a campaign of fear. Let them doubt and debate, let them panic. We will make this girl regret ever turning her back on the Banshee Queen."

CHAPTER FIVE

Orgrimmar

High above the dusty thoroughfares of Orgrimmar, Zekhan found himself face-to-face with a demanding audience. He had hoped to spend the afternoon communing at the Western Earthshrine, a pocket of peace and tranquility, humming with the power of ancient stones and pillars shining with blue flames, bright with the laughter of fledgling shaman learning their craft.

Even under the shade of a low tent, the sun seemed to scorch. Zekhan sat cross-legged on the ground, wiping at the perspiration on his brow. He often yearned for the cool shelter of trees on the Echo Isles, the pockets of jungle there like oases, where an afternoon's work could be rewarded with a dip in the sea.

But those homey jungles had never felt farther away, and Zekhan couldn't shake the feeling that he had done something wrong. For one, he couldn't stop sweating.

"Was she really going to die!?" a young orc boy, no higher than Zekhan's knee, begged to know.

His interrogators were fierce indeed. Word had spread of his proximity to the assassination attempt, and every child shaman shirked their lessons to crowd around Zekhan and herd him into a corner. Now they stared at him with wide eyes, hands tucked up curiously under their chins.

"I bet she's the most beautifulest troll ever!" a pandaren girl murmured.

"I heard you got stabbed!"

"Let us see where they stabbed ya!"

"Children, children . . ." Zekhan chuckled, tamping down their flurry of questions with both hands. "Zekhan will tell ya the tale, though it might be too shockin' for your young ears . . ."

"Pfft, no! We can handle it," the orc boy, Aggu, cried. "Except maybe Yu Yi. She's a big stupid baby."

"Am not!" Yu Yi stuck out her tongue at him, her dark fur ruffled with irritation.

"Are too!"

Zekhan laughed again, taking a scrap of linen from his pocket to wipe at his brow. "I won't be tellin' ya nothin' if this bickering keeps up."

The future pride of the Earthen Ring fell silent, though Zekhan remembered his youth well enough to know retaliatory pranks would come later. All six of the children and Zekhan jumped as a tear forced itself open in the bushes near the tent. The portal widened, crackling with electric blue energy, a pair of purple-silk-clad legs appearing an instant later, and then the whole nightborne as he emerged from the portal, dusting off his pristine livery.

Zekhan recognized the white-haired, narrow-faced elf; he often ran errands or delivered messages for the First Arcanist. If Zekhan had been nervously sweating before, now he was practically drenched. Whatever the man had come to say, it must be urgent, else he would have simply walked the distance from Grommash Hold to the shaman enclave.

"Sorry to interrupt," Lorlidrel smirked. He did not look very sorry. "The council requires your presence, Zekhan. Now."

"Noooo!" Yu Yi whined, turning and scowling at the nightborne. "You can't take him now!"

"He was just getting to the good part," Aggu added. "Let him finish the story!"

"I will not." Lorlidrel's lip curled as he matched Yu Yi's frown. She glanced away, frightened. "Zekhan has more pressing matters to attend to than the whims of children. I suggest you all return to your studies and forget this foolishness."

Zekhan hurried over to the elf and his portal, telling him in a low voice, "There's no need to scare them, yah? They're just kids."

The nightborne said nothing, and Zekhan knew better than to argue. Every bit of him wanted to stay at the shrines and entertain the fledglings, but he didn't dare keep Thrall and the others waiting. He squared his chest and stepped into the portal, bracing for the yank in his stomach that felt like it was pulling him inside out as they materialized in Grommash Hold an instant later.

Their arrival interrupted nothing. The hold sat strangely still and quiet, a sign, Zekhan thought, that they had been waiting only on him. The full might of the Horde Council sat before him in a half circle: the short, pointy-eared green goblin Gazlowe, followed by Baine Bloodhoof, First Arcanist Thalyssra, the hunched Forsaken Lilian Voss, Huojin monk Ji Firepaw, the former warchief Thrall toward the center, then finally the blood elf Lor'themar and Rokhan of the Darkspear trolls to Thrall's left.

They made for an intimidating sight.

"Thank you, Lorlidrel," First Arcanist Thalyssra told him smoothly. "Efficient as ever."

"Welcome, Zekhan." Ji Firepaw, speaker for the pandaren on the council, extended his hand graciously. Firepaw's red leather tunic shone brilliantly in the torchlight. Zekhan's interactions with the pandaren monk were limited, but Firepaw had always treated him with respect. "You performed a great service yesterday by protecting the Zandalari queen, but now, I'm afraid, we must ask even more of you."

"I only did what felt right," Zekhan said, a bit nervously. He felt his youth then, faced with the combined power and wisdom of all the Horde leadership. Even if he counted some of them as friends, his knees shook and his gut tightened, as if he were no more than one of those tiny shaman fledglings being disciplined for oversleeping or lighting a rival's hair on fire.

"And I told ya already," he went on, "it was mostly just an accident."

A chuckle of amusement rose from the eight assembled leaders. Thrall, sitting near the center of the crescent of chairs, rested his elbows on his knees, leaning forward. "Perhaps. But when that troll drew a knife, you did not hesitate to put yourself between that blade and the queen. An honorable instinct. An honorable *act*."

Zekhan smiled a little, releasing a pent-up breath. So he wasn't exactly in trouble, then. That was good. Maybe they wanted to give him a commendation of some kind. Or a promotion.

"No good deed goes unpunished," Lor'themar said, reclining with relaxed grace back in his spiked chair, fingers tented.

Zekhan gulped.

"P-punished?"

"Don't terrorize the boy," First Arcanist Thalyssra chided gently, her eyes sparkling as she gazed across the room at Lor'themar. "We are extending a great honor, an opportunity to prove yourself to the council, and to serve the Horde as ambassador to Zandalar."

Ambassador? Him?

Zekhan snorted, but nobody laughed along with him. "Oh. Oh, you're serious."

"Serious as an assassination attempt." To his left, Gazlowe, the goblin trade prince, did at least humor him with a chuckle. "Yes, kid, we're serious. Pack your bags, you're going to Zuldazar."

His immediate instinct was to look first to Thrall, then to Rokhan, the two council members he knew best. Rokhan held his gaze for a moment; the old veteran shadow hunter with his massive tusks and beady black eyes gave him a single nod of confidence.

"I've never been an ambassador before," Zekhan replied, squeezing his hands together behind his back.

"We need Talanji in this accord," Thrall explained to him steadily, slowly, as if the shock of the appointment had addled Zekhan's wits. "She has lost faith in us, but you . . . you risked your life to protect her. Your youth and inexperience will be an asset, Zekhan."

"She will most likely underestimate you. Use that to your advantage. Be our eyes and ears," First Arcanist Thalyssra suggested.

"Report to us as often as you can," Lor'themar continued. "Any shifts in mood, any strange happenings in the city, any information at all you can gather on her is useful. We cannot lose her as an ally; her city is strategically vital as a resupply point for our ships."

Zekhan listened so carefully he felt his ears twinge. The room fell silent again, and he forced himself not to shrink back.

"Do you accept?" Thalyssra pressed. "We would know your answer. Time is of the essence."

Did he have a choice? Zekhan didn't ask, but he knew that question lingered between them. Making his way to Orgrimmar and earning the favor of Thrall had seemed like the accomplishment of his life. The war had carried him so far, from crumbling battlements in the company of a legendary soldier like Varok Saurfang to the cruel mak'gora before the gates of Orgrimmar that finally took the orc's life.

It felt like a lifetime had passed between his first taste of battle on the fields of Tirisfal Glades and the moment when he watched Saurfang fall to the Banshee Queen's foul magic. He wondered what the grizzled old veteran would say if he could see Zekhan standing there before the council, struggling to accept an honor he might have earned but was not sure he deserved.

As if in answer, he felt, as he sometimes did in moments of confusion, the echo of his ancestors, a voice and a presence there with him, bolstering his spirits. A heavy hand with a heavier gauntlet landed on his shoulder, but it was not his father's energy urging him to hold his head high. Instead, he felt Saurfang's presence, his strength and his experience solid as a bulwark. Even if he had sometimes spied weariness or regret in Saurfang's eyes, he had never sensed weakness.

"Is . . . is this all right? Talanji is our friend, no? But now we're spyin' on her?" Zekhan asked, fidgeting.

"We do not send ya to do harm," Rokhan assured him. "We cannot help her if we do not know her mind."

Zekhan stared at him for a long moment, but Rokhan looked so calm, so confident. There wasn't a glimmer of mischief anywhere in his eyes. "Then I accept."

"The council is dismissed," First Arcanist Thalyssra declared. "We wish you all haste and good fortune, Zekhan. We know you will not fail us."

Before he could respond, everyone was standing. After Talanji's unhappy exit from the summit, the leadership had locked themselves inside Grommash Hold, no pages or advisers or assistants allowed. His mother would do something similar to him and his brothers when they bullied one another, forcing them to sit down in the family hut and argue and scream until all of it was out, and life could go on. They were in the hold for hours and hours, but apparently all the screaming and arguing had worked.

One by one the leaders walked by him and out of the hold; some clasped his forearm in a show of confidence, others simply nodded. Gazlowe gave him a wink.

Thrall and Rokhan of the Darkspear came last, staying a moment with him as the hold grew empty and the only sound inside became the blood pounding in Zekhan's ears and the spit and crackle of the torches. Rokhan heaved a great sigh, then shot Thrall a sidelong glance.

"Ya think he can do it?" he asked, as if Zekhan were not there at all.

"I think the young queen will find his presence less revolting than mine or yours," Thrall said, half teasing.

"Why?" Zekhan's mouth had gone bone dry. "Why can't you go? I'm . . . I'm nobody."

"Saurfang didn't think so," Thrall replied. "I don't think so, either. There are things I must do, places I must go. Yukha brought dire news from the Earthen Ring, and while you take your place among the Zandalari, I will be taking my own journey. The council has decided that some of us must join Yukha in Nordrassil, to better understand the unrest in the spirit realm. There I . . . well. It is best simply to go and not to hope."

Thrall put his hand on Zekhan's shoulder, and it felt almost exactly like the grasp of the presence that had joined him just a moment before. Then the orc left, braids swaying with each heavy tread, his chest canted forward slightly, as if the mantle of burdens and exhaustion he wore had finally grown too heavy to shoulder.

"Take this." Rokhan produced a dagger from his belt of many blades. It was light and well balanced, with a series of enameled runes along the crossbar. "We sendin' ya into a pit of vipers, boy. There will be more assassins, more danger. Ya might have a shaman's powers, but a blade on ya belt means ya are never unarmed, even when ya strength is spent."

Zekhan took the dagger, cradling it carefully in both hands. “Thank you, Rokhan, but I don’t know how to fight well with it.”

The Darkspear troll took his thumb and pressed it hard to Zekhan’s temple.

“It’s instinct, all instinct. Think like a shaman, boy.” He nodded to the dagger. “Fight like a soldier. And for your sake: Blend like a shadow.”

CHAPTER SIX

Stormwind

"How many?"

The king of Stormwind listened to the final cathedral bells tolling, the day's last rays of sunlight spearing the stained-glass windows above, casting mournful blue and purple shadows across the high altar. It was a melancholy image, one that only widened the pit in Anduin's stomach. He waited in the echo of the bells while the soft-spoken Bishop Arthur, clad all in cream, black and gold, unlocked the door leading to the crypts beneath the Cathedral of Light.

"Six." The answer came from Anduin's close friend and trusted adviser, Genn Greymane, king of Gilneas. "Or rather, SI:7 discovered six. No one can say how many were washed away by the tides."

"More could be in hiding," High Exarch Turalyon pointed out. He stood tall and broad, his Light-forged armor a polished and impressive silver and gold. Bearded, scarred, Turalyon looked every inch the tried and hardened warrior. The two men followed

Anduin down the winding path that snaked into the catacombs. "Shaw sent at least a dozen to monitor the waters between the Zandalari coast and the Eastern Kingdoms."

"Let us go where there are no curious ears," Anduin told them in a whisper.

Though the cathedral had largely emptied out after the evening service, a few brothers and priests remained. Of course they looked; who would not be eager to see the king of Stormwind present, and accompanied by two such illustrious warriors? To the people of Stormwind, Turalyon in particular was practically a myth. His noble likeness had been forever commemorated as a statue in the Valley of Heroes, rising above the bridge leading into Stormwind. He had helped forge the Knights of the Silver Hand, companion to heroes of legend and song like Uther the Lightbringer and Tirion Fordring.

All three stowed their conversation, making the long, sober descent into the crypts. Anduin hurried, though he dreaded what awaited him below. Yet he went, for it was his duty to see what had befallen troops dispatched in his name.

The air grew colder, the scent of mud and brick reminding him of rainy autumn days. The fetor of stale air and dust followed, then a light perfume of dried flowers and herbs, a weak defense against the unmistakable odor of fresh rot. Fresh death.

At the very bottom of the crypts, where it was chill enough to bother even a man dressed all in furs, they found a row of bodies. Each was laid out and still in their sodden clothing, skin discolored, lips twisted in the agony of a mortal scream. Turalyon snatched a torch off the wall and charged ahead, sweeping the light over the corpses, his stoically handsome face pinched with concern.

"Look at the precision," he said, standing before one young dwarf, his reddish beard full of sand and bits of seaweed. "One shot directly to the heart."

Greymane joined the paladin at that body, carefully inspecting the arrow left sticking from the dwarf's chest. "They are all like this. A single deadly shot. Mark the fletching on the arrows here and here—it has been shaved down."

"That was why Shaw ordered them brought here," Turalyon continued, his eyes fixed on the deceased dwarf lying between them. Anduin had never seen the war-forged paladin look afraid, and it was not fear in the man's eyes then. Not fear, but rage.

"What am I not seeing?" Anduin asked, frowning.

"Zandalari arrows," Turalyon replied. "But these are not Zandalari tactics."

"I should think not! This is some mischief, some . . . some dark mischief I do not yet understand." Greymane paced, lips curled as if a low worgen's growl might emanate from his throat at any second. "There are few archers in the world that could make these shots, my king. The only sort I know are allied with the infernal Banshee Queen."

"Dark rangers?" Anduin murmured, eyes darting between the two men. "Can we be certain?"

"Certain? No, but I've seen a damned mess of their arrows in my time, and the style matches, and so does the accuracy," Greymane huffed, pacing faster, every bit the caged and furious wolf.

"What would the dark rangers be doing in Zandalar? The Zandalari are allies of the Horde, and that would not make them friend to Sylvanas or her rangers." Anduin had nearly put his hand down on one of the soldiers' boots. Distracted, he had forgotten they were in the presence of the dead. But now he looked closer and felt keenly the stab in his chest. *By the Light, they were all so terribly young . . .*

He took small, cold comfort in the thought that at least the soldiers were home and protected in a sanctuary of the Light.

"It could be a warning from Sylvanas; perhaps she sent her

rangers to punish the new queen. The Dark Lady was still warchief when they made their alliance, but our spies believe Queen Talanji has pulled her support and remains largely independent. We all know how well Sylvanas takes betrayal . . ." Turalyon said gravely.

Anduin nodded, considering the paladin's point of view, but Greymane had other ideas, tossing up his hands in frustration.

"This is our opportunity, Anduin, don't you see it? Where Sylvanas goes, her dark rangers are sure to follow. She may be close at hand, and these murders her critical mistake. We should gather what forces we can spare and sail west. Whether she is in league with the Zandalari or moving against them matters not, we must not squander a chance to *finish this*."

He ended with a resounding note to his already galvanizing baritone, but Anduin didn't move. Instead, he stared resolutely at Turalyon, who appeared unconvinced at best. The paladin shifted in his heavy golden plate armor, a crease of worry between his brows.

"Now is the time to think, my king, not the time to react. There are still spies unaccounted for in the field, and we must not forget the armistice. Zandalar is a vast continent, certainly, but the eyes there are friendly to the Horde, not to the Banshee Queen." He tucked a fist under his chin thoughtfully. "The Horde wants her dead as much as we do. The armistice you signed is meaningless if we cannot rely on the Horde to share intelligence of this nature."

"The armistice," Greymane hissed, obviously not enthused. "We can rely on the Horde for nothing. How many times must we learn this lesson, Anduin? I know you know better."

Anduin did. He did not necessarily trust the Horde, but he did weigh their actions. Were they untrue to their words, they would have assassinated him and his Alliance generals outside the gates of Orgrimmar before or after the mak'gora.

He waited a moment, hoping Greymane would calm down, but the man's face had turned red with fury, his thick white whiskers bristling.

"Genn." Anduin tore his eyes away from his adviser and friend, instead raking his gaze across the bodies laid before them. "Rash action has harmed us far more often than care and caution. I will not overcommit to what could be a diversion."

High Exarch Turalyon nodded his agreement.

"We must ask ourselves: Why would Sylvanas go to Zandalar? What would she want there?"

"What does it matter?" Greymane thundered. "You said it yourself, Turalyon, the Zandalari queen pledged herself to Sylvanas first. Perhaps that vow remains true. Perhaps she has turned her back on the Horde and even now shelters the traitor and her soldiers." He gestured to the fallen spies. "Perhaps these brave few were killed for discovering the truth."

Anduin had a duty to the truth, whatever it might be. Both men provided opinions he valued, but he could not deny that Turalyon offered the more tempting take. Still. *Still.*

"I am reminded, my noble friends," Anduin began softly, "of a day not so long ago, and not so far from here. A placid place in the Arathi Highlands. A gathering meant to be peaceful, a gathering meant to reunite families torn asunder by forces they could never have foreseen . . ." He sighed, leaning forward, resting his knuckles on the edge of the stone slab. "Human and Forsaken families met in good faith, trying to find common ground and common love, and many did. For their trust, for their grace, they received only slaughter." He lifted his gaze to Greymane, who had gone mercifully still, the flush in his face fading. "I give your recommendations equal weight. Turalyon, take Alleria Windrunner and investigate these deaths."

Standing tall again, Anduin pressed his hand over his heart, finding that Turalyon regarded him with a sure smile. He approved. "I name you Lord Commander of the Alliance forces. Your task—your only task—is to find Sylvanas Windrunner so we might bring her to proper justice. Hunt her day and night; use whatever means you must."

Turalyon bowed his head with practiced gentility, accepting the honor and the charge with a humble, "My heart and my sword to the cause."

Together, the kings of Gilneas and Stormwind watched the paladin go, his mail and plate clanking quietly, the torchlight gilding him from head to foot as he left on his sworn mission.

"A wise choice, your majesty." Greymane clasped his hands together when they were alone in the gloom and chill. "Who knows what devil's tricks Queen Talanji learned from Sylvanas. There are insects under every rock in every kingdom, even your own."

"I pray you are wrong," Anduin replied. He strangely wanted to stay in the crypt, to sit there among the dead and know their pain, their stories. It seemed easier than facing another day of frustration and failure. But the bodies had to be washed and the proper rites given. "By the Light, Genn, I will see them given all due honor. How can I write the name of every soldier in stone, on the stars, so that they are never forgotten?"

"They knew what it was to serve, Anduin. They were not expecting the life of a baker or tailor," Genn said, placing a mollifying hand on Anduin's back. "They knew."

Anduin turned away, shrugging off the man's hand. He felt the cold in his marrow as he left the safety of the torches. "No, Genn, I don't think they did know. None of us do. None of us know what awaits us in death, what awaits us in the dark without a dawn."

CHAPTER SEVEN

Dazar'alor

"The petitioner's request is hereby . . ." Talanji felt every onlooker and gawker inhale with anticipation. She let the moment hang, enjoying the undivided attention. Of all the many tasks assigned to a queen, this might be her favorite. "Granted."

The word rained down from the throne like a handful of generously tossed coins. The audience in the council chamber erupted in cheers. And then there was the petitioner in question, a young girl no more than seventeen years old. She blushed at the resounding appreciation of the crowd, her family rushing to embrace her. Her father, Bezime, hugged her tightest of all, having just given a heartfelt speech in his daughter's defense. "If you must, punish me, Queen Talanji, but do not punish my daughter. She is my light, she is the heart of our family, and all of our hopes go with her."

His clear devotion to his daughter's happiness moved Talanji, reminding her of her own deeply missed father. Soldiers and ships

Talanji might not have had to give, but gold she possessed, and gold the girl had needed.

The girl now beaming ear to pierced ear, Nav'rae, bowed several times toward the throne, carried out of the chamber on a tide of good will. She belonged to one of the struggling noble houses that had been punished and shamed for their ties to the traitor Yazma. While Talanji traveled to Orgrimmar to treat with the Horde, the Zanchuli Council, comprised of warriors, priests, and advisers loyal to Talanji, had found the family cleared of any wrongdoing. That pronouncement did not, however, fill their depleted coffers with gold, and left the young troll Nav'rae too impoverished to honorably marry her love, whose rich and admired family had avoided the stain of betrayal.

Outside on the balcony, Nav'rae's betrothed, Khila, waited, hands clasped nervously under her chin, her shoulders draped in a beautifully beaded cloak, preemptively celebratory. Now nothing stopped the two young girls from marrying, and Talanji felt a blossom of warmth over her heart as the petitioners made their triumphant exit, flowers and seeds tossed joyfully in the air. Khila had worn the right cloak after all.

"Fortune and health to them both," the first and only tortollan on the council, Lashk, murmured.

"Happy small things," Jo'nok, Bulwark of Torcali, added. The dire troll, far too large for any of the council seats, simply stood to Lashk's side. "Good to see. Boring, but good."

Two dozen or so Zandalari mingled still in the council chambers, separated from where the council itself sat by tall steps. A series of more manageable stairs ran up the center toward where Talanji and the others heard cases and claims and handed down decisions. A spotless blue sky fell like a curtain behind the petitioners, the chamber open to the outside and to the skyterrors circling majestically over the city.

It had been a long day. A grueling day. Petitioner after petitioner, request upon request. A queen's time was never truly her own. It was a sacrifice she made gladly—her people were her greatest pride.

"The light of the loa shine on us, I think that was the last one." High Prelate Rata sighed, standing with a stretch. Yellowed bones protected her rib cage and shoulders, an unwashed spill of blue hair tumbling over one eye. Talanji had watched her nearly doze off as Nav'rae presented her case. Minor house love stories were not the compelling cases Rata enjoyed adjudicating.

Yet the crowd below them parted, a cry going up. Someone forced their way through, arms waving over their head as they shouted, grabbing the attention of all those left milling in the chamber.

Wardruid Loti sighed, slumping back in her chair, her tusk-adorned pauldrons clacking against the gold-enameled seat. "Gonk carry me away, it never ends . . ."

"Is it true?" The troll shoving his way forward was tall, thin, four spikes of green hair jutting forward from his head. He had the sunburned, coarse look of a laborer, a heavy pack strapped to his back. "Is it true what they say? The Horde tried to kill the queen! They want to depose her, take the city for themselves!"

Whatever peace they had hoped to bring to the chamber was broken. To her right, Lashk audibly groaned, his green beak falling into the cushion of his palm.

"Justice!" someone below shouted. "Is it true? Justice!"

"Horde defilers! Traitors!"

Talanji leaped to her feet. "Silence, now. Silence. These rumors are just that. Rumors." Tired, exasperated, she fought for the right words. The quelling words. The last thing she needed was more unrest in the city. General Rakera had greeted her that morning with dire news—word of the assassination attempt had reached

Dazar'alor, and worse, whispers of missing patrols, violence encroaching on the northern borders.

"But we part of de Horde!" a voice carried from below.

"Who tried to kill our queen?" came another.

"You want me to stab them all?" General Rakera whispered with a snort.

Talanji glanced her way, managing a wry smile. "Yes, we are part of the Horde, but only if they support us as we deserve." She raised her voice, but the irritating gossipy whispers persisted. They smelled scandal, more potent than blood. "They will meet our demands, the demands of Zandalar. We will not serve them unless they serve us, too."

"There!"

"Look! One of them, not our kind, not Zandalari . . ."

"An assassin!"

The cries and shocked calls crested again, an indignant tide, the petitioners below swarming, forming a shifting barrier around a new arrival. Talanji squinted, trying to make out just who had entered the council chambers. He had come flanked by two royal guards, their armor as embellished and beautiful as the stranger's clothes were simple and nondescript. Yet something about him scratched at Talanji's brain. She knew him. How did she know him?

"Horde! He's from the Horde! Make him explain! You did not protect our queen, why did ya not protect her!?" The troublemaker who had come with the pack and sunburned face turned quickly on the stranger. He shoved him, making the troll's shockingly red hair sway as he stumbled to the side. The guards intervened, but that only made the crowd rowdier. Soon, all Talanji could see of the new arrival was the top tufts of his hair and the royal guards' halberds towering above the throng.

A strangled cry came from within the swirling mass of bodies. Talanji could not afford to have the death of a Horde ambassador on her hands. A rebellion grew in her city, and the death of her father had not yet been repaid. She might yet need the Horde, as much as it chafed her pride.

"Stop!"

Another cry. Even her own guards seemed swallowed by the chaos.

"*Stop*. Let him pass."

At last, Talanji's voice had the desired effect, freezing everyone in the room, resonant with a queen's power. The crowd stilled, then parted, and a narrow lane appeared, allowing the Horde troll to hurry forward. He brushed off his shoulders and arms, throwing a wary backward glance at the swarm before taking a few shuffling steps toward the council stairs.

"I know you," Talanji said softly, her memories of him at last becoming clear. She gestured toward the guards still stationed behind him. "Remove the petitioners. This meeting of the council is at an end. I will meet with this . . . this traveler."

She had left Orgrimmar in such a hurry that she had never learned the troll's name. Now it struck her as a mistake, for while her relationship with the Horde Council remained in flux, this one jungle troll had saved her life.

"Come," she called down to him. "State your business."

The red-haired troll bowed artlessly but with enthusiasm. "I am here to serve as ambassador to the Horde. My name is Zekhan. A-Ambassador . . . Zekhan."

Talanji lifted a brow.

"Ambassador?" General Rakera spat. "Try *spy*."

Zekhan nodded, pointing to the stunned general. "Yes. Spy. Ambassador. Spy. Eyes. Ears." He shrugged, laughing helplessly. "Nose. Mouth? The Horde worry about ya. More than that, they want your friendship, Queen Talanji, and they won't be givin' up."

"Evidently," she drawled, looking him up and down. "Well. They could have sent worse."

They could have sent Thrall. Thrall, whom she might never trust for his stubborn loyalty to Jaina Proudmoore.

The troll below her let out another nervous guffaw. "I'll take it."

"You want Jo'nok smash him?" Jo'nok offered, more than capable of doing so, his bulk making him look like a direhorn among ants.

"No, Jo'nok, he is under my protection."

Talanji pressed her palms together, inspecting the "ambassador" for a long moment. Her instinct was to send him away, but then what courtesy would that show when he had knocked the poisoned cup from the assassin's hand and then tossed himself in front of a deadly blade? She felt the burning gaze of her father spear through her. Burning and disapproving. He had trusted her judgment when she invited the Horde to Zandalar, believed her even after she went behind his back to do so. Even if it pained her to admit as much, Zekhan deserved a chance. The troll fidgeted, nervous, young. She could find some use for him or simply use his inexperience to gain information about her allies that he did not mean to give.

"Approach, Ambassador Zekhan, if you are going to serve in this palace, then you must know its many twisting halls." She clearly heard General Rakera inhale with disgust through her teeth. Talanji ignored her. "Come, climb the stairs. I will be your guide."

"I thought Orgrimmar was impressive but this . . . this . . ."

Talanji smirked, watching the jungle troll spin in a circle, his mouth open in a perpetual O of wonder. Sometimes she forgot the beauty of the palace, its halls of gold and turquoise, the restful pools filled with fragrant lilies and the tiles underfoot that sparkled like cut gems. And she was not immune to the delight of seeing a provincial jungle boy step into halls of ancient splendor.

"Nothin' like this in the Echo Isles," Zekhan added. "Ruins, sure. This be like somethin' from a dream!"

The lower halls of the palace retained a cavelike shaded cool, away from the glaring sun that provided light for the upper chambers and throne room. There, shallow gutters trickling with water ran alongside them, colorful mosaics spreading out below their feet. The jungle troll possessed a seemingly endless capacity for astonishment, and more than once Talanji felt the urge to reach over and clack his lower jaw shut.

"The palace has always been my home," Talanji told him. Two royal guards flanked them, maintaining a cautious distance. "I forget what it must look like to outsiders."

"Ha." Zekhan clutched his belly and laughed. "My palace was sand and shrub. My whole village could fit in ya royal closet."

Talanji grinned as they rounded a corner and, distracted, she had not realized they had reached the heart of the pyramid. Her steps stuttered, and she struggled to keep her smile plastered on. She did whatever she could to avoid this wing of the palace. Just glancing down the corridor and into the tall, golden hall filled her heart with dread.

"Somethin' the matter?" Zekhan asked, frowning. "Your majesty?"

"I remember loving this place. This hall . . ." Talanji forced herself to take another step and then another, trembling as memory overtook her, plunging her into darkness. The floors had been cleaned, of course, and the mess long ago sorted, but the place where her father died would forever be tainted. She could still feel the warmth leaving his flesh as she held him, the star-bright strength in his eyes fading, his hand becoming limp as Bwonsamdi claimed his soul.

Holding him there, the cold tiles biting into her knees, rage making her choke, she knew true loneliness. All her life, Rastakhan had watched over her, taught her, loved her, fighting to protect their legacy and their land, afraid, she came to see, of only one thing: disappointing his daughter.

And in the end . . . In the end . . .

"I played here as a child," Talanji said softly. Other memories came, happier ones. Her tutor strumming a harp while she held her breath and tried her best to hide under the water of the pools. "With my friend, Parri. She and I would chase each other here for hours. Play hide and seek. She always won, always held her breath under the water longer . . ." She sighed and shook her head. "I think I was that little girl again when my father died here. It made me feel small, a child taking a crown, just playing at being a queen."

The ambassador said nothing, staring at her.

"This is where I learned the true cruelty of the Alliance and their cursed witch, Jaina Proudmoore. She has always been a snake, treacherous and selfish. I spit on this armistice your council has negotiated. It ignores the pain of my people, it ignores our suffering."

Wringing his hands, Zekhan hesitated, then rushed into his speech. "B-but Proudmoore helped us free Baine. And she was there to stand with us against Azshara. You said you felt like a little girl when you took up your father's crown, but you changed. Folk . . . change." Zekhan hung his head, hands clasped loosely in front of his belt. "You be a real queen now. I saw it with me own eyes. The way you commanded your people, the way you speak . . . your people listen. The Horde be listenin', too."

Talanji spun to face him. "And you will tell them about this, then?"

The jungle troll shrugged, walking slowly toward her and then deeper into the chamber at the heart of the pyramid, his eyes turned up to the ceiling as he gazed around. "No, ya majesty. Your grief is your own." He stooped to push his hand through one of the crystalline pools. She thought she saw a far-off smile flash across his face for an instant. "I lost people, too. One father, and then another."

"Another?" she asked.

"Our high overlord who fell at the mak'gora to the Banshee Queen's magic. He . . . he wasn't perfect, he was a killer, I know that. Not *just* a killer. What he did to the elves, to their tree, that is something too big for me to judge. But he taught me how to be a soldier. How to stand tall. His lessons are firm, but me? I . . . I'm not so steady: I see the mak'gora over and over again in me head, and each time I be wonderin' if it could be different. If I could have changed things." Zekhan stood, wiping the clean water on his face. "But Saurfang is gone and nothin' will change that. I only hope Bwonsamdi helped him to his rest, maybe you could ask. He is close to ya, after all."

Talanji stiffened. "Not that close."

"No?" Zekhan tilted his head to the side. "Ya throne is tied to the loa of graves, or that's what they say."

"And who is *they*?"

The troll's eyes widened in confusion. "Everyone, ya majesty. Everyone."

The queen sagged, tired. It was foolish to argue with him, to rage against the truth. She only wondered just how much the Horde knew of her blood pact to the loa.

"Hm. You're smarter than you look, ambassador," Talanji said, eyeing him closely.

Before the troll could respond, she noticed movement over his shoulder. The two royal guards stationed at the open doorway to the chamber snapped to attention. One slid into the corridor, tall, bladed weapon at the ready.

"What is it?" Talanji demanded, pushing past Zekhan and toward the guards.

"My queen—"

The spear struck the guard in the unlucky gap between helm and breastplate. The protector still living swiveled to block the entrance to the chamber, keeping well clear of the sightline that had been her partner's doom.

Talanji shrieked. Her first thought was: *How?* How could rebels make it so deep into the palace? The thought immediately following was one of determination. *I will not fall here, not where my father breathed his last . . .*

"Stay behind me!" the guard called back to them. Talanji scrambled to recall her name. She scrambled to remember anything. *Breathe. Breathe.* Her name was Mah'ral, and she had stood in the vanguard during both the blood troll invasion and later the Alliance raid on the palace. A veteran. Reliable.

Talanji sprang forward, joining Mah'ral at the door, and Zekhan followed, close on her heels. The corridor filled with voices, bloodthirsty whoops that quieted eerily into a single, unified chant.

"Hunt the queen! Hunt the queen! Hunt the queen!"

"Is there another way out of here?" Zekhan murmured, glancing over his shoulder several times.

"No." Talanji closed her eyes, gathering her powers to her hands. The loa would protect them. This was her ground, her territory, and the strength of her ancestors and their gods would fly to her side. "We stand here and we fight."

"As the queen commands." Zekhan was not without defenses, pulling a dagger from his belt, the blade igniting with lightning as he held it high, imbuing it with power.

"They're comin'!" Mah'ral shouted.

Too many, Talanji thought. *There are too many!*

In the chaos she wasted no time counting, but at least a dozen lightly armored, spear-wielding trolls barreled into the chamber. The first two slammed hard into Mah'ral's halberd, jolted back, falling into their brethren and creating an opening for a counter-attack.

"Loa protect us!" Talanji cried, a shimmering shield bubbling forward from her open hands, enveloping her, Mah'ral, and Zekhan. A spear bounced uselessly off it, clattering to the floor.

Mah'ral swung her halberd down and out, striking the first two trolls, their faces streaked with white and black paint, to the floor. Blood leaked around them. It was no deterrent to the others, who did not hesitate to step on their fallen brethren and leap toward the royal guard. They dropped their weapons, both clinging to the long, sturdy handle of Mah'ral's halberd, twisting against her until her grip failed and she was forced to retreat behind Talanji's protective shield.

"Watch ya head!" The flames building on Zekhan's dagger shot forward, taking one of the halberd thieves by surprise. The other kept hold of the weapon, using it like a spear to jab at Mah'ral, but she dodged, grabbing a small knife from the golden belt around her waist.

Furious shouts echoed from down the hall and Talanji's heart sank. They might hold off these few rebels, but if reinforcements arrived, they would surely be overtaken.

But the rebels did not rally, and they did not cheer. She watched them try to scatter, panicking as royal guards from elsewhere in the palace descended. The halberd thief swore, darting forward, trying to clear a path, but Mah'ral disarmed him, taking back her weapon and using the handle to swat him hard in the forehead.

Talanji called out to her guards before the slaughter could begin. "I want them alive!"

But none surrendered. They hurtled toward the guards, impaling themselves on the sharp and ready halberds aimed in their direction. Talanji gritted her teeth, furious and frustrated, then gasped as the final rebel left standing careened toward them. He wore a curious black mask streaked with white, his eyes flashing crazed behind the slits as the edges of his body erupted in strange green flames. Her protective shield cracked down the middle, and with another stride he was upon her, jagged little knife pressed to her throat.

"The Widow's Bite be here, traitor queen," he whispered, tackling her roughly to the ground. "They be all around ya!"

A sudden plume of blue smoke rose behind him. The room grew colder, a strange rattling exhale like a final breath . . . One huge, bony finger tapped on the masked troll's shoulder and he jumped, turning.

The gruesome visage of Bwonsamdi hovered right before the troll's face.

"*Boo.*"

As abruptly as he had come, he was gone. Bwonsamdi vanished. But the distraction was enough. The troll's mouth twisted, hanging open, the light in his eyes extinguished. Talanji heard the squelch of a dagger, but it was not slicing into her own throat, rather into his. His mask sizzled with lightning and then his hair, Zekhan's blade jutting out from the rebel's neck.

Talanji pushed him off, rolling, gasping for air as the heavy body slumped lifeless to the floor.

The Widow's Bite. She shook her head, disbelieving. They were followers of Shadra, of Yazma, but both the loa and the high priestess were dead.

"The queen!" her guards were crying, swarming to her side. "The queen!"

"*Pah.* I'm fine," she grunted, sitting up. "Tell me there are survivors."

"None." Mah'ral offered Talanji her hand. "They all rushed our blades, killed themselves."

Talanji climbed to her feet with the guard's assistance and glared around at the blood and death heaped once more on the floors of the Heart of the Empire. Thrall was right. Bwonsamdi was right. The assassins would not stop coming. How could she call herself a true queen of the Zandalari when her people remained divided? While the insurrection remained, all that she had hoped to protect and build remained in danger.

"Just like the assassin," she murmured, kneeling to inspect the masked rebel. The fire had gone out, but not before consuming half of his face. "They die for their cause. Die . . . to kill me." She inched back from the dead troll's blood pooling toward her. Slowly, she turned and regarded the ambassador of the Horde. The Horde. When her father died in that chamber she had been alone, but now she saw an ally staring back at her. One who had now protected her twice.

"Double the patrols. Seal the palace. I must speak to the council, Zekhan, and then we have much to discuss."

CHAPTER EIGHT

Dazar'alor

"Now look at us! We make quite a team, little zappy boy."

Zekhan flattened himself against the council chamber door. Instinctively, he held out the dagger to the loa before him, a meager but last-minute tribute. He trembled. Did . . . did the loa of graves just call him *zappy* boy? Who was he to argue? Especially with a god. Voices drifted out from inside, but his only concerns at the moment were the blood drying on his hand and the loa of graves, Bwonsamdi, levitating with a smile in front of a golden flowerpot. Talanji had commanded Zekhan to wait outside while she addressed the Zanchuli Council's concerns about the attack; she had not warned him that a god would be keeping him company.

"You're . . . you're Bwonsamdi. What c-could ya want with me?" Zekhan stammered. Bwonsamdi didn't seem interested in his dagger, and it felt weird to hold it out to him still, so Zekhan gingerly tucked it back into his belt.

"Ah, so ya mouth does work. And ya eyes. That's good, boy. I *could* want one thing from ya, and that's to give my thanks."

Zekhan wasn't certain he had heard him right. "Thank me? For what?"

"Protectin' my investment."

Zekhan's mouth felt bone dry. A high whining noise in his ears sounded a constant warning, and so he resorted to staring, worried he might say or do the wrong thing. He was, after all, speaking to a loa. Growing up with tales of the trickster god had not left Zekhan prepared to deal with the real thing. He was gigantic, and Zekhan felt slightly nauseated in his presence, an aura of rot and darkness swirled around the loa.

Bwonsamdi snorted and then sighed dramatically. "Ya lives are all so adorably fleetin'. Ya come and go, but some of you be comin' and goin' in more interesting ways." He tilted his head toward the council chamber.

Talanji.

"I don't know if that's true . . ." Zekhan scratched nervously at the back of his head, then remembered his hand was covered in blood and stopped. "It feels like I'm just in the right place at the right time."

"And?" Bwonsamdi bellowed out a laugh. "How do ya think the powerful become that way? It ain't always their smarts, let me assure you."

Zekhan shook his head, still pinned against the council door. The voices from within grew louder, more agitated. "I don't want power, I just want to make the Horde Council happy. They sent me to watch the queen, that's all I aim to do."

Stroking his chin thoughtfully, Bwonsamdi leaned closer to the flowerpot to his left, the flowers there recoiling, wilting. "So what do you think of her, then, our queen?"

Zekhan held out his hand, the one still coated in the masked assassin's blood. "I think she's in trouble."

"Ya see clearly, boy," the loa replied. His blue fire eyes burned hotter, and Zekhan felt that sourness in his gut worsen. "There is trouble everywhere. A sickness festers. Here, with ya Horde, and in me own domain . . ."

Zekhan swallowed around a bundle of thorns. The loa drew closer, sizing him up; the stench of decay followed the god, clinging to him as strong as a blood elf's perfume. His eyes must have betrayed his fear. The loa chuckled softly, bearing down on the troll until they were nose to nose.

"Ya eyes tell me everythin', boy," Bwonsamdi growled. "'Tis time I showed you my gratitude. Ya helped save the queen twice now, and that deserves a gift. Will you accept?"

The ringing in Zekhan's ears intensified. Never in his life had he expected to be dealing with a loa directly, but he could practically hear his wise granny screaming at him from beyond the grave. How many stories had she told him that featured Bwonsamdi's legendary talent for tricks?

He swallowed noisily again and glanced at his feet. "What's the gift?"

"Can't tell you that. But I can tell ya this: 'Tis a vision of death. A vision ya will be wantin' to see. How about a gift for a gift?" Bwonsamdi's skeletal grin chilled Zekhan to the bone. "Take this vision of death from me; in return, ya make sure one thing happens."

"If I have to give you something in return that's not a gift," Zekhan muttered.

"Do ya want it or not, boy?" Bwonsamdi thundered. The corridor shook, the meeting inside the chamber silent, as if they too had heard the loa's outburst.

"W-what do I have to do?" Zekhan asked. For the second time in as many days he found himself thinking: *Do I have a choice?*

"The Zandalari must remain with the Horde. She must sit on the council. Use all ya considerable charms, boy, and make her see that this is the only way. It be best for Zandalar, and even better, best for *me*," the loa said, nodding slowly as if hoping to fool the troll into nodding along with him.

Maybe it wasn't a trick after all. Zekhan was in Zuldazar for exactly that reason, to watch Talanji and hopefully sway her into trusting the Horde. It seemed, he thought with a grimace, too easy. A vision of death . . . Who would it be? His father, Hekazi, or maybe his mentor, Saurfang? Both were tempting.

"Why can't you convince her?" Zekhan pressed.

With a sneer the loa floated away, glancing at the flowers that had wilted from his proximity. "The queen doesn't like to take advice from old Bwonsamdi just now. But she might listen to you, mm?"

Inhaling deeply, he hoped his granny couldn't see him from the beyond, or she would be deeply disappointed to hear him say, "Show me this vision."

Bwonsamdi grinned, and the world went dark.

Is this death? Did he kill me?

For a long moment all was quiet, and he squirmed helplessly in a void that stretched indefinitely around him. Something cool and damp tickled the backs of his arms and his nape, and then in a blinding blink the sun appeared, detonating like goblin dynamite, blowing a hole in the inky nothingness above. The muted sounds of somber voices and clanging spears came and went, and then all was the comforting din of nature. Insects whirred, wings clicking delicately against a sea of grass as vast as the formless void it had replaced.

Standing, Zekhan reached out to brush his palm over the coarse, tall grass, finding it was not his hand at all, but one much larger, stronger, and scarred from war. Ahead of him, a smattering of mountains grew out of the ground, then settled, and across the horizon a herd of talbuk scattered, startled by something . . . someone . . .

"Father! That was an easy shot. Don't tell me age has made you soft!"

A tanned orc with a shock of black hair jogged up to meet him, his golden eyes wrinkled at the corners from smiling. His face, while that of an orc in his prime, was terribly familiar to him. *Wonderfully* familiar.

"Dranosh . . ."

The orc reached for another arrow in the leather quiver slung over his shoulder. "Wake up; another herd approaches. Mother will have our hides if we return empty-handed."

"Mother, Dranosh . . ." Memories flooded him, not his own, not Zekhan's, but Varok Saurfang's. These plains—each rock, each divot in the earth and hidden pool—were as known to him as the grip of his favorite axe. *Home*. He had come home.

"Remda," he whispered, his chest flooded with pain that flared and then ebbed, turning sweet. His wife. Saurfang's. They would be reunited, and beside the glow of a laden table and hearth, he would touch her face and run his thumb over lips long missed and almost forgotten.

"Father?" His son waited, eyeing him as if he might be wounded or dull.

"Yes. I'm ready, Dranosh, lead on."

Father and son turned toward the orange sun half eaten by the horizon, bows drawn, strides matched, the hunt awaiting them on the broken plains of Draenor.

That same sun blinded him again, devouring his vision, plunging Zekhan back into the shapeless void that had held him before. It thumped with a heartbeat, lazy but rhythmic, and then with a nauseating snap he felt the stone tiles of the palace slam into his feet. Reeling, Zekhan touched his own face, finding it troll-shaped once more, and feeling tears there that he hadn't known were falling. To return to his body, to the realm of the living, felt like a warm embrace. Relief overcame him, and he leaned back gratefully against the chamber door, Bwonsamdi staring at him with the palpable impatience of a prisoner awaiting the judge's verdict.

"Will it be like that for me?" he finally asked. "Will my fa'da be waiting for me?"

Bwonsamdi wagged a bony finger at him. "Now that would ruin the surprise. Did ya see what ya needed to see?"

Zekhan nodded. "I . . . think I did."

And in accepting the vision he had also taken Bwonsamdi's deal. Zekhan shuddered.

Chuckling, the loa gave him a theatrical bow. "Little Zekhan, walkin' in the footsteps of giants. But keep ya eyes up, eh? Even giants trip."

CHAPTER NINE

Arathi Highlands

"I know it's you, sister, do not hide. Sylvanas. Do not try to escape me, not this time. *Not this time.*"

Blazing red eyes skewered the shadows, hunting Alleria Windrunner. She wandered a sickly forest, withered trees with broken branches scratching at her cloak, scraping her cheek, breaking skin and drawing blood. She had thought herself the huntress, at last sensing the presence of her ignominious sister and following her trail, but now she was not so sure.

Now she had come to see that she was the hunted.

Thick tendrils of purple smoke curled at the edge of Alleria's vision. The forest, her sister—her own blighted vision—fought her. Yet she persisted, dodging from tree to tree with precise leaps, catching a glimpse of a cloak hem ahead. How many times had they played this game as children, giggling their way into the silver forests of Quel'Thalas with their sister Vereesa, all of them eager to play the huntress. All of them eager to prove their wit and their stealth.

"Close, now," she heard Sylvanas whispering to her through the knotted snarl of the brambles and trees. Her voice was little more than a silken thread leading her onward. "So very close, sister . . ."

"I will not stop hunting you," Alleria murmured. "I will never stop."

"Then what are you waiting for?"

Her voice filled Alleria's head like a clap of thunder. Sylvanas no longer raced ahead of her through the forest, but appeared directly behind her. Whatever foul magic she had used to win the mak'gora she utilized once more. Her Forsaken sister screamed, shadows pouring from her mouth, filling the woods, twisting around Alleria, smothering her with an icy grip.

"The whispers were right," Alleria managed to say. The shadows squeezed, robbing her of air. Every breath felt like sucking down shards of glass. "The Void, it told me to kill you. I should have done it. I should have listened."

Sylvanas stepped away, just a calm, scarred face framed by darkness. "You could never best me, sister. The end will come quickly now, you'll see."

Death crept nearer, and the Void called out to Alleria, begging her to give over her soul entirely and become a manifestation of power even greater than her sister. It was tempting. Oh, it was tempting.

Abandon your flesh, came the whispers. *Abandon your flesh.*

She gasped, desperate for one last breath to make her decision. That chance was stolen from her. In agony, two figures emerged from the shadows wreathing Sylvanas. One, lithe and blonde, shared Alleria's same small nose and pointed chin, a half-elf with long, golden hair, and eyes like the sun. The other was a human man, broad and bronzed as a paladin's shield.

"Arator! Turalyon!" If these were her last words, at least they were the names of those she loved most.

Half-elf and man didn't see her at all, staring straight ahead, their eyes glazed over with terror. Black veins spidered up their necks and across their faces, their skin going gray and ashen, their eyes hollowing until they were nothing but empty pits. Once hale bodies shriveled until their armor swallowed the pitiable skeletons, and then, in a blink, they were dust.

The shadows surrounding Alleria tightened until her eyes bulged. There would be no victory over this, no thrill of the hunt.

Sylvanas. There was only Sylvanas and the cruel delight dancing in her scarlet eyes.

"Did your little whispers tell you this, Alleria?" her sister taunted, stepping away, disappearing into the night. "Did they warn you that this would be the cost of standing against me?"

"NO!"

Alleria screamed herself awake, jerking hard to the right in her saddle, startling a neigh from her horse. A strong hand steadied her, clasping her shoulder, and Alleria shook off the delirium of her dream. Turalyon. His touch was soothing, and for an instant the terror of the dream dissipated. They walked separate paths—his of the Light, hers void-touched and dark. Their lives had grown only more complicated when N'Zoth the Corruptor invaded Azeroth, his efforts to spoil the planet for his own ends narrowly thwarted. Many mistrusted her even more now, and Alleria could not blame them. Turalyon doubtless had his concerns, but he was there, alive despite the nightmare's lies. He watched her closely, understandably grimacing with alarm.

"We've been riding all night," he told her. "You fell asleep in the saddle, Alleria. You were so quiet that I did not notice until now. That must have been some nightmare."

She sighed, wishing she could tell him more, knowing neither of them was ready for it. "You have no idea."

"We should stop soon," Turalyon said, gazing ahead. His skin seemed to absorb the moonlight that filtered through the midnight clouds, giving him a pleasant glow. They had just returned to the Thandol Span, having combed the highlands with two dozen soldiers searching for Horde travelers fleeing Stromgarde Keep. As they journeyed, she and Turalyon slept in separate tents, Alleria lying awake at night measuring the space between them, finding that when they were apart she missed him, but now that he was near she had no idea what to do with him. She had once wondered if the legacy of the Windrunners was death, but with Turalyon she had created new life, and she would always hold that like a shield against encroaching doubts.

He didn't acknowledge her sudden faraway look. "The men are exhausted, and a brief rest will lift their spirits. I could use a moment's stillness myself."

"No," Alleria replied, stony. "They can rest after we find these refugees."

"Alleria—"

"We ride on." She tossed a glance in his direction, and whatever Turalyon saw in her gaze convinced him to drop it. That was why their love had even a chance of enduring, that he could see the darkness in her and accept it. Many would consider their relationship an impossibility—Turalyon, forged in the exalted light of the naaru Xe'ra, and Alleria, imbued with the void energy of L'ura, were for all appearances too different to coexist peacefully. But Alleria saw the poetry in it. There was no Light without the Shadow, and a bond like theirs, fashioned in the fires of tragedy and strife, was not easily sundered.

"My lady! My lord!" The void elf captain Celosel Nightgiver appeared out of a spatial rift just down the road, accompanied by one of Turalyon's loyal lieutenants, a Light-forged draenei of uncommon beauty who simply went by Senn. She kept her distance from Nightgiver and shuddered with disgust as she quickly left the rift behind; the Light-forged probably thought that it would never spit her back out again.

"What have you found?" Alleria demanded, spurring her horse to meet them. The riders at her back joined, but more slowly, no doubt weary from nearly eight hours of patrol.

The purple light of the rift still clung to Celosel and Senn as she met them in the middle of the road. He gestured to a rise of hills north of the span. When Alleria squinted into the night, she noticed a thin ribbon of smoke rising toward the moons.

"Just as Trollbane instructed." She heard Turalyon canter up to her side.

"Are they on the move?" Alleria asked.

The draenei, her pearlescent hair swept into a crown of braids behind her horns, strode back toward the column of riders, seeking out her mount. "No, they look entrenched. Not much of a watch set, mostly women and children. These are not soldiers, my lady."

"Then we take them now, before they can scuttle into the hills."

"Should we not be careful?" Turalyon pressed, matching her speed as she spurred her horse into a gallop. The wind tore at his voice as he called to her above the rising din of hooves. "If there truly is a dark ranger among them . . ."

"A dark ranger would know to hide better," Alleria called back. "And if by some chance *she* is among them, then we must strike and strike hard, before she can run."

The strike was swift but not hard. They stormed north, veering along the edge of the hills until they came upon a shallow clearing. There they found a ramshackle encampment of tents and dugouts nestled against a mountain, cleverly hidden from the road and the span but near enough to fresh water to be useful. Sagefish and meager raptor haunches dried on a makeshift rack, mounds of hare bones all that remained of a paltry supper.

Captain Celosel overcame the one sleepy troll on watch, a precise, focused frost shard striking him in the chest, incapacitating the troll but not doing any real harm. These were, as their scouts assured them, farmers and families, not a trained fighter among them. Half of the Alliance detachment dismounted while the other half formed a tight circle around the camp, cutting off any avenues of escape while Turalyon, Alleria, and the draenei Senn approached the central fire, recently out and visibly smoking.

"None of you will be harmed so long as you remain calm and answer our questions," Alleria shouted over the shrieks of fear. She watched a robed Forsaken man stand guard in front of a family of frightened orcs, mother and child, the baby wailing inconsolably. A toddler crouched beside the orc mother, a boy with most of his teeth yet to come in. Their eyes were wide, sunken with hunger.

Alleria fell quiet, letting the refugees whisper among themselves for a moment while Turalyon stood beside her, his weight to one side, left hand resting on his sword hilt.

"This may be a dead end," he said in a low tone.

She shook her head, resolute. "Danath Trollbane assured me his outriders spotted a cloaked woman, red eyes, armed. She was with a group of civilians." Subtly so the refugees could not see, she pointed to the southwest. "The Alliance spies washed up not far from here, and Trollbane's riders glimpsed what sounds remarkably like a dark ranger in the region . . ."

"Yes. It *would* be one hell of a coincidence."

"One of them knows something," Alleria stated, swiveling to examine the nervous faces spread out before her. "One of them will talk."

"Alliance dogs!" The Forsaken in heavy black robes shuffled forward. He had once been a tall, large man, but the curse of the undead and time had put a pronounced bend in his spine. The remnants of a black beard clung to his exposed jaw. "Where is your compassion? These are innocents, homeless and starving, just pawns in your endless war."

"You speak for all, then?" Alleria asked, her gaze sharpening on the Forsaken. She noticed flecks of herbs sticking to his collar, his bony fingers discolored by some sort of green paste.

The whispers began, as they always did, cold and hissing, as ephemeral as shadow.

Twist his brittle bones until he speaks. Crack them open, find the marrow, spill his secrets . . .

"I speak, that is all," the Forsaken grumbled. "If someone must stand up, it will be me."

"We have no intention of shedding blood here this night," Turalyon told him, calm but firm. "Give us the information we seek, and we will send you on your way with what blankets and provisions we can spare from our packs."

At that, the assembled civilians exchanged looks, some of them hopeful, others suspicious.

As Turalyon dealt with the mouthy Forsaken, Alleria's gaze fell again on the mother orc and her children, drawn there by some tendril of curiosity. The Void often guided her in this way, always seeking deception, always on the hunt for the darkness every creature harbored within. At first she had only seen the woman's hunger, but now she saw something else. The orc huddled close to the ground, rocking back and forth, never daring to glance at any of the soldiers surrounding her. Furtive. Nervous.

Distracted, Alleria almost didn't see the little orc boy jump up in his loincloth, a thin blanket around his shoulders flapping like a cape as he dashed toward them, tiny tusks bared in a warrior's roar.

"Zun! No!" the mother cried.

Turalyon knelt, grabbing the orc around the waist and swinging him around, depositing him back on the grass with a low chuckle.

"Not today, boy."

"Spare him! Please!" The orc mother squeezed her infant, weeping into his wrappings.

Alleria crouched and placed both hands on the orc child, steadying him, waiting until his big brown eyes snapped to hers. He was afraid, certainly, but imbued with a wild and young courage.

"Can you understand me?" she asked.

The boy, Zun, gave a single nod.

"I will tell you, Zun, what I told my own son when he picked up his first blade and played at being a soldier," Alleria said gently. She remembered the moment as if it were happening all over again—the frosty winter day, the shards of pale sun brightening the courtyard in Stormwind Keep, Arator's mischievous smile as he swung the wooden sword high over his head, aiming for a frog but swinging into a pillar instead. Another woman's heart might have swelled with pride, but Alleria had felt only sadness. "Whatever your elders have told you, war is not glory. War is seeing people at their very worst and choosing to protect them anyway. Go back to your mother, and do not forget what I told you."

She spun Zun around and sent him racing past Turalyon and the Forsaken, into the grateful arms of the waiting orc. At last she gazed up at Alleria, and the whispers grew louder, more insistent, all but deafening Alleria with their certainty.

Her, her, her.

"She is the one," Alleria said coldly, just for Turalyon. "I will speak with her privately."

"Alleria, wait—" Turning to Celosel, Turalyon motioned to the captive refugees. "See that everyone remains calm. Give them food and drink if you must. I must speak to her ladyship briefly, captain."

Celosel saluted and took a place at the head of the crowd.

"Leave us in peace!" Alleria heard the Forsaken shout as she and Turalyon retreated down the hill until the voices dimmed and they stood more or less alone under the veiled moonlight.

Turalyon sighed and passed his hand over his face, his eyes

fixed on the scene playing out up the hill. "How do you think we should proceed?"

"However we must," Alleria replied at once. The dream that had come to her while they rode through the Arathi Highlands returned to her, a chill running through her body that felt like the very fingers of death trailing up her spine. "The mother knows something. You were too quick to offer them food, we might have bartered for information. The king was quite clear—our orders are to find Sylvanas at any cost; her dark rangers will lead us to her."

Turalyon nodded, grim. Something dark, something like doubt, flickered in his eyes. "The Light compels me to have mercy, Alleria, but I hear you. I do. I also heard what you said to that young boy. Is this us at our very worst?"

She sighed, staring straight ahead. "I see visions, Turalyon. So many visions. A thousand futures in which we fail to stop Sylvanas. Each one more monstrous than the last, and I would become more than my worst self to stop it."

"Yet the Void often lies," Turalyon pointed out.

"Of course it does, I do not blindly believe—I question and I wonder what the Void seeks to tell me, what wisdom is buried in the deceit. And after peeling away the layers of horror and destruction, I have come to a single conclusion: that no matter what, complacency and inaction will be our doom. We have our orders. It gives me no pleasure to interrogate civilians, Turalyon, but what choice do we have?"

"Let me talk with her, please. Give me a chance to pursue this the right way. Though time be short and our task dire, let us not forget who we are, what principles separate us from Sylvanas and her ilk."

He reached out toward her, and Alleria felt him close the distance between them, in word and bond, and she relented. Were she in void form, that touch would have burned him like a brand. In that moment, it felt like a balm. "Very well. Speak with the mother."

Turalyon managed a vanishing smile, then marched back toward the orc mother, crouching, his back to Alleria as he began speaking to her. Moving a little closer, Alleria pretended to inspect the perimeter, instead listening intently to their exchange, though it proved not to be a discussion at all, but rather Turalyon beating his head against a stubborn brick wall.

"Tell me your name, please," he said gently. "You may have mine first. I am Turalyon, Lord Commander of the Alliance. But you need not fear me, or any of us; we have no desire for bloodshed, only information. Now, please, madam, your name?"

The orc hesitated for a long time, then muttered something Alleria couldn't hear.

"Thank you. May I ask you some questions?"

"Ask," was all she said.

Turalyon did. Several times. Nicely, more directly, then with growing impatience. He tried bribing her with an escort, volunteering to give her safe passage to wherever she and her family pleased. Nothing. He called over Senn, having her take the mother a measure of wine and fruit from the soldiers' supply. The orc refused to talk, avoiding even his most mundane questions. She drank her wine and munched her fruit, and stared at Turalyon as if he were dimmer than a kobold candle. Irritated, Turalyon reminded her that the Alliance would be gone and stop bothering them the moment she chose to cooperate. The orc had nothing but a shrug for him. When nearly an hour had passed with no change or improvement in the orc's attitude, Alleria watched Turalyon rise, knees creaking, and then return to her. He looked as if those fifty minutes had aged him as many years.

"Her mouth's clamped shut tighter than a darkwater clam."

"I noticed," Alleria muttered. "What do we do?"

Alleria knew what she wanted to do—no, what needed to be

done—but she had to hear it from Turalyon, too. He glanced at her from under his lashes, rubbing his stubbled jaw.

"It's easy to say, 'what we must,' but that is not so, is it?"

"Turalyon . . . How many more hours should we waste? It is her. Her stubbornness only proves it. She refuses to speak because she knows she will incriminate herself or the others." Alleria gestured broadly to the troops still watching over the Horde refugees.

"We could question the others," he scrambled to say. "Or . . ."

"Or take the information we need," Alleria replied. "Take it now."

He glanced at her askew again. "Is this who we have become?"

Under different circumstances, under a different moon, his words might have wounded her, but Alleria shook them off without hesitation.

"My sister has not known a worthy adversary for a time now," Alleria whispered. "She has outsmarted, outplayed, and outwitted us because she is not shackled by good or evil, she is freed by her own willingness to pursue the mission, no matter the cost."

"Was that admiration I heard in your voice just now?"

Alleria sighed distantly. "There is nothing left of my sister to admire. Were she here now I would fill her head with visions of terror until it burst like a boil."

That settled it for Turalyon. He turned and began the plodding journey back up the slope. "Whatever the cost, then," he said.

"Whatever the cost."

The refugees had been given a few horse blankets and hunks of bread by the time they returned to the camp, but the soldiers maintained a tight perimeter, torches flaring, illuminating the ten nervous faces of the refugees. They smelled strongly of unwashed bodies and smoke, but Alleria quashed her pity, approaching the orc mother and looming over her.

"What is your name?" Alleria demanded.

She handed a small piece of black bread to her boy and then

shooed him away. The Forsaken apothecary hurried over, glowering, taking the babe from the orc's arms and sheltering the young boy behind his robes.

"Hmph," the orc refused to reply, sitting cross-legged at Alleria's feet.

"Her name is Gowzis," Turalyon informed her.

"Tell me what you know about the dark ranger that traveled with you recently," Alleria said, feeling a rush of dark energy flood from her toes to her fingers. The Void called; it wanted her to ferret out the secrets. It wanted her to poke and pry and do so with her Void-given powers.

Gowzis grunted and glanced away, but her knee bounced erratically, betraying her. "What would a dark ranger want with us?"

"An excellent question," Alleria replied. "What did she want with you? And where is she now? Answer us and we will be on our way."

Gowzis growled again and spat on the ground, narrowly missing the tip of Alleria's pointed boot.

"Wrong answer."

The Void invaded the orc's mind easily, readily, commanded by Alleria's experienced hands, guided by her knowledge of its capabilities. The Old Ones could use the smallest thought to drive a person mad, to wrench any information they wanted from an unwilling, tormented subject. Gowzis clutched the sides of her head, gasping, her eyes snapping open, suddenly glowing with eerie light.

"Hold her," Alleria whispered.

Turalyon did as she asked, reaching out with one gloved hand. Golden cuffs, glittering with the Light wrapped tightly around the orc's wrists and ankles, chains bursting forth and securing her to the earth.

The world fell away, leaving Alleria within the orc's mind.

She sifted through memories and thoughts like fingers combing through sand, each second that passed plunging the woman into greater agony.

This is the cost, this is the cost . . .

It would haunt her forever, but that was the cost. Alleria didn't know if it was her thinking such things or the Void that seethed within.

A pair of red eyes caught her attention, a clear memory of a pale-skinned woman with curling blue hair and red flowers tattooed around her eyes. A kaldorei twisted by her sister's undead touch. Teldrassil had burned, and then the kaldorei rangers had died trying to defend it, and then they were not even allowed the dignity of peace.

No, they were raised to serve a monster.

The orc woman shrieked, tears pouring down her face, her back bending at strange angles as she fought the pain tunneling through her mind.

"Stop! Stop it! For pity's sake, let her go! I will tell you of the dark ranger. I swore an oath of silence, we all did, the ranger demanded it, but I will tell you whatever you wish to know!"

Alleria stumbled backward, ripped away from the work and the woman, her breath coming in short, fast blasts as she regained her own sight, and the shadows slipped away. A comforting hand grazed her lower back. Turalyon. Catching her breath, she whirled on the Forsaken with the beard, the one who had interrupted.

Gowzis collapsed in a heap, her young son running to tug on her sleeve.

"She traveled not half a day with us a week past," he hurried on, throwing concerned glances at the trembling orc. He still held the woman's babe. It had ceased crying, snuffling into the armpit of his robe. "Please, do not hurt her again. I will tell you anything. Anything!"

"Just the truth," Alleria said coolly, collecting herself.

"Where did she happen upon you?" Turalyon demanded.

The Forsaken pointed to the north. "Off the road near Stromgarde, she was coming from Hillsbrad, or so she told us. Had some trouble with her steed; it threw her and she hurt her wrist badly, then the raptors tried to have a nibble." He reached into his robes, and every soldier in the vicinity touched their weapons. But he only drew out a small, red pouch. "I'm a healer, you see. An apothecary. Apothecary Cotley, I look after these people you see here, and I looked after her."

Alleria nodded; this was good. This was progress. "Go on. What happened after you healed her? Did she say anything?"

"A woman of few words, but I set the bone and wrapped it, and then she was on her way," he explained. "Had to go south, she said, and quick-like. Faldir's Cove. She was chartering a boat."

"Any names?" Alleria could hear the excitement in Turalyon's voice. She felt the same. This was a solid lead if the apothecary was telling the truth, and she sensed no deception in him, only fear.

Apothecary Cotley frowned and rubbed at the bald skull on the back of his head. He bounced the baby in his right arm absentmindedly. "Only hers. Vis-something. Vis . . . Visrynn."

"Thank you," Turalyon told him, inclining his head respectfully. "You have been most helpful, apothecary."

They turned away, and as soon as they did, the Forsaken rushed to the orc woman, kneeling and feeling for a pulse. She groaned and thrashed, babbling incoherently. Her body would mend at once, and her mind would recover in time, but the process would be slow and uncomfortable. There would be scars. Alleria had no room left in her heart for regrets, yet somehow it wormed its way in, cold and steady, paining her every step.

Captain Celosel approached, his torch bathing them in heat. "Your orders?"

"Give them more food and blankets, whatever water we can

spare," Alleria replied, beginning the short walk back to their mounts. "Urge them to find somewhere else to go; the Witherbark will find and raid them otherwise."

"And the apothecary?" Celosel called after them.

"Take him to Stormwind. He may know more, and we cannot afford to miss a single detail."

CHAPTER TEN

Nazmir

Apari lit the final stick of incense, wafting the fragrant smoke toward her face and breathing deep. Her lungs ached, but the pain was part of her ritual.

The deep throb in her right leg was constant now. Nothing eased her suffering, but she let it fuel her, just as the blood of traitors would fuel her magic. Tayo swore she knew a vulpera sawbones talented enough to remove the leg cleanly at the knee, but Apari refused. Instead, she let it wither and grow mottled with dark blotches, a reminder that time was short, that not a single moment could be wasted.

How much longer she could walk on it, she could not say.

"Is everything ready?"

Tayo's voice cut clearly through the winds whistling above Prisoner's Pass. The tar pits bubbling below stank, but the incense mellowed the reek. Apari struggled to her feet, ignoring the stubborn pain in her leg. No help came from Tayo, for she knew Apari would reject any assistance she offered. The followers of the

Widow's Bite gathered around them in a loose circle, and they could not be allowed to witness their leader's weakness.

"I stand ready," Apari told the taller troll, Tayo's hair painted as black as the tar pits. "Our assassination failed, Tayo; the Horde will come looking for answers. We attacked the queen on their soil, but we cannot allow them on ours. Their numbers are too great, and they will overwhelm us and the pale rider before our justice is had."

"The storm will keep them at bay, Apari; this magic is old, old as the empire itself," Tayo assured her. "We will not fail. All is not lost."

Apari snorted. "When the pale rider sees this, he will not doubt us again. He thinks he is powerful, he knows nothing of our real power. This . . . this will stop all of his complainin', and show the reach of the Widow's Bite."

Then Apari gazed around at her assembled rebels. Their numbers grew each day, slowly but surely more of the Zandalari in Dazar'alor and the surrounding villages leaving homes behind to join their ranks. News spread of their attack on the palace. Talanji had made an appearance in the marketplace afterward, quelling rumors that she had been killed in the assassination attempt, but many reported she looked unwell.

If the Widow's Bite could threaten the queen herself, then they were not just an upstart insurrection but a true danger to the crown. They could not allow her to gather any allies to her side. Zandalar must be cut off, isolated, made vulnerable so that it could again be made strong.

"We all stand ready." Apari raised her arms, and the members of the Widow's Bite grew silent with awe. "It will take all of our power—all of our considerable might—to shake the seas and command the clouds!"

Before her, a nobleman from the palace lay on a flat, polished piece of black rock. He squirmed. Daz, Apari's dreadtick, perched on his chest, fangs chattering. The old troll, his eyes big and round as moons, had been tightly gagged, and his muffled protests were drowned by Apari's voice. They had taken his fine robes and jewels to trade with passing merchants for food and weapons.

"Chant with me now, brothers and sisters, I need your voices! Let the heavens hear ya, let your will be known!"

Thirty or so trolls sat perched in that circle around Apari, their backs to the vultures circling over the pass. The moon flashed bright and red, drenched in blood as if it had predicted their purpose. Her followers wore loose black tunics and loincloths slashed with white stripes to mimic a spider's many legs; some wore carved talismans, and others fearlessly allowed fat, furry tarantulas to crawl freely over their shoulders.

The chanting began slowly, Apari conducting her followers with broad sweeps of her arms. Tayo walked the circle painted on the dark, flat stones, the narrow plateau above the pass serving as their ritual altar. Not far below, hewing closely to the rocks, they had made a temporary camp, pushed out of their swamp caves by increasingly paranoid royal patrols.

She beheld her faithful followers, hungry, tired, hunted from one end of Zandalar to the other. Many had eaten only bone broth and paper-thin bat wings for days now. It did not matter. They would not stop. Their starved bellies made them wild and reckless, and that suited Apari just fine. The pale rider Nathanos would join them soon with his rangers to plan the final blow against Talanji and her cursed loa, and then there would be no escape for the traitor queen.

Even the seas would churn with the fury of the Widow's Bite.

Apari limped to the old troll at the center of the white circle while Tayo lit the eight ritual torches. White flames blossomed like pale flowers, the acrid smoke mingling with the incense and the stink of sweat pouring off the noble. Apari paused, dagger at her side, wondering what the sacrifice must think of her. She knew him, knew his family, but that did not matter. Once, Apari had been just as rich and noble, as beautiful as the old troll's young daughter, held to be even more desirable than Talanji herself. Her hair had spilled like a clear silver waterfall over one shoulder, braided intricately, pink flowers and beads winking out from between the strands. General Jakra'zet had often praised her smooth green skin and slender arms.

"Arms made for dancin'," he would say, teasing her as she flitted down the palace halls.

But those comments, those smooth, slender arms and flowery braids felt like a cruel joke. Now she never washed that silver hair, her eyes hidden behind a half-mask. The wound in her leg festered and oozed, pungent with malodor. The infection was like nothing she or her physicians had seen, resistant to magic, and to poultices, a wound more of the heart and mind than the body, some shaman told her to her face, as if she were the one responsible for its refusal to heal. Only months had passed since her world was shattered, her future stolen from her, and her body broken, but those had been the truest months. The months that defined her. No more frivolities. No more games. The Widow's Bite was her purpose now, her mother's legacy her only concern.

"You won't be needin' this anymore," Apari said, kneeling with difficulty. She snatched the gag from the troll's mouth, and at once he began pleading.

"You do not need to do this! Do you want gold? I can give you gold! P-please! Please, Parri, I know you! It is me, Bezime! You . . . You must know me! There is no need for all of this I will give you whatever you want! My daughter is to be married soon, let me live to see it!"

"Ah," Apari teased cruelly. "Ya gave ya daughter away. Then this be a mercy. Keep ya gold and ya promises, sacrifice, but don't be stingy with ya screams."

Apari raised the ritual knife and then brought it down with a true strike, piercing the heart, bringing forth the blood. The fuel. Magic had its cost.

"Nav'rae . . . forgive . . . me . . ." His thin voice ebbed as his eyes rolled back and the fuel for the storm began to run into the rivulets carved in the stone.

The pain in her leg no longer bothered Apari, a surge like lightning throwing her to her feet. Those arms made for dancing were raised to the moon, and the thrilled cries of her followers felt as intoxicating as the blood magic.

"By flowing, foaming blood, we call the sea to rise!" Apari thundered. Tayo lifted her torch, the flame hitting its zenith each time the crowd chanted, "Blood, Blood, Blood . . ."

The blood racing toward the painted symbol ignited, crackling, then the ground all around Apari's feet began to hum and glow.

"By wind from dead lungs, we call the clouds to seethe!"

"Wind, Wind, Wind . . ."

"Blood be fire, fire burn bright, light the skies and show us your might!" Apari closed her hands into fists, the white flames rising around her traveling from the runnels in the stone to the white painted symbol and back to the sacrifice at the center of it all. Her clothes caught fire first, curling. Tayo held her torch high, and the chanting became erratic, her followers leaping and dancing, laughing and twirling one another as the flames abruptly snuffed themselves out. The wind died down. All was quiet until the fire burned anew, now in Apari's hands.

A distant rumble to the east announced their success. Soon the skies above the Zandalari coast would thicken with black clouds, the waves below towering taller than ships.

Apari brought her palms together, smothering the magic until it hissed and dulled, and for a moment, with that power still rolling through her veins and her followers celebrating, she knew happiness.

The body before her, charred and still, was nothing now but a gift for the buzzards.

Tayo brought her torch and a smile to Apari, putting her free hand on the troll's shoulder. Hers was a more reserved jubilation. "Yazma would be proud."

Nodding, Apari watched her dreadtick pace listlessly next to the still smoldering body.

"I know." Sighing, she clucked her tongue, and the tick buzzed up into the air, then flew a crooked path to her shoulder, landing there with a nip at her ear. "Patience, little one. Don't be sad now. When the traitors lie dead at our feet you will have your feast."

CHAPTER ELEVEN

Arathi Highlands

"Alleria! Turalyon . . . Have you found anything?"

The whistling vortex of the portal twisted shut behind her, and Jaina Proudmoore stepped out onto the sand, salt and spray greeting her. She had come with all haste, sent by the king of Stormwind, Turalyon and Alleria's lack of progress concerning him. Days had passed with no word from the pair, no indication that the tip sending them to the highlands had borne fruit. Jaina had tried to counsel him toward patience, but none of her assurances, none of her arguments, eased his troubled heart.

A human man, sprawled on the ground, shook helplessly as a dark, shadowy cloud enveloped his head, golden shackles holding him against his will.

Turalyon was the first to turn and face her, the paladin's concentration breaking, the glittering chains pressing the man into the sand vanishing in a puff of light. Jaina Proudmoore knew that some wielded the Light and Void seamlessly, but she had never seen such methods used as coercion. *Horrible*, she thought. *What has possessed them?*

Perhaps Anduin was wise to send her after all.

"This man and his family sheltered one of the Banshee Queen's dark rangers, then smuggled her to a shipping boat," Turalyon told her.

Alleria did not acknowledge her presence, apparently too busy drawing agonized screams from the smuggler to stop and answer Jaina. A small outpost had been built not far from the shore, and a smattering of Alliance soldiers waited there, lingering in the doorway. Down the beach, a handful of void elves kept solemn watch over what appeared to be the rest of the smuggler's family, all of them on their knees cowering.

"And you know this how?" Jaina pressed, joining Turalyon and Alleria on the damp and shifting sand near the surf. "Did he resist?"

"The father refused to answer our questions, but he possessed a suspicious dagger." And here Turalyon produced the blade, its handle finely wrought with a raised silver skull, purple gems glittering along the hilt. "A dagger that would look more fitting in a Forsaken scabbard, don't you agree?"

Jaina took hold of their evidence, examining it closely. She could not deny that it resembled the weapons used by Sylvanas and her chosen guards.

"A group of refugees led us here. Their apothecary treated the ranger for wounds and then she left for the coast. Visrynn is the ranger; do you know her?" Turalyon asked.

A cutting wind streaming up from the south bit at Jaina's skin, fluttering her blue-and-gold cloak. It might have given her a chill, but she already shivered, mistrustful of the Void, disgusted by what she now watched Alleria do to the smuggler.

Many looked on, including Turalyon's Alliance forces; some even squirmed, seemingly sharing Jaina's discomfort.

"I don't know her," Jaina replied, returning the blade.

"That is no matter," he said with a shrug. "We will find her soon enough."

The smuggler went silent and limp, perhaps dead, curled into a ball on the sand while the foamy waves lapped at his boots. Alleria inhaled deeply, her eyes lit with strange excitement as she at last ended her cruel work and turned to address them.

"Yes, we will find her soon." Alleria nodded, satisfied. "They provided a skiff sturdy enough to sail deep water. The fool ranger was quite specific. It must get her west." Alleria glanced between Jaina and Turalyon. "The only thing worth sailing to directly west of here is the Zandalari coast."

Jaina could not argue with the results of their use of both Light and Void, but she certainly could argue with the method. They seemed distant, numb, as if this was something they had reluctantly done before. Jaina was left hoping it was a desperate measure taken in response to limited time, not their new normal. And time *was* limited. Searching every corner of Azeroth remained a massive undertaking, and the longer they looked, the less likely they were to find Sylvanas before she caused more death and mayhem.

"Does the king know you are employing these . . ." Jaina groped for a diplomatic word. "Tactics?"

At last the poor man on the ground moved, his hands clawing listlessly at the wet sand. The wind carried the full-bodied sobs of his wife and son toward them.

"The king was quite clear," Alleria answered. "We were to use whatever means necessary to extract information. Now we know Sylvanas has her sights set on Zandalar. Our scope has narrowed, and I can only imagine King Anduin will be pleased."

"If this is how we must behave to achieve victory then he is not pleased," Jaina assured them in a hiss, gesturing to the broken smuggler. "Nor am I."

"I assure you, all will make sense in time, Jaina." Turalyon spoke before Alleria could spit out whatever she had ready, though the Void-touched elf's face froze on a snarl. "Alleria did not harm him overmuch, and the Light will soothe whatever now ails him. I will see to that. I would never let the void within her rage out of control."

"And I would never need him to control me."

"Indeed." Jaina pushed past them both, kneeling beside the trembling smuggler. Carefully, she rolled him onto his back, cradling his head with one hand, her eyes seeking along his face for any hint of recognition.

"He has told me everything," Alleria continued impatiently. "To dawdle here with him is to waste precious time."

"I'm sorry . . ." The words dribbled out between thin, bluish lips, as if Alleria had stolen the last trace of warmth from his body. "My family . . . I couldn't f-feed them, the storms have k-kept the fish away—"

"And a dagger that fine would fetch a tempting price," Jaina finished for him. "When it comes to those we love, we always do what we must. Your honesty is your penance, sir. So I tell you now: If you have anything more to say—"

Alleria sighed. But the smuggler in Jaina's grasp pawed at the air, nodding frantically.

"She . . . the ranger . . . she must reach her destination before the White Lady is full," the man whimpered, his eyes rolling back. "After . . . no ships will pass."

"What did he say?" Turalyon demanded, his heavy boots making sand fly as he hurried to join them. "What did he say about the sea?"

Jaina frowned, gently placing the man's head back on the unforgiving pillow of the shore. *No ships will pass.* It was compassion and not torture that produced the final warning. Perhaps the man might have told them all he knew willingly if only a bit more patience had been utilized. "When is the next full moon?"

Taken aback, Turalyon whispered something under his breath, frowning as he made the quick calculations. "Six days."

Careful not to disturb the smuggler further, Jaina stood and marched back to Alleria, who had crossed both arms across her chest, watching the mage with naked suspicion—one feathery eyebrow cocked, her lips pulled into a crooked smile.

"We have but six days to reach Zandalar safely," Jaina repeated. "I will return to Stormwind at once and relay all of this to the king."

Not missing the subtle emphasis she placed on "all of this," Alleria shifted to her right, standing exactly where Jaina had meant to place her portal. The two women locked eyes, and Jaina felt a chill prickle in her palms, a warning from her own instincts that if she did not leave soon they might descend into a true argument.

"Is this truly our highest priority, Jaina?" Alleria whispered, mindful of the soldiers observing them. "Tattling?"

Jaina tossed back her long braid of hair and conjured her portal, summoning it uncomfortably near to Alleria's back.

"All will make sense in time, Alleria," she said, using Turalyon's own condescending placation. "I go only to apprise King Anduin of your progress." *And to tattle.* Jaina waited until the elf stepped aside, allowing her to stride quickly toward the portal. She did not trust the Void, and she could not trust anyone practically possessed by it.

Anduin couldn't possibly know the extent of what Alleria and Turalyon were doing in his name, and he would never condone it. They were setting a dangerous precedent. She returned to Stormwind City with all possible haste, though her thoughts only grew darker along the way. How could they justify abusing Light and Void together in such a way? A paladin of Turalyon's experience and wisdom ought to know better. Alleria ought to know better, too. And yet . . . And yet, through their strange alchemy of light and shadow, they had found the most usable information thus far in the campaign to hunt down Sylvanas.

When she arrived in the city, her priority remained Anduin. Jaina stormed into the throne room of Stormwind Keep, finding the king was not there to hear petitions. Two armored sentinels in blue-and-gold livery near the throne directed her to the map room. Jaina Proudmoore was, after all, a fixture in the castle, both friend and adviser to the young king. Her cloak billowed behind her as she skirted around the ever-present crush of nobles, soldiers, and visitors filling the throne room.

She was not at all surprised to find Anduin hunched over the immense, yellowed map of Azeroth strewn with books and smaller charts, the king of Gilneas at his side. She was, however, loathe to tell them both what she had witnessed, as Genn Greymane's temper flared readily, even more so since the armistice. But Anduin brightened at her appearance, his blue eyes twinkling with what seemed to her like much-needed hope.

"Please," was his first word to her. She braced. "Please tell me you bring good news."

Jaina produced her crystal-topped staff with a wave of her right hand, snatching it up deftly and pointing with its brass end to the sea separating the Eastern Kingdoms from the troll continent of Zandalar.

"We have six days to catch a fishing boat headed for eastern Zandalar," she told them with clipped efficiency. The macabre fate of their smuggler source could wait. "When the full moon comes, the waters in that pass will become impossible to sail. A dark ranger called Visrynn told all of this to the smuggler that outfitted her with a ship."

Anduin's eyes danced even brighter, and he slammed a joyful fist down on the map table. "At last. At last! We will summon Mathias Shaw—he will be the best choice to give chase. His sea legs are stronger after our long campaign in Kul Tiras."

Greymane expressed his gruff agreement. "I have no objections. But should we not send a larger force?"

"We cannot risk alerting the Horde to our presence there," Jaina replied. "Zandalar is under their protection. Our ships in the area would be one thing, but making landfall might be seen as an act of aggression."

"Jaina is right. The armistice is too fragile, and we cannot survive another war right now. Precautions must be taken, and Mathias can be but a shadow when he desires." The king clapped Genn Greymane several times on the back. "Go. Find him. With his cunning and a tidesage's magic, we may yet catch this dark ranger. We must pray for good fortune and haste."

Greymane bowed to Jaina on his way out, leaving her with a hurried, "Lord Admiral."

She fiddled with the anchor charm dangling around her neck, picking her next words carefully while Anduin leaned excitedly over the map, nearly touching his nose to the Great Sea.

Time to dash this brief lift in his spirits.

"Anduin . . ." She spoke softly, cautiously, wary of any prying ears and eyes that might be lingering outside the door. "I have concerns."

"We all do, these are concerning times." Anduin almost laughed, but then he craned his head back, still half embracing the table. "Jaina, what is it? You look truly troubled."

Jaina sighed through her nose. There was little point in stalling. He had to know what she had witnessed. For all the lion's strength Anduin possessed, he was also gifted with a compassionate heart, a rare combination in a leader, and so it pained her to speak ill of those he respected.

"Alleria and Turalyon tortured that smuggler in front of me. She used the Void to infiltrate his mind while he held him prisoner with chains made from the Light. It looked unspeakably painful." She rounded the table, searching his face. "My king . . . I worry that their tactics represent you poorly. Every one of us, every soldier, is in service to your crown. We stand under your banner, and if their actions are sanctioned by your rule, what does that say about us?"

Anduin did not speak for a long while, though his smile diminished. He shook his head, turning away from her, pacing back and forth across the lush green carpet beneath their feet. Finally, he crossed to a large brazier in the corner belching healthy flames. Flattening his hand, he passed it back and forth just above the reach of the fire.

"What does it say?" he echoed. He sounded almost offended that she had to ask. "It says we will do whatever we must to bring murderers to justice. It says we will not forget those lost in war. It says we will not forget Teldrassil, or Lordaeron. It says we will not forget the mak'gora. It says that we will not forget the flames blazing over the Veiled Sea, or the fires reflected in the eyes of a thousand mourning children." His hand closed into a fist, with every word his determination grew, rising and rising, a crescendo that nearly reached a shout. Then he glanced at her out of the corner of his eye, and his voice dropped to a whisper. "There was a time not so long ago when you were not above swinging the harsh hammer of retribution. I have not forgotten, Jaina. Have you?"

Oh, great lion, your heart is becoming steel. Hers had once done the same, hardened by the bomb that destroyed Theramore, and that rigidity had ruled her for a time, not only her powers but her heart and mind encased in frost. Vividly, sadly, she remembered telling Varian in no uncertain terms that the Horde must be utterly annihilated. It had taken a long time for her to thaw, and remnants of that icy anger still lingered, making her all the more able to detect it in others. She saw it then in Anduin, a grief like all-encompassing cold.

"Jaina," he prompted her, but she felt no rush to answer him.

Jaina held fast to her staff, the red light of the brazier burnishing Anduin's face. Silently, she turned and regarded Azeroth spread before her on the table. How well a map represented lands, but how poorly it described the people, the little, tiny things that truly made up a whole entire world.

"I have not forgotten," Jaina murmured, eyes fixed on Zandalar. "But I also remember that your father once warned Vol'jin to uphold honor or be ended. I wish more than anything, my king, to see your reign endure, and for it to be *remembered* fondly. And more than anything, for you to be remembered in the same breath as your father."

"Difficult decisions have to be made, and I trust Turalyon and Alleria to know where the line of decency is and not to cross it." Jaina had thought the argument over, but Anduin stood firm, watching her intently. His gaze never wavered. "Would their statues preside over our city because they are without honor?"

Jaina need only blink to feel as if she were standing in Thunderbluff again, flush with victory and the optimism that often came with it. After all, they had just managed to rescue Baine Bloodhoof from the dungeons below Orgrimmar, a nigh impossible feat. And yet they had done it. Thrall had not shared her optimism, wary of her desire for a temporary alliance.

What's different this time?

We are.

"People change," Jaina said heatedly. She rolled her shoulders back, proud of that change, proud of who she had become, and who she believed him to be.

Anduin considered her words but withdrew further into the corner, holding out his hands to the brazier as if her words had somehow chilled him. The thick curtain of his yellow hair swung before his face, concealing his expression. "People do change, but I trust Alleria and Turalyon, despite what misfortunes have befallen them. Stormwind would not exist without them, they are woven into the very fabric of our kingdom's tales."

There would be no swaying him; that much had become clear. She turned to go, leaving him with one last murmured plea. "Clarity and time are the final editors of that story, Anduin, I would know."

CHAPTER TWELVE

Atal'gral

"What do you think of her? The *Bold Arva*! Say it with me: The *Bold Arva*. Has a certain ring, doesn't it?" Flynn Fairwind cackled, slapping the mainmast vigorously as he turned his chest to the wind and breathed deep, a serene, almost religious glow about his face. "Christened her myself. The old name was—to be frank—rubbish. The *Prowse*. Can you believe it? I mean, I'm sorry. Pardon me? The *Prowse*?"

Mathias Shaw stared straight ahead, convinced that if he said nothing at all and ignored the sailor like a basilisk desperate for a glance then Fairwind would be forced to cease his blathering.

He was wrong.

"What even *is* a prowse? Blimey. Sounds like something you pick out of your teeth. No, it's much better this way. Can you believe I won her in a dice game? Who would be stupid enough to wager this gorgeous girl?"

"You," Mathias said without thinking it through. Well, in for a copper, in for a gold. "And you would be soused."

"Yes. Yes! Absoluuuutely hammered! Ha!" Fairwind dissolved into further ridiculous laughter, doubling over as he gallivanted up and down the deck. "Well, well, well. You know me well, Shaw? Do a bit of digging before we came aboard? What does the dossier on me say, by the way? Devilishly handsome? Irresistible in every conceivable way? Crack sailor? Deadly with a blunderbuss?"

The significantly less glamorous answers would have to wait. *Ca-crack.* A fork of lightning, white as alabaster, split the horizon. A moment later, waves rocked the *Bold Arva* so hard, Flynn wrapped an arm and a leg around the mast to stay upright. Sailors began their calls. Whistles blew. Clouds the color of slate gathered thick and threatening just a few miles from the bow. Shaw tumbled to the railing, an old break in his shin screwing up tight enough to squeal. They were in for one hell of a storm.

"We should have another day," Shaw spat between gritted teeth.

"Survival weather!" Fairwind was sober enough to shout. "Grigsby to the helm! Keep speed, my lads and ladies, aim for the flats! Rig out the storm sails and watch the decks, nobody overboard on my watch!"

Mathias didn't dare relinquish his grip on the rail. He had seen his share of storms while posted in Kul Tiras, and they had taught him that only the cautious and wary survived. Light, but he despised sailing. Give him a good old solid office tucked away behind a false bookcase, a roaring fire and plenty of desk space the only true creature comforts a spymaster required. His stomach churned, his jaw clacked, his entire body protesting the sudden lurch of the ship as a particularly nasty wave broke against the bow.

"Tides be kind, I hope they're quick enough." Fairwind slid to the railing beside him, his lately acquired parrot pet struggling to flap to his shoulder, tossed hither and yon by the oncoming storm.

"Honestly, this is very, very bad. If the storm sail isn't up soon then we're all well and truly f—"

A wave knocked the words out of Fairwind's mouth, and both men found themselves shocked across the ship, Fairwind landing against the opposite railing with a pained grunt while Mathias had far less luck, his fingernails scratching along boards as slick as ice before he bypassed the railing and slid right off the edge of the ship, nothing but churning water beneath him. He watched a gnome holding a sail line soar overhead, mouth open in a scream, the sound of it drowned out by the thunder of twenty-foot waves.

Before Mathias could make the steep fall into the sea below, Fairwind managed to clamp a hand around his wrist and began to pull, but his chest slamming into the side of the hull left him breathless and seeing stars. Mathias collected himself, scrambling with his free hand for some purchase on the seams in the hull while Fairwind braced a foot on either side in the gap in the railing, heaving and sweating, cursing as he at last found the leverage to hoist Mathias back aboard.

"Below deck!" Fairwind shouted. "Now! You don't have the sea legs for this, and I'm entirely too drunk. See? Nobody overboard on my watch."

It was an undignified retreat to the stairs. The threat of another wave meant that crawling on all fours was the safest option. Mathias sprang to his feet the moment they reached the relative safety of the sheltered corridor leading below deck. Water washed across the boards at his feet, spilling down into the stairwell, though there seemed to be no signs yet of flooding.

When Mathias had traveled down the stairs a ways, Fairwind grabbed a passing sailor. To Mathias it seemed like chaos, yet every man and woman aboard went about their job diligently, even if it appeared as if they were all running in random directions.

"The flats . . ." Fairwind shook the sailor by his coat.

"The mist is thick, but Nailor up the crow's nest spotted a gap. We're bringing her around and threading it, then we should have a safe stretch heading north."

It was a screamed conversation, but both men kept their calm.

"And Melli?"

The sailor grinned and nodded, sodden from head to foot. "Never seen speed like that in me life, captain."

He was referring to Melli Spalding, one of the finest tidesages in Kul Tiras, transferred urgently from the Proudmoore fleet. At first she didn't seem to fit in well with the crew, keeping to herself, a head taller than the average sailor aboard. But then Grigsby had produced a flute one night and Melli had come out of her shell, beguiling them all with a run of shanties so beautiful it left almost everyone in tears. Her voice rang out as crisp and haunting as a gust whistling off the Waning Glacier.

"Are we to survive this?" Mathias demanded, ducking out of the cramped stairwell and into the marginally taller corridor. He flattened himself against the wall to let a sailor pass. Fairwind jogged down the stairs to meet him, following as Mathias shouldered open the captain's cabin, the view from the windows nauseating as the ship crested a wave and barreled back down.

"No, no, it's all fine, Shaw. Completely fine. We live for storms like this, keeps us all on our toes." Fairwind gave a barking laugh then wiped the saltwater out of his ginger mustache. "Hard to find a crew this fit. Melli and Nailor will bring us through, you'll see." Predictably, he crossed to the well-stocked liquor cabinet in the corner, carefully fishing out a bottle while the ship tossed like an enraged shardhorn.

"Just something to settle the gut," Fairwind assured him, tossing back a healthy gulp from the bottle.

"I'm sure," Mathias sighed. "We should have had more time."

Smacking his lips, Fairwind kept the bottle, ambling over to the windows and watching the furious crash of the waves. It made Mathias sick to even glance at it.

"Maybe your source lied."

"Maybe." Mathias rubbed at his stubbled chin. "Or maybe this is just the opening act, and the real show hasn't even begun."

"I . . . hadn't considered that." Fairwind clutched the bottle. "Well, if your source was right then this is indeed just a taste. The seas were meant to be impassable, yes? And ta-da! We have passed!"

His final word was punctuated with a crack and then an ominous scattering of shrieks and voices, finished with a desperate pounding on the door.

"I may have spoken too soon."

"Enter!" Mathias roared.

The sailor they had passed going below deck skidded into the cabin, his clothes just as wet but also somehow singed.

"Fire!?" Fairwind slammed down the bottle and rushed to the sailor. He was a short lad, hardly more than twenty, with a pockmarked face and small but quick-moving blue eyes. "Fire, Swailes? How can there be fire?"

"L-lightning, captain, a-and—"

"Never mind!" Pushing him aside, the captain stumbled out into the corridor, and Mathias chased after him, curious to know just how a ship in the midst of a cataclysmic storm could also catch on fire. Lightning, obviously, but surely the waves would take care of any flames?

Above deck, they found fires spreading from the charred mainmast to the barrels piled below it. They had come through the rain and the waves, leaving the ship damp but vulnerable. Mathias himself knew how much gunpowder and pitch waited aboard to ignite and blow them sky high.

"Well, the fire was a surprise," Fairwind admitted, tucking a curled forefinger under his chin.

Mathias might have warned him of the oncoming footsteps but didn't, dodging as the woman batted Fairwind aside like a sack of feathers. Melli Spalding slid across the foam-slicked decks, back to them as she dropped her head, raised her arms, and with her curious tidesage magic brought water streaming up the sides of the hull before it cascaded gently across the deck. One by one the fires went out, cheers erupting from the sailors as the *Bold Arva* slowed, sailing smoothly out of the black-and-blue squall behind them.

"Well done, Melli! Well done!"

Mathias didn't feel in the mood for celebration. He surveyed the damaged mast, the burned sails and smoking provisions, as well as the thickening storm growing like a cancer across the sound. They had passed into Zandalari waters, and he couldn't help but think that the storm had been specifically summoned to keep them out. Who possessed magic like that? And where would they find them?

"Sir! Message for you, sir! Er, I mean, a shark . . . A thing for you, sir!" Swailes again, this time wet, singed, and carrying a wind-up shark, gnome technology fit for passing covert messages even at sea. Much trickier to spot than a carrier pigeon.

"Is it always like this with you?" Fairwind chuckled, watching Mathias crack open the shark, revealing a bundle of tiny rolled notes.

"These are fraught times," Mathias muttered. "I don't cease being spymaster simply because I'm on a boat."

He trusted the seafaring sorts to see to the damaged parts of the ship, retreating back below deck to see what his spies had uncovered abroad. This was not the business one conducted in front of prying eyes, and while Anduin assured him that the entire crew had been carefully vetted, Mathias knew the operation had been put together hastily, not allowing much time for lengthy observation of the crew.

"Bit paranoid, are we?"

Fairwind had followed him and not subtly, banging into every door and wall available with his drunken weaving. He was going to use up all the usable air if he kept sighing so much, so Mathias simply charged ahead into the cabin, desperate for a relatively stable chair and a long think.

Taking the seat far, far away from the liquor cabinet, Mathias seated himself comfortably, tucked beneath the painted portrait of a one-eyed, four-toothed goblin. Bold Arva herself, the ship's namesake, one of Flynn Fairwind's goblin first mates, killed—allegedly—in a tragic harpooning accident.

Mathias listened to the return of the familiar mundane noise of the ship sailing at a relaxed pace, gulls crying outside the windows and the waves forming an almost hypnotizing rhythm that one had to lean into or risk seasickness. Unrolling his messages, Mathias found that Fairwind was not put off. No indeed, the pirate made himself comfortable, leaning back in a chair until the edge tapped the windowpane, his boots kicked up casually on the table.

"That from your girlfriend?"

Mathias snorted. "Hardly. Intelligence reports from my agents within the Horde."

"Oooh, very spicy!" Fairwind giggled, nursing his beloved bottle again. Finally putting down the booze, Fairwind cleared his throat, reading the room. "Very paranoid."

He regarded the pirate dryly above the first unrolled message. "Just because we signed an armistice with the Horde doesn't mean we aren't watching them. Only a fool mistakes peacetime for complacency."

"So, then, what's new with the Horde? Any betrayals a-brewin'?"

Mathias skimmed the messages quickly. They were written in a code illegible to anyone not trained in his specific style of shorthand. Efficient and cautious. He hadn't been able to successfully embed enough agents to cover every single member of the new Horde Council, but had trusted them to choose their targets once they reached Orgrimmar.

Narsilla Keensight, codename Lancer, had chosen to focus her attention on Lor'themar Theron. Lancer, an old blood elf contact from the Uncrowned, had no loyalties to the Horde or Alliance, but only to gold, which Mathias provided her regularly. Her intelligence always proved worth the price. With a captive audience, Mathias read aloud the message, speeding along.

> Lor'themar spends his days at study, though I often observe him gazing listlessly at nothing, then scribbling something in the margin of his book. Reading. Reading.

This was the way an agent marked down time when nothing of note occurred.

> Another five days of reading. Still reading. No progress. At last I managed to access one of his tomes when he left to dine. It appears he is either composing poetry or notes of a more intimate nature. Beside a passage about holy energy he writes, "My dusk lily bends more each day toward the sun."

Fairwind broke into laughter. "Dusk lily? Hm. I am . . . confused. Confused yet enchanted. Is there more?"

"Not about the flower, sadly. But she does describe an incident at the Horde Council meeting with the Zandalari queen. Something of real substance. An assassination attempt by a troll . . . So somebody within the Horde wishes harm against Queen Talanji." Mathias set the message aside, pleased that he had managed to have eyes on the assassination.

"Could explain the storms," Fairwind mused, running his finger idly in circles around the mouth of the liquor bottle.

"How so?"

"If someone wants the queen dead then maybe she put the whole continent on lockdown. Nobody out or in until they find the assassins."

Mathias frowned. "That is . . . annoyingly reasonable."

"Why, thank you."

"This one is from a goblin contact, Krazzet the Bishop—"

Fairwind spat out half his swig of booze. "Krazzet? *The* Krazzet? I know Krazzet! Spooky little fellow liked to gamble in Freehold! Called himself the Bishop 'cos he would get three sheets and say, 'Oh, lads, I'm a bit slopped' but it just sounded like 'I'm *abrrshop*!'"

Calmly, Mathias clacked his teeth together and forced himself not to kick the table out from under Fairwind's feet. Problematically, the pirate was right. That exact fact existed in Kraz's dossier.

"I miss that guy!" Fairwind went on. "Lost my old parrot Bongbong to him in a card game. Always wondered what happened to that bird . . ."

"Yes, well, Kraz thinks the assassination attempt really gummed things up for the Horde," Mathias informed him, scanning the message and translating it. "The queen left in a huff. They've sent their own spies after her, a troll shaman called Zekhan. Interesting. They must not be as solidly loyal to the Horde as we thought . . ."

"How did you get Krazzet to turn and snitch for you, if I may ask?" Fairwind smirked, derailing Mathias's thought.

It had been so long ago, he struggled to recall. "Parrots. A weird amount of parrots."

Shrugging, the pirate hugged the liquor to his chest. "He hasn't changed a bit. Hang on, isn't it a bit crass that they've sent a spy after that troll queen? She nearly died and now they don't trust her? Maybe she's in cahoots with Sylvanas, eh? That's what we're here to investigate, right? And if the Horde don't trust her then maybe we're all on to the same thing!"

He really didn't have time to give an introductory espionage class, or time to point out that "we" weren't on to anything, but Stormwind Intelligence was. But then again given their situation there was little to do but wait and strategize. "The Horde might not be our friends, but they're not stupid. In my experience, a conspiracy is easy to spot once you know what to look for. They probably just sent a spy as a precaution. A smart one."

There was a soft, nervous rapping at the door.

"Who wishes—"

"Yeah?"

Mathias glared at the pirate, but Fairwind was already grinning ear to ear, bouncing his boots gleefully on the table. The tidesage Melli poked her head in. Tall and sturdy, she had neatly braided her reddish brown hair in a crown across her head. Points of sunburn reddened her dark skin.

"Beg your pardon," she murmured. "There's another storm comin' on. I wanted to talk to you about it, about this weather . . . It can't be random, and this is no magic I know of. It's like they know where we are, it's like they sent these ragers just for us."

CHAPTER THIRTEEN

Nazmir

"What a pit," Sira Moonwarden sneered, pulling her foot up out of the mud and listening to the resounding squelch. "A blessing that this post is only temporary."

Beside her, Nathanos stood stalk still, ignoring the visible cloud of flies gathering around his head. He often wore a subtle cologne to ward off the scent of being neither living nor dead. Many found the complete absence of scent unnerving. Sira had only just grown accustomed to it herself. She did not handle the bugs as gracefully, batting at them while they gathered in ever thickening swarms.

"Where are they?" Sira added, annoyed.

"Patience, Warden. Patience."

She had little on a good day, even less when she was forced to stand knee-deep in rotting mud, the Frogmarsh a strangely painful reminder of how undead she truly was. Here, life roared at her from every direction, from the damp trees draped with green curtains of moss to the crabs clicking their way up and down the shore behind them, to the deafening chorus of frogs and insects robbing any chance of a peaceful thought.

Life. It was everywhere there. Brash, audacious life. It probably *smelled* green. Not an inch of it went uncovered in vines or nests or pond scum. Through the trees ahead, a herd of riverbeasts snorted and huffed, the brass section of the teeming band of chittering, birdsong, and ribbets.

It was, in a word, loathsome.

"We'll be eaten alive," she huffed, swatting a dozen bugs before all the words had left her mouth.

"There." Nathanos pointed to the same trees that concealed the riverbeasts. Long, dripping strands of moss made the beach feel claustrophobic. The four dark rangers spread about to stand watch dutifully endured the stinging of bugs and stinking of the bog.

"Do you see them?" he asked.

Sira squinted.

"They move like shadows along the forest floor, and being shadows they will continue being very useful to us."

She marked movement among the tall roots jutting out from the base of the trees. Trolls cleverly smeared in mud crept toward them, nearly invisible in the jumble of bushes and fallen logs in the swamp. Sira would not argue about their usefulness—they had already had to move the *Banshee's Wail* out of deep water to avoid the deadly storms raging along the coasts.

"They can come out of hiding," she snapped. "They called for this meeting."

"I happen to agree." With a smirk, Nathanos whistled with his fingers in his mouth, alerting the Zandalari rebels that he had noticed their presence. They stood one by one, their leader among them, slowly making her way to their location with a pronounced limp. Sira somewhat liked the witch, Apari, for they had both been betrayed by the one thing that had always defined their lives.

For Sira, it was her worship of the goddess, Elune. For Apari, it was her loyalty to the Zandalari crown.

For the seriousness of her injury, Apari navigated the swamp deftly. They met in a clearing not far from the sands, the Widow's Bite leader arriving with her bulbous tick pet on her shoulder, a small entourage of twelve or so guards, and her ever-present lieutenant, the tall, black-haired troll called Tayo.

Apari's white hair had been streaked with mud to hide her identity. None of the trolls wore the distinctive white-and-black robes of the insurrection but rather nondescript rags and bits of armor.

Only Apari and her bodyguard Tayo broke away to speak with them. The troll witch leaned her weight onto her good leg and pressed her palm to her heart. "Greetings, pale rider."

"At last," Nathanos replied shortly. "I realize it must have been difficult, given your limitations, but next time I expect promptness."

Her eyes flashed. "I've no limitations ya need worry about, pale rider."

"Indeed. At least you have understood our need for secrecy. We cannot risk venturing further inland. If Zandalari loyalists lay eyes on us then our plans are forfeit."

The witch waved away his words impatiently. "Have ya brought our payment?"

"You are hardly in a position to make demands." Nathanos snorted. "But I am eager to be out of this swamp."

He twisted at the hip and gestured Ranger Visrynn forward. The dark-haired ranger brought forward a small enameled chest, silently placing it on the neutral ground between the trolls and Blightcaller. Aboard the ship, Sira had seen them preparing the payment, a collection of gems, jewelry, beautifully hammered metal necklace plates, small flagons of rare spirits, and daggers. It struck Sira as slightly excessive given their dwindling resources, but Nathanos had made clear that this was the price of a successful mission.

"Soon," he had assured her aboard the *Banshee's Wail* not an hour earlier, "where we will be going none of these trifles will matter at all."

Sira slapped at another swarm of insects buzzing around her head, watching as the witch's bodyguard knelt and flicked open the chest with one finger. No smile. No thanks for their generosity. No reaction at all. Sira simmered, looking to Nathanos, who revealed as little as the black-haired troll.

"This is not what I want." Apari shook her head, sneering. "This is not what we agreed upon."

Clearing his throat, Nathanos calmly signaled for Visrynn to return. She did and with equal serenity picked up the chest and returned to her sisters behind them.

"Insulting," Sira murmured. Perhaps she should not have. At once, the witch fixed her piercing turquoise eyes upon Sira. An instant later, Sira felt a sensation like a thousand spiders skittering down her back. She shivered but refused to tear her gaze away. Just a witch's trick, she told herself, nothing more.

"Now, now," Nathanos intervened. "This is a simple misunderstanding. What would you have from us instead?"

Apari grinned, showing a set of yellowed teeth sharpened to points, the ends blackened by the foul, strong spirits the Zandalari distilled in charred vats. She hobbled forward, looking Nathanos up and down as if he were a prize cut of meat. Whatever came next, Sira mused, would not make him happy.

"Your messenger said ya want to kill a loa." Apari nodded. Her eyes lit up, the idea clearly exciting her. "You *want* to kill Bwonsamdi, but ya can't, not without us. 'Tis no easy thing, what ya ask. He must be weakened first. Believers and tribute keep him strong, but without faithful followers he be vulnerable. His shrines be protected by powerful magic, the tribute I need from ya will dispel that magic."

Nathanos hurried her along, at last reaching a state of visible impatience. "Go on."

"It will require somethin' precious," she continued. Pointing to Visrynn and the chest, she flapped her hand and shrugged. "That might be precious to some, but not to *you*. Ya must give up somethin' painful, somethin' irreplaceable."

"What we offer should be more than sufficient." Nathanos stood firm. "You are not in a position to bargain."

The witch was stunningly bold, Sira could give her that. With a theatrical sigh, the troll witch began to turn around, avoiding her bad leg and refusing help from her bodyguard as she began rounding up the members of the Widow's Bite. For a moment, Sira remained certain it was just a bluff, but no, the trolls regrouped and slowly disappeared back into the dense foliage of the swamp.

"A moment."

The trolls paused, looking to their leader. Apari waited, only offering a glance over her right shoulder. Before Nathanos could relent and submit to their demands, Sira took him by the elbow, lowering her voice and tilting her head toward him. "Wait . . ."

But he was already pulling a chain out from under his heavy black coat, a green-and-gold badge, warped and faded with time, hung from the tarnished necklace. An officer's badge? A remnant from a war long since forgotten? Sira couldn't say. Nathanos and Sylvanas had once served Silvermoon, he so tactically gifted that he had been raised to the rank of ranger lord in the Farstriders, an achievement no other human had managed. The Dark Lady herself had been the one to give the promotion, the dark rangers serving Sylvanas had told the tale many times at sea. It seemed to be a favorite. Was this the badge recognizing as much? Though his eyes always pulsed with the same steady crimson glow, Sira saw that dim for a moment, fading just like the old, etched memento.

"What are you doing?" Sira whispered. "We cannot simply give in to every demand and roll over like trained dogs. They will think you weak."

At that, Nathanos curled his lip, eyes now as hot and bright as his flaring rage. He seemed to collect himself, breathing hard. His strength, it seemed, was not to be questioned. Sira nearly recoiled, but he only pushed the hair back off his forehead, his gaze burning into her with the same furious intensity.

"You will learn the value of silence, or I will teach it to you." That seemed to satisfy his fury, and when he looked at her again it was as if she were no more than a pustule on his foot, something he loathed to notice but must.

Sira stewed in indignant silence as he pulled at the chain around his neck, breaking it, before closing the gap between them and the troll witch, holding out the badge for her to take. Apari might have been severely injured, but she moved swiftly then, her arm but a blur as she tried to snatch the necklace from his palm. Nathanos, however, was ready for her, and quickly trapped her hand there before she could take the payment.

"This is no trinket, witch. If you fail to destroy the loa's shrines as you have promised, then there will be severe consequences. You may have conjured a few clouds off the coast, but payment this dear demands results."

Sira grinned. There. That was the Blightcaller she knew. While the witch threw back her head and laughed, Sira noticed a shadow moving just behind Apari and her bodyguard. Had that always been there? Sira moved her hand to her side, tucking her fingers around a dagger, preparing to strike. The thing suddenly propelled itself up into the air and then flopped back down, landing in a puddle with a *plop*. Sira smirked. Just a frog. It waited for another moment before taking another graceless leap.

"This . . ." Apari nodded, a serene smile concealing her sharpened teeth. Even her tusks were yellowed and muddy, but she seemed strangely beautiful in that moment, almost angelic, as if by just touching the necklace she had been imbued with a new bloom. "This is what the spell requires. There be the power of longin' in it, of pain. It will do, pale rider, it will do. We assault the first shrine tonight. Bwonsamdi's effigies will burn, and every loss hastens his final hour."

She turned to her bodyguard with a cackle, showing her the badge and necklace.

"What was that?" Sira asked, following Nathanos as he rounded up the dark rangers and headed for their dinghy. He could threaten to teach her the value of silence all he wanted, she was not going to stop speaking her mind. His shoulders were slumped forward as if he had suffered a defeat.

"It doesn't matter now."

"It belonged to her, didn't it?"

Nathanos stopped and sneered, adjusting the quiver buckled across his chest. "Remind me when this is over to drown the witch in this bog."

A rustling in the swampy undergrowth made them both freeze, and all eyes fell on the tumbled shrub in the muck not far from Apari's feet.

"Assassin!" one of her followers shouted. Sira drew her blade, the rangers nocked arrows, Nathanos reached for his immense carved longbow.

Then a single spear soared across the reeds and into the bush, loosed by Tayo with perfect, deadly aim. She stalked over to the spear and tore it out of the undergrowth. A fat, wet toad hung limp from the sharp end.

"Krag'wa the Huge inhabits these swamps, and he be sympathetic to the traitor queen," Tayo spat, lifting up the skewered frog for all to see. "His little spies are everywhere. Could be this one is just a toad, could be he hoppin' away to make mischief for us." She snickered and licked her muddied lips. "Either way? Lunch."

CHAPTER FOURTEEN

Orgrimmar

Thrall pushed away the platter of steaming roast meat in front of him, losing his appetite the moment Yukha arrived at his table. Already he had received word from Zekhan in Zandalar that the assassins who had come after Queen Talanji at the council feast had struck again. They were organized enough to have taken a name, the Widow's Bite, and they had managed to wound several guards at the palace before kidnapping two civilians.

The message from Zekhan lay curled next to his untouched plate of food. He had taken a small residence in the Valley of Spirits, little more than a lodge to keep his belongings and a bed. The other council members had agreed to more luxurious accommodations, but Thrall preferred the modest house; a larger home would simply amplify the emptiness, the absence of his wife, Aggra, and his children, Durak and little Rehze.

No, a simple hut would do until his family could join him or the Horde no longer needed him.

"Not going to eat that?" Yukha leaned against his carved shaman's staff, twirling his gray beard thoughtfully.

"Have you come to steal my supper or do your job, Yukha?"

The shaman smiled, but it didn't reach the wrinkles at his eyes. "Old friend, your missive reached Nordrassil and I carry with me the reply. The Night Warrior bids you come on one condition."

Thrall shifted, even less hungry than before. "And? Spit it out."

"She says you must bring what is owed."

Frowning, Thrall scratched his chin. "What else did she say?"

"Nothing." Yukha shrugged and reached for the haunch of boar growing cold on the table, tearing off a piece of charred skin and eating it. "She claimed you would know what that meant."

"I see. And how does she seem?"

Emboldened by Thrall's disinterest, Yukha tore off a larger piece of boar meat. "Her rage has not lessened, if that is what you mean."

Of course not. Were it me, my rage would simmer for a thousand years.

"Very well. I can linger here no longer waiting for messengers and quelling council squabbles." He sighed. "And this will only cause another one."

Thrall pushed himself up from the table, lumbering over to the door. "Boy!" he called.

The head of a skinny orc page appeared, shoving aside the leather curtain protecting the doorway.

"Run to the hold quick as you can. Summon Calia Menethil and Baine Bloodhoof—we depart for Nordrassil before sundown."

"Right away!"

The boy vanished, and Thrall crossed to the large, ancient chest of his belongings next to his spare bed. He fished out a clean leather harness and a woven red cloak, one Aggra had made while teaching their children to weave. A subtle design of yellow and darker crimson ran along the border, and Thrall traced it with his fingers. *Home.*

He shrugged on the harness and draped the cloak around his

shoulders while Yukha rubbed his chin. "Hm. The undead woman and the high chieftain. Are you certain that's wise? Will they not both remind her of the Banshee Queen in their own ways?"

"Baine despises Sylvanas, and the feeling is mutual," Thrall replied, leaving the hut with the shaman trailing close behind. It was well known that Sylvanas Windrunner considered Baine a softhearted liability, even before he sought to overthrow her. Her hatred of the tauren struck Thrall as a ringing endorsement, and now that he had come to know Baine better and witness his devotion to the Earth Mother and to the spirits, his respect for the chieftain only grew.

Sunlight dampened by a haze of dust roasted the city, and Thrall found himself longing for the cool, shaded pools dotting the land on his farm in Nagrand. He could almost hear the laughter of his children splashing in the water . . .

"And the woman?" Yukha asked.

"Calia Menethil wishes to bridge the divide between the Forsaken and the kaldorei that have recently found themselves raised into undeath. I see no harm in it."

They stood side by side, the old shaman leaning heavily on his staff while Thrall surveyed the warren of streets under the shaman's quarter packed with shops and forges, anvils ringing day and night as blacksmiths tried to replenish the deficit left by the Blood War.

Yukha cringed at his words.

"You disagree?" Thrall's eyes followed the page, Gunk, as he wound his way through the mundane chaos of the commerce below.

"It would be better if you came alone."

"Half the council is already convinced that I will be ambushed in Nordrassil; some small concessions must be made," Thrall said. At last, Gunk vanished, bare little feet flying, out of sight and well on his way to the Valley of Strength. "Go back inside and finish the rest of my supper if it bothers you so."

At that, Yukha barked with mirth. "Ha, Earthbinder, to go without me would indeed be your downfall. I have negotiated safe passage with the druids protecting the World Tree, I am to escort you and your chosen companions."

Thrall flinched at the old title. It did not fit him anymore. "Well. I feel safer already."

Yukha ignored the jab. "Tiala assured me that passage to the World Tree would remain safely open for us. I am to guide you there and then to Tyrande's location. After that? After that, you're on your own."

You must bring what is owed.

Thrall was no fool. Surely Tyrande Whisperwind and Malfurion Stormrage desired some gesture, some remuneration for the war crimes visited upon Teldrassil. Even in Nagrand, even cut off from his connection to the powers of a shaman, he had felt the moment the world shifted and the wrath of Sylvanas Windrunner set the kaldorei capital ablaze. It was quiet, it was distant, but he heard a collective cry, and for a brief, terrifying moment he tasted smoke on the air where none had been before.

What did he owe?

How did he answer that? He had not been part of the Horde war that led to the atrocity and that, perhaps, was why Tyrande and Malfurion were willing to meet with him at all. Innocence in one specific crime felt like a weak shield. But perhaps he had more. He gazed over the raised plateaus and flying banners of Orgrimmar and imagined it aflame, imagined the city that had been the source of so much life and joy and war and pain reduced to smoldering rubble. What would he want if such a thing were to happen? What would he need?

What possible balm could soothe a wound so impossibly deep?

They exchanged mounts at Valormok, leaving behind their long-maned wind riders for four saddled and restless hippogryphs, their feathers a brilliant rainbow of blue, purple, and green. Fortunately, the largest of the beasts was able to accommodate Baine's considerable heft. Thrall spent the exhausting ride in subdued contemplation, hardly noticing the open scar of the strip mines outside Orgrimmar and then the far more placid view of the Southfury River. The burnished trees of Azshara diminished into just a smear of blood across the land as their hippogryphs lifted them higher, higher, following the path of a churning waterful until at last Mount Hyjal sketched itself in behind the evening mist.

The skies darkened to a striking imperial amethyst, and the first glimpse of the World Tree came, roots gripping the mountainside like gnarled hands.

"Oh," he heard Calia Menethil say softly to his right. "Oh, but it is *beautiful*."

"Nordrassil," Baine Bloodhoof added, echoing her delight. "The Crown of the Heavens. What a gift, to walk in the shade of a World Tree."

"Look!" Calia pointed at a pair of playful faerie dragons chasing each other across the surface of the lake below Nordrassil. They flew in a spiral, then dashed back toward the hills and the clearing where Thrall, Calia, Baine, and Yukha made their descent. The dragons passed within inches of Calia, their purple-and-pink wings ruffling her hair.

They dismounted, safe as Yukha had promised. The hippogryphs were wrangled and taken away while they waited in the almost oppressive calm.

"The light here is so different, the way it strikes the leaves . . ." Calia murmured, gazing up at the World Tree, its top unseeable in the clouds by even the keenest eyes. "And the flowers! Have you ever seen blossoms of truer blue?"

"By my father's spirit, it is truly a blessing from the Earth Mother." Baine knelt, the beads adorning his horns and armor twinkling as he admired one of the flowers, inhaling its fragrance.

Thrall watched the gloom of night crawl toward them, encroaching on the clearing, stone pillars topped with bright azure flames the only wards against the darkness. For all the fresh air and pretty flowers, Thrall couldn't allow himself to be at ease.

"There is a pall over this place," he said softly. Under the eaves of the inn nestled against the roots of the tree, a Hyjal warden, cloaked in the brown and green sigil of Nordrassil, kept vigil.

Only Yukha heard him. "We should move quickly. Come."

The shaman led them, skirting the gray-timbered inn and taking them down a shallow slope to the banks of the crystal-clear lake. With a tap of his staff against the damp earth, the water ahead of them turned sturdy enough to hold them all. Yukha pressed on as swiftly as aged legs would carry him.

"Take care with your words," Thrall warned Baine and Calia.

"Perhaps it is better now to listen," Baine replied with a solemn nod. "Chatter will not help heal old wounds."

"Yes, you sense the darkness that hangs over this place?"

"Mourning . . ." Calia spoke gently, her footfalls as delicate as raindrops on the watery path. "I did not at first realize, the beauty of the World Tree is overwhelming. But Thrall is right, this is a place in mourning, and we are trespassing on their grief."

Thrall nodded, heartened that they both understood the gravity of the situation. He had chosen his companions wisely.

"I would not have come at all but that the spirit realm is fractured and our shaman cannot find a cause; that is too dire to ignore," Thrall said, reiterating an argument he had made before the council when justifying this very journey to Nordrassil.

On the other side of the lake another hill rose, this one crowned with three silver tents, the poles intricately carved with leaves and painted moons. Thick blankets and furs were spread before the tents, along with a low, cushioned bench, the arms carved into owls. Seated beneath the bench, a night elf girl plucked dolefully at a lute.

Thrall hardly noticed the somber music, gripped instead by the two regal figures seated on the owl bench. As they neared, one of the figures stood, observing them but refusing to bow or give any respectful sign of recognition. Archdruid Malfurion Stormrage made an imposing impression, tall and strong as timeworn timbers, the antlers of a stag growing from his head, feathers sprouting from his arms, and an emerald beard longer and finer than Yukha's hanging from his chin.

And where Malfurion embodied the forest and its creatures, his wife, Tyrande Whisperwind, was a sublime manifestation of Elune, the goddess of the moon. Her white enameled armor chased with silver might have been woven from starlight itself. Two even turquoise braids framed her face, the clean loveliness of her garb and hair making the blackened pits of her eyes all the more unsettling.

Malfurion and Tyrande were not alone, and Thrall was surprised to find both Maiev Shadowsong and Shandris Feathermoon joined them. The two night elves had been in whispered conversation behind the bower, but grew silent at the Horde's approach. Maiev's cold steel helmet, winged and sharp, stood in unsettling contrast to the harmonious natural beauty all around them. Only her emerald green cloak, trimmed in cloud-soft fur, blended into their serene surroundings. Shandris Feathermoon had come as armed and armored as her companions, a fall of dark blue hair spilling from the top of her leather helmet, her eyes hidden, though he hardly needed to see them to know they were unfriendly.

Yukha stopped them several feet from the edge of the carpets, and Thrall stood shoulder to shoulder with him. Nearly two heads shorter than Thrall, Calia waited beside the orc, Baine to her left.

Expecting a chilly reception, Thrall bowed deeply, relieved to find that his council counterparts did the same.

"As promised." Yukha also demonstrated his respect for the kaldorei leadership. "Thrall, son of Durotan, high chieftain of the tauren, Baine Bloodhoof, and Calia Menethil, princess of Lordaeron and councilor of the Horde Forsaken. They have come to discuss the disturbances noted by the shaman of the Earthen Ring and the Moonglade druids."

Tyrande merely tapped the musician on the shoulder. The girl strummed one last time and then grew still. The insect nightsong of the glade began, though it did little to assuage the awkward silence. Thrall kept his attention on Tyrande, as she had locked her eyes on him and did not look away.

"Thank you for agreeing to this meeting," Thrall began, his voice unexpectedly ragged. He cleared his throat and pressed on. "Yukha and others feel a sinister interference in the spirit realm. Our dead are not passing on as they should, and they are heedless of the shaman attempting to guide them."

Nothing. None of them so much as blinked, though it was hard to say with Maiev and Shandris wearing their helmets. He decided it was a safe bet.

"Yukha tells me your priestesses have made similar discoveries," Thrall continued, growing a little angry. His cheeks burned with the indignity of their reception. In different days, younger days, he would not have abided the insult. "We have come seeking answers. Will you speak with us?"

Nothing. Frosty, rigid silence. At his side, Calia shifted nervously.

Thrall collected himself before saying something rash. He looked into Tyrande's eyes once more, into the hypnotizing aura of darkness in the never-cool embers of her eyes. That moment in Nagrand returned to him, when he tasted smoke and sensed a far-off pain. That pain was not so far off for her, it was constant and as potent as the day Teldrassil burned. They had once stood together, he, Tyrande, and Malfurion, all three of them defending Nordrassil. That tree they had managed to save, but now the crime of its sister burning must be answered. They had even witnessed his marriage to his wife, Aggra, there in the shade of Nordrassil's venerable branches, though that seemed many lifetimes ago now. Perhaps Tyrande's rage had obliterated those memories altogether.

"I brought what you wanted, what is owed," Thrall said, and at last he saw a spark of life in her eyes. "I bring you the sincere apology of the Horde. We are not a single voice now spoken through the mouth of a warchief, but a whole host of voices. We have formed a council, so that never again will one take power and abuse it as Sylvanas did. As . . . as Sylvanas used that power to slaughter your people."

He could swear the moon above glowed brighter, as if the mere mention of the Banshee Queen's name had ignited its anger.

"Calia Menethil has come, she stands as an example of how we hope to change," Thrall soldiered on. Calia nodded, but mercifully kept silent. "Lilian Voss now speaks for the Forsaken. Both women seek to reforge themselves anew, free of Sylvanas, free of her poisonous influence. Those who are sympathetic to the traitor have been exiled, her loyalists torn out by the roots. Baine Bloodhoof even sought to overthrow Sylvanas and remove her as warchief; it is only a shame that he did not do so sooner, and that more did not listen."

Was he speaking to a wall? Would nothing move Tyrande? Even Malfurion gave him the smallest nod of understanding, perhaps only indicating that he was listening.

To his surprise, Shandris Feathermoon removed her helmet, revealing the red tattoos and startling white eyes beneath. "You will understand our hesitation, Thrall. Even promises made by our own allies have been broken. I would hear more of what you have come to say, but only because I crave justice as dearly as I crave healing for our people."

Maiev scoffed. "Have a care, Shandris. Listen to his honeyed words at your peril, believe him at your peril, join the Horde to hunt Sylvanas at your peril, for once the deed is done, you will again find their daggers at your back."

At that, Tyrande almost smiled.

Shandris's wispy brows met in frustration. "I believe justice is action, Maiev, I have told you as much before."

"Whose action?" Maiev demanded, her sharp voice shattering the peace of the glade. "The Horde's? Whose action? What justice? For I will not be content with only Sylvanas Windrunner receiving her due. She was not alone when Teldrassil burned."

"Baine was imprisoned for opposing Sylvanas," Thrall reminded them. "Not all of the Horde stood with her that day."

"And yet she spoke for your side, acted for your side," Maiev shot back. "The warchief is the voice of the Horde, the hand of the Horde, but now you have scattered yourselves to a council, dispersing the blame, hiding behind cowardly revisions of a history that will not be forgotten!"

She punctuated her anger with a step toward him. Carefully, Shandris drew her back.

"I doubt you would like to be held accountable for every mistake and crime committed by the Alliance," Shandris said in a soothing tone.

"Aye," Baine spoke up. "What is justice to you now? Must Thunderbluff burn? Must Orgrimmar? Will the deaths of our innocents appease you? Do you think pain does not simply bring more pain?"

"High Overlord Saurfang engineered the siege with Sylvanas, though he had no intention of destroying the World Tree," Thrall added. "His part cannot be forgotten, but he is now in the grave, put there by his own warchief."

Calia Menethil glanced between the far taller, larger Baine and Thrall, then softly joined her voice to theirs. Quietly, but no less firm and sure. "These disagreements are a distraction. Our divided sides only keep us from apprehending the one who gave the order."

Maiev swiveled, watching for Tyrande and Malfurion's reaction, but neither of them replied. In the lingering silence, Shandris ventured her opinion once more.

"If we agree to . . . to a temporary understanding," she said, obviously picking her words with care, "then we do so not to exonerate the Horde entirely, it is but the strategy of a moment. I see no reason why this cannot be."

"I see many reasons," Maiev muttered.

Tyrande, it seemed, still did not care to speak.

The elf began plucking her lute again, but Tyrande slammed her hand down on the owl-shaped arm of the bench, demanding a return to silence. Had the moon grown bigger in the sky? Was it somehow closer? Threatening?

"It was not yet time." Malfurion's grave baritone filled the clearing. He leaned down toward his wife, placing a furred, clawed hand on her shoulder. "This was folly. Let them go."

Tyrande uncrossed her legs and sat back on the bench, shaking off her husband's hand with a tight grimace.

And then, all at once, she cared very much to speak.

"When you have washed the bodies of a thousand kaldorei burned and broken, when you have fallen to your knees and kissed the feet of a thousand mourning souls, when you look into their eyes and tell them 'our Horde has changed' and they *believe* you, only then will I accept your apology and treat you as my equal." Tyrande's voice, edged as steel, pulled the air out of the clearing. "My brethren here may be willing to entertain your empty pledges of justice and aid, but I know better. I have learned better."

Then she stood, and Thrall worried that the moon might truly fall from the heavens and crush them at Tyrande's command. Her eyes, though black, somehow glowed, Elune's fury blazing colder and brighter along her skin with each word. The glade itself grew gray and almost dead, as if by her will she had sapped the life out of everything around them, withering the trees and obliterating the flowers and grass to dust.

"How many orphans did your Horde create that day?" Tyrande sliced the flat of her hand diagonally across her body. "Those children will grow, they will wake each morning tasting ash, and one day they will come for you. Oh, they will come for you, and they will make you taste that same ash, and then you will know their justice." She sat down again, as if winded. Light returned to the clearing, and the plants around them were green and vibrant once more.

"Quickly," Yukha muttered, trying to gather them. "We must go. This was a mistake; I should not have brought you here."

Baine and Calia allowed Yukha to corral them back toward the path of glittering solid water. Thrall remained, only taking slow, careful steps, never showing Tyrande his back. For his trouble, Tyrande directed her final words to him and only him.

"You will find that justice less sweet than the sorry excuse for punishment you faced, and when this justice comes, there will be no armistice to save you."

Thrall felt Yukha grab him by the arm and yank. But he did not agree with the shaman's assessment; it was important and right that they had come. Thrall had thought he knew what Tyrande wanted, that what was owed was his remorse, but now he realized his error.

He easily shook off Yukha's hand and pressed his fist to his chest to prove his sincerity.

"I will bring what is owed, then. I will not bring words or promises, I will bring you the head of Sylvanas Windrunner."

The faintest trace of a smile appeared on Tyrande Whisperwind's face. "Do it, then, or never seek to speak with me again."

CHAPTER FIFTEEN

Dazar'alor

The nightmares had come frequent enough that Talanji could reconigze them for the falsehood they were. Recognizing them was different from escaping them. Still, as venom dripped from fangs as thick and white as riverbeast tusks, the first corrosive splash landed on Talanji's shoulder. She screamed, helpless to protect herself as the spider hovered over her, jaws descending. Razor sharp. So, so close . . . Thrashing, kicking, twisting, nothing helped. No hope.

The creature in Shadra's own image pinned Talanji to her bed, its eight legs trapping her like a living prison. Its abdomen heaved, silk threads filling the chamber, the threads that would form a deadly cocoon and Talanji's mausoleum. The giant spider opened its dripping mouth wide, and Talanji cried out once more. Inside, struggling to get out, she saw the face of Bezime, the inconsolable father who had come to beg for a queen's lenience so that a young marriage might blossom. But the Widow's Bite had taken him from the palace during one of their raids on the city, Talanji's patrols finding Bezime's corpse at the edge of Nazmir, charred almost beyond recognition.

The troll clawed at the spider's insides, desperate to get out.

"Help me! My queen! My queen, help me!"

"I cannot." Talanji thrashed harder. If this was the end, if she was to be visited by all her failures, then she would not simply lie still and die without a fight. One name might save her. One cry for aid might actually banish the nightmare. Tears streamed down Bezime's frantic face, and then his skin began to blister and burn, his pleas buried in the spider's thorax as the beast clamped its jaws shut and lunged for Talanji.

"Bwonsamdi!"

The image of Shadra stilled then broke apart, fragmenting into puffs of blue smoke that gradually faded, rising to the ceiling like candle smoke. Just another dream. Another *nightmare*. It didn't matter; Talanji gasped for breath, leaping out of bed and grabbing up the blanket, wrapping it around herself while she wiped at the very real sweat on her brow. As she pulled her hand away from her forehead, she saw deep lines carved into it, wrinkles that had not been there the day before. How could that be? Was ruling leeching the life out of her so quickly?

"Ya called?"

She exhaled and sat back down on the edge of her bed, knowing Bwonsamdi waited just on the other side of the immense golden platform. A merciful breeze, humid yet cool, blew in from the open balcony window. Talanji turned her face toward it, greedy for the relief it brought.

"It was . . . it was only a nightmare," she said. "Shadra wanted me dead, and the poor father they stole from the palace was inside her. It felt so real."

"Because ya guilt is real." Bwonsamdi appeared before her, the azure fire eyes behind his mask glowing dimly. "Take a look outside, my queen, ya nightmare is not over. Somethin' must be done, and soon."

Talanji hissed, clutching the blanket to her chest and padding on bare feet to the balcony's edge. She tried not to look at her visibly withered hands. The loa of graves spoke true. Fires burned bright in the jungles below, eight pinpoints of light in the darkness. Either she was still emerging from sleep or Bwonsamdi appeared shaky, translucent, as if he were only half present.

"How is it possible?" Talanji bit down hard on her lip, a rage building inside that would soon spill out or consume her. "My soldiers patrol the jungle tirelessly, yet somehow they slip by. They raid my city, attack my palace, attack *me* . . . How did they grow so strong so quickly?"

Bwonsamdi floated beside her, surveying the work of the Widow's Bite. Talanji had not been idle, meeting with her council each day to discuss new approaches, new tactics. They had the superior force and superior resources, but their own land worked against them. The Widow's Bite could use the jungle to stay hidden, their scattered numbers an advantage against an army spread thin by the size of Zuldazar. And many even in the city, she knew, remained suspicious of her rule. Those sympathetic ears might become sympathetic mouths, spreading the lies and terror of the group, eating away at the stability of Talanji's rule.

"What do we do?" Talanji murmured. "How do I stop what I cannot see? They have no fortress, not even camps. By the time my guards find them, they are already gone. We are chasing vapor, fighting fires that are already smoldering coals."

"They attack you because of the pact ya fa'da made," Bwonsamdi told her, waving his hand toward the chaos below. "They think I control ya, and they fear what my queen, a queen of death, might become."

Talanji glared. "I am *not* your queen."

"Tell them that." He gave a dark laugh. "They be burnin' my shrines, breakin' the magic that protects them, killing my priests where they stand. If they burn many more, I won't be much help to ya. A loa is nothin' without believers and prayers."

"It's harming you," Talanji gasped. "You're growing weaker."

The loa nodded gravely. "And you."

"Me?" She collapsed back against the balcony wall, hopelessly frustrated. Holding up her hands to the light of the braziers, she forced herself to look at them. "My . . . my hands. What is happening to me, Bwonsamdi?"

"We share a bond, little queen." He sighed. "We share a fate. If I have no followers, if there is no tribute and no faith, then I will be all but gone. My strength weakens, and tethered together, yours weakens with it."

Talanji swore, stuffing her hands under the blanket to hide them. "Then these shivers, this pain in my chest . . ."

"It will get worse, Talanji, unless ya protect me. Ya *must* protect me."

She heard the true fear in his voice, and wondered how she was to stand tall and courageous when even a god was afraid. "I . . . I cannot accept this."

"Accept it or not." Bwonsamdi bowed his head, the flames in his eyes even dimmer. "It is the truth."

Talanji inhaled shakily. "If true, if, then . . . then how do I fight these rebels? Can you not help me?"

The loa chuckled, but it was utterly mirthless. "You have the soldiers, Talanji, and ya could have many, many more. I think ya already know how to fight the rebels."

The Horde. Of course. That ambassador Zekhan wouldn't stop pressing her to return to Orgrimmar and accept a place on the new Horde Council. A position that would give her what, exactly? She needed troops and ships, not empty promises. But her stubbornness wouldn't put out fires, and the Zanchuli Council had offered no solutions, just repeated concerns. It was up to her. It was *always* up to her. And now her life was on the line.

"I will never accept peace with the Alliance," she said, stony. "But I will ask for the Horde's help. This is . . . this is growing beyond us."

"Good, good." Bwonsamdi grinned at last. "An attack against me is an attack against you; if they destroy us both, who will protect Zandalar?"

Talanji narrowed her eyes, suspicious of that grin. "This is no small thing you want from me. The Horde is working with the witch that killed my father. The Horde is content to ignore the crimes of Jaina Proudmoore, but I never will be. So if you get what you want, loa, I will not go empty-handed."

"Empty-handed?" Bwonsamdi cackled at her, an unkind sneer twisting his mouth. "Ya get a kingdom and ya life, I'd say that's more than fair."

"*And* I am rid of this bond between us, Bwonsamdi. *Rastakhan's* deal. I want it no longer, and if I am to abandon my pride to the Horde then you will abandon this pact. My life is my own, tied to no other's."

Talanji felt her breath catch in her throat. It wasn't often she gave an ultimatum to a loa. And from the grimace on Bwonsamdi's face, he clearly disapproved. But she did not back down from the loa of death. If he needed her so badly, then he could compromise. It was only fair. It was time, at last, for her to be making the deals.

"Ha. I don't think so, little queen."

"Why? It cannot be undone? Our pact?" she asked. "Will it kill me to break it?"

"No, Talanji, but ya would regret it. Ya have the loa of graves on your side, the loyalty of a god—did ya really think there would be no drawbacks?"

The breeze whistled between them, then a crackle as the flames spreading through the jungle claimed a stand of trees and sent them toppling over. Screams punctuated the night.

The room behind her grew frosty and fogged, a blast of energy sending her toppling against the bed as Bwonsamdi mustered what little strength he had, thundering, "Foolish girl, nothin' to say?"

Talanji whirled to face him. She did not cower. She did not speak. Let him throw his tantrum, the high ground was hers to keep.

"Reckless child of a reckless king! Consider yaself lucky you be workin' with me and not another loa," Bwonsamdi spat. In his rage he had expanded to fill the room, his hair brushing the ceiling. Then he diminished, his eyes once again dimmer and less blue. "Mueh'zala would eat ya alive."

Even the mention of the other loa's name made Bwonsamdi's image waver and blur.

"I would tell him the same thing," Talanji stated, defiant. She might have only been a young troll in a bed sheet without crown, without jewels, without a weapon, but she was still the queen.

"Ya will regret this," Bwonsamdi assured her, shrinking further. "Consider the deal struck, girl. Protect my shrines, keep us safe, and when I am strong again our pact will be no more. Ya will have your life back, all your own, but ya may not like what it means to be all alone."

CHAPTER SIXTEEN

Dazar'alor

Zekhan hopped lightly from foot to foot, waiting for his moment to speak. The Zanchuli Council had put him down on their schedule, an emergency meeting called at dawn to address the growing threat of the Widow's Bite.

He had never before presented officially in front of a crowd of important strangers, and the pressure squeezed him from every direction. The answer, he felt, was plain. Talanji needed help from the Horde, the Horde wanted to give it, and she simply had to be convinced that her personal vendettas mattered less than the safety and security of Zandalar.

However, the likelihood of swaying her to his point of view seemed less and less as she paced before the council in their lofty golden chairs, her voice clear and decisive, the council nodding in agreement with nearly every word.

"The Widow's Bite would have us believe that they are everywhere and nowhere," Talanji was saying. "But this is not true. They have made a mistake. Now we know what they want: They want to weaken Bwonsamdi because they believe it will weaken *me*."

Servants in glittering headdresses and feathered skirts took vigorous notes behind the council members, scribbling frantically on tablets while Talanji continued her speech to the silent, enthralled audience.

"They will continue to target places of Bwonsamdi's power. His shrines, of course, and more importantly, the Necropolis. It must not fall, but knowing where the rebels will strike means we can put a stop to this now." She stilled, facing her council with her head held high. "We protect the shrines, we protect the Necropolis, and the Widow's Bite will be forced into open conflict."

Zekhan began to applaud, moved, but realized he was alone in doing so. Not only that, he was not there to support her plan, not really; he needed her to ally with the Horde, that was the primary reason Thrall had sent Zekhan in the first place. He cleared his throat and slipped further into the shadows behind the pillars of the great council chamber.

The chieftain of the Darkspear tribe had arrived just hours before dawn, alarmed by what he had read in Zekhan's messages. A brutal storm had begun to rage off the coast, the way unpassable by sea, air the only available route. Even that was dangerous. One of Gazlowe's flying machines had been able to safely drop him off in the harbor, but only just, damaged by the electricity brewing in the clouds, crashing offshore the moment Rokhan set foot on dry land. Zekhan had greeted his arrival with relief, thrilled to have support from not only a member of the Horde Council itself but a close friend of the queen's.

Chieftain Rokhan stood, blood-red tabard and leather armor a stark contrast to the blue- and purple- and gold-clad council members.

"I agree with ya assessment, Queen Talanji," he said. "But we best send those patrols now. Sentiment in the city is not good, ya majesty. These attacks make you look incompetent and weak."

To her credit, Talanji did not flinch.

Wardruid Loti, enameled armor blazing under the brazier hanging above the council, stood and grunted her agreement. "The rebel threat ends today."

"Then let a force be assembled," Natal'hakata, blue-haired and golden-tusked, roared. "The Necropolis is vast, with many tunnels where little spiders might hide; it will take a great deal of resources to secure it."

It was time to step in. Zekhan wasn't on the schedule until after Zolani was slated to speak, but he knew this was his one opportunity to intervene before their enthusiasm and certainty grew too powerful to overcome. He not only had a duty to the Horde to represent their interests, but the loa of graves himself had bid him change Talanji's mind.

No pressure whatsoever now. Ancestors protect me.

"I-if I may?"

Zekhan swore he heard a parrot flap its wings six miles away in the abrupt, chilling silence. He tiptoed around the pillar concealing him and stood in Talanji's shadow, her arms crossed expectantly.

"Ah, Zekhan. Come forward, boy. What do ya have to say?" Rokhan gestured him forward. "Let us hear from our Horde ambassador."

"Do we really have time for this?" Natal'hakata muttered.

"I can be brief." Zekhan hurried to the center of the great chamber. It reminded him of the grandeur of Grommash Hold. How many great decisions had been made there? How many executions decided? How many wars declared? Just a jungle boy from the shores of the Echo Isles . . .

Varok Saurfang had taught him to see war differently, to see it as the preventable horror it truly was. Zekhan made a fist, holding that thought in his hand like a talisman. What he said next might save the lives of many Zandalari warriors, and further on down, it might save lives in the Horde if Talanji were to join her strength to theirs.

"Speak, boy," Natal'hakata demanded, impatient.

"Don't send your soldiers to the Necropolis," Zekhan blurted. Bad start. He winced and tried again, this time slower. "The queen is right. Bwonsamdi must be protected, and all the people of Zandalar, too. But you can't do it alone."

"This is a Zandalari problem." Talanji stalked up to him, nearly butting against his tusks. "I am not unreasonable, I can bend. The Horde may send their troops, if and when they agree to lend me those same troops against the Proudmoores."

"No, no, no, they will never agree to that!" Zekhan countered. "And what then? Ya people think ya weak now, what will they think when ya can't protect ya own shrines and temples from a band of rebels?"

Rumbling from the council. *Interest* from the council.

Zekhan pushed on, sensing his moment. "You will get one chance to write the endin' of this story. So far your people have only witnessed defeat, can ya stand to show them one more? Why take that chance? The Horde is willin' to stand with you. With their help, with their strength, we can write that endin', a victorious endin', right now."

Talanji looked ready to throttle him, but she kept her temper, her chest rising and falling faster and faster. "This is propaganda!"

"The boy has a point." Rokhan stroked his chin thoughtfully. "The only propaganda I be seein' is what the Widow's Bite spreads against us, my queen. That tide is turnin' and without a decisive victory the rebels could raise the whole city against you."

"If the queen's rule is truly threatened," the tortollan, Lashk, spoke up, head craning farther out of his shell, "then inviting the Horde forces back here could be a mistake. I mean no insult to you, Rokhan, but what if your generals see an opportunity to invade?"

"Lashk speaks wisdom." Talanji nodded, reiterating, "There are already rumors of such in the city, if the Horde is to come then we must have certain promises in return. Justice for our city, revenge for the Alliance siege."

"These rumors . . ." Standing, the chieftain Rokhan stepped down from the raised platform where the council members sat. He regarded first Talanji and then Zekhan, his voice low with weariness. "I have my doubts about these rebels. They be too fast, too smart. Maybe a loa be helpin' them. Or maybe somethin' else."

Zekhan blinked. "Like what?"

"I don't know yet, boy. But I intend to find out." Rokhan pushed by them both, separating them, leaving the council chambers with slow, deliberate steps. On his belt, his red dagger flashed with cunning magic. "Ya won't have my support either way until we know more, Queen Talanji. The ambassador here be right—we only get one chance."

Talanji went after him and then the others, arguments erupting between the council as they adjourned without any official call to do so. Everyone and everything was in an uproar. Zekhan stared, speechless, buffeted this way and that by the leaving council, trying to drop a word in on conversations he was not welcome to join. Before he could think of something that might keep them all there, the chamber was empty, even the note-taking pages fleeing.

Scratching his head, Zekhan tried to piece together what had just happened. He had persuaded some of the members, at least a little, but Talanji remained impossible to reach. And here he thought she was growing more sympathetic to the Horde. What would it take? What would make her see that she need not stand alone?

"Thanks for listenin'!" Zekhan called after the long-gone council. "I think."

"Oh, they heard ya, boy. They heard ya. And ya did well."

The voice wrapped around him like a vise, wringing all the joy and lightness out of his body before he could breathe again. Bwonsamdi. The loa had come to visit, his unsettling, masked presence somehow weaker, as if he was stretched thin, a well running dry.

"I didn't do well." Zekhan slumped his way to the platform, sitting on the edge of it, just below where the council chairs gleamed with hammered gold and jewels. "Talanji won't trust me, she won't trust the Horde, and we're runnin' out of time."

Bwonsamdi floated down to meet him, sitting to his right, his bones and armor rattling as he descended. His presence cast a shadow over everything; even the sun outside lost some of its heat and shine. Still, his image was thin, worryingly so, like linen breeches almost worn through. "Ya new at this. Don't be so hard on yaself, boy. Some of the council be listenin' to ya, and that's no small feat. They see somethin' powerful in you, they see what I see."

At that, Zekhan straightened. A loa, a god, thought he was doing a good job? That he was powerful? It didn't seem real. But no, he had heard the words and he felt them lift his sinking spirits. What had he done to find his way into the presence of so many influential beings? Maybe Bwonsamdi was right. Maybe he truly was powerful.

Ancestors, you never let me down.

"And what do they see?" Zekhan chuckled. "Besides a failure."

"Someone they want on their side."

Zekhan jumped up and straightened the Horde colors draped over his shoulder. "You're right. The council did listen, and if they can listen to me, then so can the queen. I can't give up."

He felt the loa walk in stride with him toward the wide-open archway that showed the carpet of green jungle blanketing Zandalar. The fires had gone out, but the smoke still rose in pillars of dire warning. The loa walked in step with him. Zekhan closed his hand into a fist again, holding on to that moment, holding on to the faith and trust of a god.

"Don't give up, boy." Bwonsamdi's amused chuckle filled the chamber, but there was a note of sadness to it. That only strengthened Zekhan's resolve. The loa needed protecting, and Zekhan would see it done.

"Don't give up." The loa's words drifted down to him as Bwonsamdi gradually disappeared, nothing but his blue flame eyes remaining in the blinding light of dawn. "That's the *spirit*."

CHAPTER SEVENTEEN

Nazmir

The sound of a flute infiltrated the captain's quarters, made thin and muted by the layers of timber separating Mathias Shaw from the crew below deck. Across from him, down the considerable length of a well-used and lacquered table, Flynn Fairwind tapped his foot to the music, boot bouncing as he sang along under his breath.

"You can go join them, you know," Mathias pointed out, studying him over the edge of his book. It was a history of Zandalar, old and somewhat out of date. Dry stuff. His companion, however, seemed more inclined to cozy up to his bottle.

Flynn shrugged. A chandelier of lanterns rocked back and forth, sending light skittering across the table toward the pirate. "Crew has less fun when captain chaperones. They need time to relax and just be themselves."

"Don't you need that also?" Mathias asked, cocking a brow.

"Everyone does." Flynn nodded to the water-damaged book he held. "Except you. Do you ever stop working?"

"Not really."

Flynn snorted. "See?"

"Fine." Mathias closed the book and placed it on the table, then stretched his stiff arms over his head, groaning a little. "I stopped working. What now?"

"You're hopeless," the pirate chuckled and rolled his eyes, but swiveled and managed to put down the bottle for a moment. "What shall we discuss?"

"This was your idea," Mathias replied.

Sometimes on the *Bold Arva,* when the sailing was smooth and the work of the day done, the crew would all sit around telling tales and singing, but Mathias kept to the captain's quarters. Flynn often joined him, ever inebriated, but most nights he would just sip to keep his end of the conversation flowing. At first, the constant company annoyed Mathias, but gradually, as he was prone to do, he built a profile of the strange and fascinating Flynn Fairwind.

He wondered if he would ever truly understand Fairwind, who seemed to him a man haunted, smiling and laughing to distract from something else. Maybe he didn't need to understand him, though the desire to remained constant. It was simply in Shaw's nature, to try and scrape away the façade and see what lay beneath—and that skill, that obsession, made him good at his job.

"My mother was a thief, you know," Fairwind blurted out then, unprompted. The ship creaked around them, a sailor's lullaby, rocking them just like a doting mother might do. Maybe that was what made Fairwind say it.

"I did not know," Mathias responded. Sensing this was going to be a long talk, he stood and fetched himself a rare tumbler of wine from the cabinet behind him.

"She was, she was." Fairwind sighed and shook his head, raking both hands through his long, golden brown hair, then fussing with the ribbon tying it back. "Always insisted she was a barmaid, but one night I hid under the bed in our cottage and waited for her. She must have thought I was out back playing, but no, I was watching . . .

Mathias couldn't help but lean forward a little, interested.

Flynn smirked. "I could only see the hem of her skirt and her shoes, worn through to the soles of her feet. She went to a loose brick by the hearth and pried it up, then stuffed a few necklaces and brooches in there."

"Did she catch you?"

"No." He shook his head. "I waited until she went back out looking for me and popped up, crawled out the window and scrambled around in a bush to make it seem like I had been out there all along. For a while I was . . . I don't know, angry, or sad because I wanted her to trust me. But then I realized: Any mother willing to do that for her son, risk her life and her liberty, must be full of love."

"And bravery," Mathias told him softly.

At that, Flynn snorted, looking at him askew. "Says the man working for the crown."

"You work for it now, too."

"Blimey, you're right." Flynn reached for the bottle, chugging liberally.

It was Mathias's turn to smirk. "So. Where is she now? Your mother . . ."

Flynn made a clicking sound with his cheek and stared at the bottle for a long moment. "She's dead. Hanged for being a thief. I think that was the day I stopped being a stupid little boy. I made myself go and watch, I remember being so small I could barely see anything in the crowd." He laughed bitterly at the memory, then gazed out the curved windows that showed the darkened sea. He kicked his feet up on the table, boots scuffed and salt-stained. "I remember the sound most of all. Everyone but me knew when it was coming, and then there was a breath in, everyone all together, and then . . ." He squeezed his eyes shut, and Mathias held his wine midway between mouth and table, transfixed. And then? "And then a crunch, like a hammer striking wet gravel. I thought I would hear her scream or cry out for me, but no, just the breath in and then the end."

Mathias flinched and put down his wine, then turned the tumbler a few times. "No little boy should know that sound."

"You've heard it before, I gather."

"Yes, many times."

"And does it always make you feel sick?" Fairwind asked.

"Always." Mathias knew they had both killed the conversation, even if unwittingly. But he didn't want it to end. "My grandmother was a thief, too."

Fairwind choked up a mouthful of rum. "Pardon?"

He should have heard the footsteps coming, but Fairwind had distracted him. There was a frantic pounding on the door. "Captain! Captain!"

No sooner had both men leaped to their feet than the *Bold Arva* listed precariously, sending book and tumbler and bottle and men careening toward the liquor cabinet. Flynn wasn't sober enough to keep his balance, arms flying out as he went along with the rest of the items not nailed down and crashed into Mathias. The spymaster caught him by the shoulders.

"Thanks," Flynn muttered, not moving away. "Sounds like trouble."

Mathias had never observed the other man from this distance. He hadn't noticed that Flynn smelled as strongly of salt and soap as he did of whiskey, and the combination was intoxicating. His leather coat was warm to the touch, holding lingering sunlight and body heat.

"Yeah." Shaw blinked rapidly, finally taking a step back. "Trouble."

"Captain!" The door burst open and Flynn tumbled toward the intrusion. "On deck, sir, now! You need to see this!"

"New plan!" Flynn Fairwind could only hope his crew could hear him above the war drums of thunder booming across the sky. "We land and we land fast! If we can land at all . . . Oh, please let there be land out there somewhere . . ."

He couldn't remember what it felt like to be dry. Good fortune had followed them for less than a full day. Choppy seas were a welcome change from the last storm, but now they faced another wall of rising, deadly waves. Ordinarily he would blame the drinking for his confusion, but even a sober man would know that these storms were unnatural. Rain poured down less like a squall and more like bucket after bucket being dumped directly on his head. The winds tore at their sails viciously, blowing in random directions that defied even the most skilled sailor's steering ability.

"Melli! Melli, if you're still aboard and alive, get us to shore!"

Flynn crashed across the main deck, using any spare piece of rigging or barrel or railing to reach the stern, where he hoped to find their tidesage and their only hope of surviving the storm. The shearing wind caught any voice and carried it away. A seagull whipped by his head, rocketing out to the sea behind him like a squawking cannonball. He flattened his hand above his eyes but it was pointless. There was nothing to see but a solid sheet of rain and darkness.

A door. Finally. He threw himself toward the quarterdeck, the stairs leading upward providing a railing to which he clung desperately. The door behind him banged open, the gale catching it and slamming it hard enough to scatter splinters across the floor.

"Shaw!"

The spymaster emerged, already shouting something, a black,

sodden cloak pulled up over his head. He yelled again, but the sound was lost. They were almost nose to nose but it was bloody impossible to make out a single word.

"What?" Flynn grabbed him by the shoulders. "I . . . I can't read lips, what are you saying?"

The wind changed direction suddenly, flipping the sails the other way with a clap, leaving a brief, swirling vortex of quiet.

"LAND!"

A warning? A jubilation? Flynn felt the *Bold Arva* lurch and heard the ear-rending crunch no captain ever wanted to hear. The hull had made contact, rowdy contact, with a sandbar, though it appeared to be intact. He and Shaw hit the boards and slid, luckily, into the quarterdeck. Unluckily, an instant later the rest of his crew appeared, tumbling toward them, until Flynn, Shaw, and a half dozen bedraggled, limp sailors lay in a groaning heap, piled at the bottom of the quarterdeck stairs.

"Land," Nailor wheezed, wedged under the bulk of a Kul Tiran gunner.

"We noticed." Flynn pushed at random hands and legs, dislodging himself from the human ball of yarn. He crawled slowly to his feet, wobbly, squinting into the heavy fog that dissipated with landfall. The storm moved off, suspiciously responsive, rain and gusts and threatening clouds retreating farther out to sea, leaving them in the stagnant, tropical sludge the Zandalari called "air."

Gradually, the crew reassembled behind Flynn. Melli stumbled down from the sterncastle, dazed and wide-eyed.

"Melli, you're fired. Wait, no, we still need a way off this damn island. You're back on the crew." He narrowed his eyes. "For now." Flynn sighed and wiped a piece of seaweed off his shoulder. Mathias Shaw, joined him at the edge of the ship.

"That storm was chasing us specifically," he rumbled.

"I'm no expert, Shaw." Flynn tossed him a weary smile. "But I think it's safe to assume we're not dealing with ordinary weather phenomena. If we don't find a way to stop whatever magic is causing this, we'll be stuck here forever."

"That won't happen," Shaw assured him. "Let's get to shore, have a look around and make camp if there's a secluded spot."

"What about the footholds you lot put down here? Fort Victory and the rest?"

"Abandoned. Once the armistice was signed, we ceded control of those encampments." With no need for a rowboat to take them in, Shaw simply swung himself over the railing and began climbing a rogue rope down the hull. "Any sign of us here will be taken as an act of aggression."

"Oh! Brilliant! Then I'm glad we shipwrecked with such catlike subtlety." Flynn rolled his eyes, motioning to the crew. "Don't get cozy, just bring enough for a meal and protection, then we find a place to lay anchor and hide the *Arva*."

It was probably wiser to stay aboard altogether, but he could read the faces of the men and women serving under him. They were tired, morale was low, and a brief stint on land always did a sailor good.

Shaw had already begun snooping around on the sand, consulting a rain-drenched map and a compass.

"Marshlands to the north, river to the west," the spymaster said, tapping the map.

Flynn nodded, surveying in every direction, grateful to finally be free of the obscuring mass of the storm. A pair of spiny diemetradons observed them a little ways inland, chewing their grass with blasé disinterest. Green mountains rose sharply behind the beasts, and farther down the beach the pointed tops of huts emerged from the mist.

"There's a village to the south," Flynn told him.

"That must be Zeb'ahari. Blast. We should be much deeper into Nazmir. I wanted to avoid veering this close to the troll city."

"Well, pardon me." Flynn stomped off toward the remnants of a campfire. "I thought we had until the White Lady was full to get there. Silly me!"

"Don't get defensive. We don't have far to sail; once the crew is back on their feet we can follow the shore north and stay close to land to avoid the storms." The blackened timbers thrown on the old fire still smoldered, and a trail of footsteps in the sand led away from it, at least three sets of prints and fresh enough to be marked deep into the wet ground. Without another word, the spymaster inspected the prints, following them.

A high, short whistle came from behind them. Flynn glanced over his shoulder to find the crew hadn't managed to unload a single thing from the *Bold Arva*. Instead, Nailor hung over the railing, a looking glass dangling from one hand, pointing toward the wall of dense jungle trees where the owners of those footprints watched in a crouch from the shadows.

"Shaw! Look lively!"

Flynn pulled his blunderbuss at once and aimed, but the powder was useless, soaked by the storm. It would have to be the cutlass, then. Drawing his sword, he charged after the trolls peering at them from the forest. Shaw calmly stuck his arm out to the side, keeping Flynn from racing into the jungle.

"They've spotted us," Flynn hissed. "What are you waiting for?"

"Spilling blood will only cause more attention. They aren't dressed in the royal colors," Shaw explained, keeping Flynn at bay. "They're moving off. Probably just foragers."

But the spymaster frowned, brow pulled down tight.

"White and black," he heard Shaw murmur to himself.

Flynn lowered his cutlass but did not sheathe it. "What about it?"

"Just . . . strange. Did you get a look at their garb? It was white and black, with some sort of design on it."

This was Shaw's mission, and he didn't seem overly bothered by the onlookers, so Flynn determined he should not be too bothered, either. Besides, the crew was apparently keeping a good lookout from the ship.

"Lots of eyes and legs," Flynn said, wandering away and back toward the campfire. "Almost like a spider."

"No, *exactly* like a spider." Shaw had, somehow, managed to fall perfectly into step with him. Unlike their artless landing, Shaw had the ability to move in complete silence. "Let's have a look at this camp of theirs. Maybe they left something behind."

Shaw drew a single dagger then, his boot knife, using it like a shovel to dig through the sand around the campfire. Little by little, the edge of a page became visible, and then the feathery tips of arrows.

"This," Shaw said, holding up a brightly colored arrow, "is worrisome."

"Why? It's just an arrow, looks completely normal."

"This fletching . . ." He held the arrow close to his eye, then examined it from several different angles. "I've seen modified fletching like this before. We're on the right track." He handed Flynn the arrow and then fished out the piece of parchment covered by the sand. "Here. Put these in your pouch," Shaw directed.

"What? Why? Why me?"

"Yours is drier. Just do it, Fairwind, I need to look around more. Get those back to the ship and be careful. I'll want to spend time with those papers later."

"All right, but only because you asked so sweetly." He nearly dropped the arrow, then carefully tucked it under his arm. The notes were trickier, but he folded them gently and slid the bundle into the leather satchel hanging off his belt.

Flynn left Shaw playing in the sand with a huff. His entire body ached from being tossed like a rag doll during the storm, and he hadn't managed to get three hours of unbroken sleep in days.

Whenever they seemed free of the magic squalls trailing them across the water, another one caught them from the side or head on. Maybe before they pushed north he could grab a minute or two of shut-eye and a swig or twelve of rum.

Nailor sat with his legs dangling over the railing, eyeing the horizon with his looking glass while Melli, Grigsby, and two gunner brothers called Harmen and Siward handed down a crate of salted cod, plopping it down on shore.

"I wouldn't," Flynn said, accepting a helping, hoisting hand from Nailor as he came back aboard, scampering up the rope ladder. "Our cheerful master of ceremonies wants us back in the water quick as you please."

A general groan came from the crew. He paused, deciding his much-needed date with a bed and a bottle could wait a moment. That grumbling and moaning from a crew, now just a scratch, could easily deepen into a festering wound.

"Now, now," he said, clapping Nailor on the back. "We won't weigh anchor far from here, and then you can eat as much cod and chug as much grog as you like. We've survived the worst bits, lads and ladies, so pull up your bloomers and let's hop to it. Melli? Can you . . . I don't know . . . tidesage us out of here?"

Melli made her way grumpily back up the rope ladder. Her crown of braids had been undone by the storm, reddish hair hanging limp around her shoulders. "Aye, sir. Tide's going out, and the waves are nice and gentle."

"Excellent! See? Good news. Fortune doesn't favor the bold, it favors the patient!"

Now to see about that rumsy slumber . . .

"Captain! In the trees! More of those trolls!"

Nailor flailed, letting out three short whistles. Flynn ran to the man's side, ripping the spyglass out of his hand and searching the edge of the jungle. Just as he said, a squad of well-armored trolls waited just inside the tree line, a single gold boot visible and reflecting the cloud-washed sun.

"Hey!" Nailor shouted down to Shaw. The spymaster gained his feet, but the trolls had already begun streaming out of the jungle, golden swords flashing. A line of archers emerged, readying their bows. "They're back! They're back, and they brought friends!"

"Run out the guns!" Flynn thundered. "Rifles loaded and ready to fire, now, now, now!"

Enough of the crew remained aboard to snap into swift action. Nailor, Grigsby, and the Kul Tiran brothers shoved Melli aside, fetching rifles from the crates stacked and lashed near the mainmast. Flynn reacted with the practiced, memorized speed of a lifelong sailor, rushing below deck to fetch a fresh barrel of powder for the rifles while the gunners busied themselves in the gallery. *Crash-crash-squeeeeak* came the heartening sound of the six-pounders being wheeled out and aimed, and the rhythmic call and response as the guns were loaded, the powder rammed down the barrel, and the wadding after, then came the ball.

"Captain! Do we fire?"

Flynn couldn't be sure who even asked, but as he cracked open the powder barrel and looked out to the shore, he found Mathias Shaw had drawn his daggers. The man faced impossible odds. Nobody could stand alone against that many soldiers and archers, let alone with only two measly daggers. The trolls charging him were not the white-and-black-clad sort they had seen before. The intricate golden armor and tactics gave them away as royal guards. They spotted Shaw and, worse, the ship.

Flynn swore. They had been made.

He watched, heart pounding, as Shaw lifted his daggers and then carefully, obviously placed them down on the sand.

"Surrendering?" Flynn whispered. He wouldn't have it. That

was their man down there, and he didn't care how many trolls he had to fire on to save him. He lifted his hand, ready to give the order to fire, but Mathias turned his back on the trolls pelting toward him, seemingly impervious to their war cries.

"Run," he said, clear as a bell. "Leave Zandalar, Flynn. *Run*."

"Do we fire, sir?" Nailor trembled, itchy.

"No . . . No, don't fire." Flynn pried himself away from the powder keg, finding Melli already dashing up toward the wheel. "Do it, Melli," he said, deadly serious. "Get us out of here."

"But Shaw—"

"He knows what he's doing, we have to trust him on that. We have to trust our own." *As much as I'd like to wring his neck right now, that is.* "Go!"

The first Zandalari arrow struck the railing inches from Nailor's arm. The others began to fall quickly after that, peppering the deck like a volley of winter hail. Melli stood tall behind the wheel, eyes closed, hands out before her as she conducted the waves like they were an orchestra and not surf and spray. Flynn didn't dare break her concentration, dodging each arrow as it whistled down toward him.

It was agony, leaving a man behind. They had spent countless hours together aboard the *Bold Arva*, not just sharing strategies but sharing their lives. True, Flynn had been tipsy for some of the more personal confessions, but he couldn't remember the last time he had told anyone about his mother. She was a sacred memory, a trove he always left buried. No X marked the spot, because he never acknowledged her existence to anyone. But somehow, Shaw had gotten it out of him. Maybe it was Shaw's quiet, listening nature. Or maybe Flynn had grown to trust him.

Shaw didn't flinch at all until he got to the part where she was hanged, a thief and a scoundrel, and the woman he admired most in the whole world. Lyra Fairwind, a thief, definitely, a scoundrel, maybe. A loving mother? Absolutely.

And now Fairwind was leaving that man behind, the only man in the world who knew about his mother, who listened and knew when exactly to give just that little wince of solidarity. That man. Gone.

The cannons and guns were loaded. They could fire. They could fire, but Shaw had surrendered and given his order. He remembered the spymaster's words. *An act of aggression.* Surely opening fire on the Zandalari would only make things worse and potentially put Shaw's life in danger.

Flynn twitched, desperate to pull his blunderbuss and show the trolls what happened when they advanced on *his* crew.

The *Bold Arva* began to slide slowly but surely back out toward the lanes. The outgoing tide caught them, just as Melli predicted, and with the bowsprit angled north they floated steadily away from the beach and toward the river pouring out into the sea. They picked up speed and Flynn ran to the railing, clutching it while Shaw became smaller and smaller, farther and farther away. No cheer went up from the crew, no one spoke a word.

Mathias Shaw was gone.

CHAPTER EIGHTEEN

Tiragarde Sound

Jaina had hosted tense dinners before, but this one was swiftly climbing to top the list.

A small dining room abutted the grand hall where the Proudmoores kept their extensive collection of maps, charts, seafaring gizmos, and nautical artifacts. That long gallery was decorated from floor to ceiling with oil paintings of the Proudmoore family, extended family, and beloved friends. A striking portrait of King Anduin Wrynn was among them. Not included, however, were paintings of her illustrious dinner guests.

Alleria Windrunner picked listlessly at her food, spending more time spinning her wine goblet than drinking from it. Despite this, a fleet of servants brought in course after course, prolonging Jaina's torment by refusing to just skip to dessert. Instead, she, Alleria Windrunner, Lord Commander Turalyon, and Jaina's mother, Katherine, endured an appetizer course of blood sausage and roasted peppers on toast, followed by a savory pie glistening with honey, nearly rupturing its crust from the sheer amount of fragrant boar sizzling within.

Currently, Jaina watched the high exarch wolf down a monumental pile of grilled fish. While Alleria's approach was to eat nothing, Turalyon instead kept his mouth as full as possible, perhaps giving him an excuse to avoid conversation. They had come at Anduin's behest, charged with concocting a secondary plan should Mathias Shaw find nothing on the Zandalari coast.

"I hear Hackney has whipped up a scrumptious ravenberry tart for dessert," Katherine Proudmoore announced in a painfully sing-song voice, one Jaina only heard when her mother was nearing the end of her patience. Jaina had to admire her mother's tenacity, her uncanny ability to weather even the most awkward supper with absolute poise.

"That is very thoughtful, but I fear it will be impossible for me to partake," Alleria murmured. "I could not possibly eat another bite."

Jaina told herself not to drink too deeply of the excellent wine, even if it was tempting. She longed to return to the strategy hall, to stand among the paintings and brass compasses and study her evolving map of Azeroth. Wherever they had searched for Sylvanas, a blue pin pierced the leather. When they at last found her, Jaina planned to drive a dagger into the spot.

But her mother insisted on being a good host, and that meant detaining them with this exorbitant, unending feast. At least if Anduin or Greymane had been there the conversation might be light enough to enjoy. Turalyon and Alleria undoubtedly detected Jaina's dislike of their methods, the manner in which they had tortured first an apothecary and then a smuggler for vital information.

It was vital, Jaina. Vital. Do not let your squeamishness cost us the goal.

She caught herself glaring at Alleria Windrunner. Once, Jaina had held nothing but pure admiration for the ranger; now, however, with Alleria infested with the Void, Jaina held her actions and her words to a higher level of scrutiny. Was it Alleria speaking to her now, lying about her full stomach, or some twisted monstrosity from the Void? Did she sit there, still as a statue, while her mind worked hard, churning with dark machinations? After all, Queen Azshara was still missing after N'Zoth's defeat, last seen escaping in a portal made from the Void. Perhaps Alleria knew where the dangerous queen had gone. N'Zoth might be defeated, but many servants of the Void remained, and they too might seek to overtake Azeroth as the Corruptor had. Would Alleria even know if she had passed the point of no return? How did one separate thought from the Void's twisted influence?

"Well!" Katherine chirped, resplendent in a deep purple frock embellished with gold admiral's fringe on the shoulders. Her iron gray hair had been coiffed into a sleek dome on her head. "I think more wine would suit us all, wouldn't it? Yes, yes, much more wine . . ."

"My lady!"

The double doors leading into the dining room from the gallery were already open, flanked by two Proudmoore guards wielding pikes. Yet a third guard slid into the room, panting, his helm crooked as he struggled to catch his breath.

"By wind and by sea, speak, Cormery," Katherine Proudmoore demanded in her precise, cool way, a former admiral even at rest. She stood along with Jaina, alarmed at the intrusion. "What's the matter with you?"

"They took him!"

Of all the people Jaina expected to come careening into her family keep, Flynn Fairwind was not one of them. But there he was, the sea dog, shoving Cormery aside and barely making it to the dining table.

"Who did they take?" Jaina asked, abandoning her wine and her plate to go to Fairwind's side.

Alleria and Turalyon joined, and soon all four of them stood circling the man, who looked as if the sea had ravaged him for months. A fine crust of salt cracked across his forehead, his swarthy skin blistering with sunburn. His auburn hair tumbled out of its ribbon in a snarl.

"We sailed . . ." He heaved again for breath. One of the servants appeared, handing him a glass of water. He knocked it away and grabbed the wine bottle off the table, swigging for ten unbroken seconds. "We sailed as fast as we could, back through the storm . . . Melli damn near killed herself, but she knew this route so well, said it was the best port to take us."

"Is Melli all right? What is going on?" Katherine pressed, snatching the bottle out of his hand.

"Here, Flynn, sit," Jaina told him, gently easing him into the chair Alleria had vacated. "Try to calm down, catch your breath, and tell us exactly what happened. Who is gone?"

"It's Shaw. They took him. The . . . the Zandalari trolls caught us, they saw our ship and Shaw was still on shore." He pulled at a satchel on his belt, unhooking it with a grunt before spilling the contents across the dinner table, spoiling Hackney's platter of tenderloin with a spiced duxelle. That didn't bother Fairwind, who began shoveling food into his mouth with more gusto than Turalyon, almost choking himself as he chewed.

"This arrow." Turalyon held up one of the items from Fairwind's pouch. At once, the Lord Commander's brow darkened, his lips turning into a firm line. "I've seen these before. This fletching . . . These are the arrows we found in Shaw's spies."

"It's all right," Jaina said, still trying to soothe Fairwind. His eyes bulged, red with tears and sunburn as he reached for the potatoes. "Mathias Shaw is a high-ranking member of the Alliance forces. If they took him prisoner then Queen Talanji will not execute him without cause."

"Read," he stammered around his food. "Read these . . ." He

shoved the bits of curled and bleached paper toward Alleria. "Because I can't."

She deftly picked one up with thumb and forefinger. "I somewhat doubt that trolls would communicate to one another in *Thalassian*. These are valuable pieces of evidence he has brought us, proof that the dark rangers are indeed infiltrating Zandalar."

"Then it's true," Jaina breathed. Thalassian. The language of the high and blood elves . . .

"Notes on the region," Alleria continued, flipping through the various messages. "Troop movements, patrol routes, nothing that might tell us what they want on the island—"

"But proof enough that the dark rangers are there," Turalyon interrupted. He sighed and pinched the bridge of his nose with irritation. "We should have acted sooner. Sylvanas could be in Zuldazar right now. She could be conspiring with the trolls."

Jaina sensed the conversation moving far beyond her control. Of course she wanted to find Sylvanas, of course these clues must be taken into consideration, but she heard the far-off drums of war echoing in Turalyon's voice. His anger, his frustration, was completely justified, but she worried now what that justification might become. Anduin had already sent his sly messenger Valeera Sanguinar to the one member of the Horde he unfailingly trusted, Baine Bloodhoof, questioning whether they might have spotted Sylvanas in Zandalari lands. Carefully he prodded, mentioning only that dark rangers had been seen departing the Eastern Kingdoms and sailing in that direction.

But Baine Bloodhoof's response had been swift and certain: They had no knowledge of Sylvanas hiding anywhere on Zandalar.

Perhaps it was naïve of Anduin to believe him, but Jaina knew Baine well, too. There would be no reason for him to lie—Baine wanted Sylvanas captured and tried as much as they did.

"I will take these missives to the king," Alleria stated, gathering up the bits of parchment. "He must be informed at once and a new strategy approved. If the Horde is harboring Sylvanas on Zandalar then we must be quick and quiet, the cunning blade never seen and only later felt."

"No."

Even Fairwind fell silent at Jaina's single word. The room stilled, Alleria gazing into Jaina's eyes with ill-concealed disdain. "You disagree that time is of the essence? The time for action is now!"

The timbre of her voice changed. Jaina heard her mother gasp and draw back. The pale blue light in Alleria's eyes flamed higher, a dark nimbus of purple vapor surrounding the ranger's body. Jaina could lose her temper, too. She could shout and rail and teleport Alleria to the very top of Mount Neverest, but she did not.

Jaina breathed in, feeling ice gather on her tongue. *No. No magic. Breathe.*

"I disagree with your conclusions," Jaina replied, voice hardly above a whisper. "Think, Alleria. Think carefully. Shaw and Fairwind were already seen by the Zandalari, so we can assume they were also identified. Zandalar will be expecting more Alliance soldiers on their doorstep. Do not reward their paranoia, do not add fuel to an already kindling fire. I beg of you: Do not risk the treaty we worked so hard to achieve."

"Then what do you suggest?" Turalyon still held the Zandalari arrow with dark ranger fletching, the sharp end pointed toward her. His other hand went to Alleria's, and Jaina saw him give a tight squeeze.

"That we put our trust in that very same treaty," Jaina murmured. An idea formed in her head, her gaze fixed on Fairwind and his stunned expression, wind-chapped lips hanging open. "All I beg of you is time. Time to let me try this one last thing. If this fails, then perhaps you are right, Alleria; perhaps then we must become the blade."

CHAPTER NINETEEN

Orgrimmar

Thrall stared in dumb wonderment at the message Ji Firepaw had just passed into his hands.

"I was only gone for two days," Thrall muttered. "Clearly I missed something."

Ji vented a tired laugh. "Forgive me for ambushing you this soon after your return, Thrall, but I believed the urgency demanded your immediate attention." The pandaren bowed, righting himself with a less tired and more mischievous smile. "That and I wanted to see your reaction."

Together they walked the long path down from the tallest heights of Orgrimmar to the seat of the council, Grommash Hold. While they waited for the elevator that would take them to the ground level of the city, Ji bounced his fingers impatiently off his own belly, one eye turned always toward Thrall.

"Well?" he pressed. "What do you make of it?"

"I cannot say it is surprising," Thrall scanned the message again, feeling the exhausted headache pinching the back of his scalp sharpen. While it was an invitation to meet with the king of Stormwind, the letter was written in Jaina's distinctive hand. The fact did not go unnoticed, and it must be taken for what it was: a brazen attempt to manipulate him with their friendship. He did not begrudge it. If he needed a favor from the Alliance, he might do exactly the same. She opened with general polite introductions to the council and addressed the missive to them as a collective—but one section in particular was just for him.

> Please, Thrall, if ever you valued our friendship then meet with King Anduin and myself. I share with you now sensitive Alliance intelligence in the hope that you will see it not only as a gesture of good will, but as a call to action.

"I had hoped to resolve the unrest in Zandalar before the Alliance could learn of it," he finally answered the curious pandaren. "But this . . ."

> Dark rangers prowl the jungles of Zandalar, and our spymaster is now in the custody of Queen Talanji. Some among us believe that the Zandalari queen may be conspiring with Sylvanas. If this is so, I refuse to believe you had knowledge of it. Meet with us, old friend, and help me protect this fledgling armistice—it feels as if it might be torn to shreds before the ink has even dried on the page.

"This cannot be ignored." Thrall folded the message and tucked it into his belt for safekeeping. There was no need to read it again; he had already made up his mind.

"May I attend the meeting?"

Thrall lifted a brow. "You want to come?"

"The letter was addressed to us all. Besides, when lightning strikes the wrong tree, the whole forest burns," Ji replied, following Thrall out onto the road after the elevator stopped at the bottom. "Zandalar is the tree. These dark rumors are the lightning. Perhaps a monk's wisdom might stem the blaze."

"These negotiations will require a delicate touch, Ji, and your wisdom generally involves acting as swiftly as possible," Thrall said. "But then I suppose going at all would be action. You know, agreeing to this might be unpopular with the rest of the council."

The monk tugged at his long black beard. With the hour very late, the streets of Orgrimmar stood nearly empty, a full moon lighting their path as vividly as any torch. "That is so," Ji agreed. "But popular or not, the Horde's previous rogue warchief almost cost my people the soul of their homeland, so you will of course forgive my insistence."

Hellscream. Thrall had defeated Garrosh Hellscream in a mak'gora, justice for his dizzying list of crimes. Hellscream's lust for power had led to him using an Old God's heart to gain unnatural strength, making him an enemy of not just the pandaren and the Alliance, but the Horde as well.

"The Vale of Eternal Blossoms has nearly healed," Ji concluded. "But the pandaren will forever wear the scars of Hellscream's cruelty."

Thrall glanced down at the stout monk master, finding a familiar tenacity in the pandaren's eyes. He had seen that same pain, that same determination, in the eyes of Tyrande Whisperwind. The burning of Teldrassil, the destruction of the Vale of Eternal Blossoms . . . It was all so pointlessly selfish and callous.

"Woes upon woes." Thrall sighed. "Trouble heaped upon trouble."

The pandaren simply made a soft sound of confusion.

A few peons stumbling home drunk from the tavern wandered by Grommash Hold, their laughter echoing off the tall, spiked towers of the city. Four orcish sentinels stood guard, braziers burning outside to aid their watch.

"The reports from our ambassador in Zandalar are bleak, Ji."

"Ah, young Zekhan. Chieftain Rokhan departed for Zandalar yesterday. He was growing concerned about the boy."

Thrall let Ji push ahead and into the hold. "The queen is being overrun with rebels opposing her rule, the Zanchuli Council is deadlocked, more assassination attempts have been made, and now the Alliance wishes to confer with us. I cannot help but think all of these things are connected."

The pandaren paused, twirling his beard with two fingers. Raised voices drifted to them through the curtain cutting off the main rotunda of the hold from view. Thrall dreaded what came next.

This is what it means to be just one voice among many. These were your conditions to return and live among the Horde again—the compromises, the arguments, the delegating . . .

"We should go in," Thrall murmured.

"We *did* walk all this way. Why hesitate?"

Thrall might have bored him with a list long enough to fill many hours; instead he simply said, "I am tired, Ji. And I feel . . . I feel so very old."

The pandaren snorted and tossed his beard over one shoulder. "We have a saying where I grew up, in Wu-Song Village—the oldest ginger is the most pungent."

Thrall pulled the leather curtain aside. "What an interesting way of telling me I smell."

"At last, there you are." Lor'themar stood at their arrival, as did all those who had been in conference with him. "Where are Baine and Calia? Hurry now and tell us what you make of this request from the Alliance."

"They will be here soon to describe our meeting with the night elves."

Tugging the message from his belt, Thrall felt the weight of their expectations fall directly on him. It was good that Ji Firepaw had managed to make him laugh, easing the burden of what might come next. Lor'themar, Thalyssra, Gazlowe, and Lilian Voss crowded toward him. As Ji had informed him, Rokhan was absent, and Calia Menethil and Baine Bloodhoof had not yet returned to the hold.

Before Thrall could continue, Ji Firepaw coughed loudly into his furry fist. "As for the message, we will go. The word from Zandalar is dire—we know this, the Alliance now knows this, and it is our duty to act. If we ignore their summons, then why did we sign a treaty in the first place?"

He was grateful to his friend for taking the arrow. The last thing Thrall wanted was to appear more like a warchief and less like a single, equal member of the council. He supported Ji's speech by simply standing at his side, still and tall, nodding occasionally to express his agreement.

Still, First Arcanist Thalyssra narrowed her eyes at them both. "Thrall, what are your thoughts?"

"Ji is right. I had hoped to put out the fires in Zandalar before the Alliance noticed, but it appears the conflict has grown too obvious to hide. I know Jaina Proudmoore well; she would not go to these lengths lightly."

"But dark rangers?" Lor'themar scoffed, crossing his arms across his red tunic chased in gold. "This sounds far-fetched, does it not? It sounds to me like they got their man arrested for trespassing and now they want our help freeing him. They are abusing our civility."

Thrall had not considered that, but he shook his head. "I have no intention of freeing their spy. I go to protect Zandalar; that is my only intent. If the Alliance decides dark rangers are working with Queen Talanji, then they will start another war, and I would have a difficult time blaming them."

"How could they think that? We have not been kind to Sylvanas's loyalists," Lor'themar spat.

"We know that," Thrall told him calmly. "But the Alliance does not. What must our turmoil look like to them? No, I will assuage their fears, and, what is more, I will *listen*."

"*Listen?* Sounds boring. How about you tell those pesky humans to stay off our lands. Last time I checked a treaty wasn't just a bunch of gentle suggestions." The Trade Prince Gazlowe, head just slightly taller than the First Arcanist's knee, made his position clear. "I say forget it. They can have their spy back when they give us something first."

Thrall breathed in sharply through his nose, but Ji Firepaw cut in, taking the tiniest step forward to place himself between the orc and the rest of the council. "They will give us something. They will give us their knowledge. Thrall speaks true—whatever we learn, we will use it to protect Zandalar."

Lor'themar, stewing over it all, tapped his boot impatiently. He tossed up his hands in frustration and gestured to Thalyssra. "Might you conjure them a portal to Zandalar, let them go to this meeting and question the Alliance for information? In truth, I want to know more of these dark rangers. If by chance Sylvanas truly is in Zandalar then we could have her in our snare tomorrow."

"Do it." Lilian Voss, who was still finding her footing at the meetings and rarely spoke, sounded unusually confident. "Any chance we have to capture the Banshee Queen cannot be wasted."

Kiro, the diminutive foxlike creature draped in beads and leather, warmed his paws at the central brazier. Just like Lilian, he was still finding his place among the council, the vulpera still a new addition to the Horde. "While many of us have left Zandalar, it is still our home. If it is sick with treachery, I would see it healed."

Optimism from Lor'themar, decisiveness from Lilian, and now the vulpera leadership agreed, too. Thrall had no idea where Sylvanas might be, but if the Alliance had information that would lead them to her then all the better. Only Gazlowe remained unsure, but his single "nay" could not overrule the decision.

But it mattered to Thrall that they reach a consensus. He stared at the goblin, patient yet impatient, a familiar knot of anxiety building in his stomach. Surviving as many battles, cataclysms, earth-shaking disasters, and invasions as he had, Thrall had cultivated a honed warrior's instinct for danger. *Time is of the essence,* his senses screamed at him, but consensus mattered.

The council mattered. Gazlowe mattered.

"Oh, fine, what the hell." The goblin rolled his eyes, waving Thrall away. "Just capture Sylvanas so we can all shut up about her already and get back to worrying about Horde problems. Our problems. Goblin problems." He winked. "Obviously."

Thalyssra tried to hide her amused smile, but Thrall noticed it. Once she had it back under control, the portal opened, slashing itself across Gazlowe's unimpressed grimace. On the other side, a ship in the middle of a strait waited, a small patch of calm at the center of a brewing storm.

Thrall did not like to be kept waiting, but his companion Ji Firepaw liked it even less. The restless pandaren stood at the edge of the ship without sails, a bobbing wreck left to float in the waters between the Eastern Kingdoms and Zandalar. Without a crew, without any means of transporting itself, it felt like the immense skeleton of some long-dead ocean beast. Scraps of rigging hung from the masts like dried entrails left to flap in the breeze, the deck as bleached as a desert corpse.

"Quite the storm . . ." Ji pointed to the west, where blackened thunderheads hung low and threatening over the sea. The waves crashing below surged high enough to tickle the bottoms of the clouds.

Thrall frowned. "Yet it isn't moving."

Ji glanced up at him. "Hm."

"Storms move. That looks more like a wall to me."

"Perhaps we should be glad. This old hulk wouldn't survive a sunshower let alone . . . whatever *that* is." The pandaren shuddered. "Just add it to the list."

"The list?"

"Of curiosities and coincidences that must be explained," Ji replied with a growl. "Of links that make up a chain we cannot yet see the end of."

There was no arguing with that. "I had at least hoped to better understand the disruption in the Spirit Realm, to remove one link from that infernal chain, but the night elves were not willing to lend us a single priestess or even discuss the nature of the disturbance."

Squinting toward the storm clouds, Ji clucked his tongue with disappointment. "Then you learned nothing in Nordrassil."

"I wouldn't say that."

The mage's portal pulled at the air around them before a reverberating *crack* split the silence on that forlorn stretch of ocean. Ji Firepaw whirled around with his hands up, his fighter's stance at the ready. But Thrall took his time, staring for a moment longer at the band of shadowy purple clouds wrapping around Zandalar like a bruised fist. Footsteps, soft ones, then a louder pair clad in armor. Just as Jaina had promised, only two had come. Thrall turned to face them wearing a thin smile.

"No ambush?" Thrall said by way of greeting. "Shame. It's a damn good place for one."

Jaina Proudmoore, redeemed pride of Kul Tiras, blonde-and-white hair braided over one shoulder, her crystal-topped staff aimed placidly at the deck, gained her feet on the gently rocking ship without a hitch. One might conclude she had sea legs while still in the womb.

"I'm full of surprises today, Thrall," she replied, echoing his expression. She dropped a leather satchel on the ground. "But not that kind."

"Thank you for coming." The king of Stormwind, by contrast, did not seem so at ease on the ship, his initial steps out of the portal wobbly before he planted himself with the expected dignity of a royal. His skin looked worn and blue around the eyes, exhausted smudges painted beneath.

Thrall knew that look well, had experienced it himself many times—the sleepless, sallow ravages of leadership. It had been mere months since he had last clapped eyes on the king of Stormwind, yet he seemed to have aged a full year.

"Ji Firepaw . . ." Jaina lifted a brow.

"Greetings, Lord Admiral. Your majesty." The pandaren bowed. "Disappointing that we meet under such unhappy circumstances."

"Unhappy isn't the half of it," the king muttered.

Before he could say more, Thrall put up his hand, interrupting. "There is something you should know. If there are to be no great secrets between us, if we are to trust, then I should tell you that I met with Tyrande and Malfurion."

Jaina and Anduin stared at him, both in stunned silence.

"O-oh," was all Jaina could muster.

Thrall bowed his head, ruffling the hair at his nape in frustration. "It . . . did not go well. I tried to put forward an apology from the Horde, but they did not accept it. They are interested only in revenge against Windrunner."

"That is also foremost on our minds," Anduin replied, impatient. He sliced his hand across the air between them. "Let us cut to the chase, shall we?"

Jaina reached into the pack she had dropped, producing an arrow that looked to be of Zandalari make and colors, and several scraps of parchment. Crossing the narrow distance between them, she handed the arrow to Ji and the papers to Thrall, then returned to Anduin's side.

"We intercepted members of the Horde aiding a dark ranger called Visrynn; she took passage from Faldir's Cove to Zandalar, warning of the storms you now see on the horizon, which speaks to organization. A plan. My spymaster and Lord Commander Turalyon are also confident that the arrow you hold has been fletched by dark rangers," Anduin barreled on. To business, Thrall approved. "It appears quite different from the fletching you see on the average Zandalari arrow. We have many left over from the war for comparison."

Thrall had begun perusing the notes but shifted his gaze to the king at that.

"The messages say—"

"I can read them," Thrall growled, silencing him. And reading them filled his heart with dread. His warrior's senses prickled along the back of his neck. More links to add to that chain. This was bad. It was bad for the Horde, but worse for Talanji. There was no mistaking the script, the language, the content. Dark rangers had written those notes, and while Thrall was not intensely familiar with the fletching those archers used, he saw no reason to doubt the accusation. The letters themselves were damning enough.

"Are you betraying us?" Anduin's voice hit the deck with the weight of an anchor. The words lingered, sea winds whistling between them for an agonizing moment that stretched on until the king broke it again. "Is Sylvanas Windrunner seeking refuge on Zandalar? I have come for answers, Thrall, and I will have them."

Beside him, Ji Firepaw straightened, huffing with outrage.

"There is no love left for Sylvanas Windrunner among our Horde, only hatred. No conspiracy exists to shelter her. Baine Bloodhoof would not abide such a gutless plot, and neither would I. Fires burn in the jungles outside Dazar'alor," Thrall began softly, his voice rising word by word as he discovered, in that moment, the true depth of the shadows spreading around Talanji. "Rebels have been assaulting the palace, attempting to assassinate the queen, and now burning down loa shrines all over Zuldazar and Nazmir. Her council does nothing, and the queen refuses to set aside old vendettas and ask for our help."

He saw the briefest flicker of relief pass across the human king's face. Thrall understood that to other humans Wrynn was said to be pleasing-looking, but to the orc, Anduin simply looked like a small, pink boy swallowed by clunky armor. At least the small, pink boy had the grace to nod and accept his words.

Jaina, however, gave no hint of her feelings. "Why?" she asked.

"Why what?"

"Why won't she ask you for help? She agreed to join the Horde ages ago."

Thrall sighed, holding her gaze and waiting until memory and pain brought wisdom. "You know why."

Jaina looked down at her feet. "I see."

"Are we to believe them?" Anduin asked her, not in a whisper.

"Yes," she said. "Yes, I think we are. What he says is true—Baine Bloodhoof would rather die than be part of some plan to hide and help Sylvanas. We must find these dark rangers and make sense of their being on Zandalar. Whatever the reason, it cannot be good."

"It appears the lightning has already struck," Ji murmured quietly.

Thrall shut his eyes tight. It had indeed. A wave of hopelessness nearly overcame him, but he stood tall. All was not lost yet. They still had Zekhan embedded with the queen and earning her favor; they now knew better what they were facing. A picture began to form in his mind, hazy and shaky, but still there, an image of Queen Talanji. She was young and brash, vulnerable because of her inexperience and her isolation, crippled by the grudge she held against Jaina, the perfect target for someone seeking to unseat a queen.

But why? What did Talanji possess that the dark rangers or Sylvanas might want? Without asking, Thrall stuffed their evidence into his pack. Anduin raised a brow but said nothing. No doubt the Alliance spies had made copies of the missives; it was what Thrall would do.

"I will go to Dazar'alor myself." Thrall looked to first Anduin, then Jaina. "We have tried the careful approach, the quill and soft words." He gave a single, grave nod. "Now it is time for the hammer and fist."

"There is also the matter of our spymaster," Anduin replied. The wreck seesawed harder from side to side, but the king managed to stay upright. "While he trespassed on Zandalari shores, he was not there without cause. His mission brought us these indelible clues, proof that Sylvanas or her agents have infiltrated the continent. We are of course willing to use all accepted diplomatic channels to recover him, we only ask that he is not harmed until order is restored to the throne of Zandalar. The Alliance recognizes this was badly done, that we should have brought our suspicions to you directly and not sought to position our spies in your territory."

Ji Firepaw rumbled with appreciation. "That is well spoken, your majesty, and the Horde Council can assure you that we do not execute prisoners without a trial."

The king of Stormwind narrowed his eyes. "We would like to have him returned. Soon."

The boat rocked again, hard, and Thrall would have toppled over if not for Ji Firepaw. The monk's superior balance kept him upright, and he caught the orc before he could tumble overboard. Jaina reached for Anduin, steadying him.

"Give me two days," Thrall said, struggling to stand with stronger and stronger waves battering the wreck. "I will see about your spy, and I will take these matters to the queen herself. Just as you said, King Anduin, there will be answers."

"If we survive to see the next two days." Ji had turned back to face Zandalar and the ring of storms shrouding it. Those storms had spread, or at least, a fragment had, a cluster of angry clouds racing toward them, bringing the misty gray fringe below that signaled rain.

Thrall could not believe the size of the waves gathering.

"That storm nearly killed Fairwind," he heard Jaina hiss. "Three times."

"A portal, Jaina, quickly!" the king demanded.

Thrall whirled to face them, taking a few precarious strides forward. "Two days; do not invade before then. Trust that we will see to Zandalar. *Trust*."

Ostensibly he asked them both, but he looked to Jaina.

"Granted!" King Anduin shouted. The storm rushed upon them with unnatural speed, hurling the wreck from side to side, tossing it like a piece of driftwood. "Two days, Thrall, but we cannot afford to lose the Banshee Queen's trail!"

"Thrall!" Ji pointed frantically at the thunderous waves, the drumming of the rain like a hail of arrows upon the sea. "Thrall! We are stranded!"

"Jaina!"

She had already begun channeling her magic, opening a portal to whisk herself and the king to safety. But she heard him above the din of the storm and turned, her blonde halo of hair stirred by the shock of winds from the west. Without another word, she swiveled, the portal she had been making for herself and Anduin sputtering out into a single blue sparkle.

"Where?" she screamed.

"The shore!" Thrall thundered, cupping his hands around his mouth. "Dazar'alor!"

The portal opened, a shimmering mirage of the golden city there in its depths. Thrall grabbed Ji and tossed him inside, then watched the mage cling to her king before he too escaped the murderous sea, the wreck disappearing from under him as they plunged toward Zandalar.

CHAPTER TWENTY

Zeb'ahari

Apari felt the storm inside her. She carried it like a child, and thought of it just as fondly. It kicked and it raged and it drained the life out of her, but it remained strong. And hers.

She could not have children the usual way, not after the pillar crushed the lower half of her body and pulverized the bones in her leg, but that was all right. Apari had never wanted children, never understood the appeal, something she and her childhood friend had shared. New mothers often brought their infants to the gardens of the Great Seal to sit among the waters, where it was said the pools were formed from Rezan's own tears and blessed one with health and longevity.

"All they do is cry and stink," Talanji had said, then only eight. "But Father says it's a queen's duty to continue the line." She had made a disgusted face, poking out her tongue.

The troll girls had crouched behind a vase taller and wider than them both, spying on the mothers cooing over their babies.

"When you are queen," Apari had told her solemnly, with the confident wisdom of a child, "you will make ya own rules."

"An' you will be there with me." Talanji had reached for her hand and squeezed it. "Nobody will tell us what to do."

Apari had believed her. She always believed Talanji. She believed her when Rastakhan's own advisers turned on him and Talanji begged for Apari to remain loyal. She believed her when she said the Horde could be trusted. And she believed her over her own mother, Yazma, who consumed her loa to cut off the head of the royal family. Apari had pressed her mother again and again, afraid of what would happen if Yazma went against their king and failed. In the young troll's eyes, Talanji was all goodness and light, how could someone like that have an evil father? How could Yazma justify such rash action?

"Loa are meant to be used, Apari. Manipulated. They care not for our lives," Yazma had said to her with the utmost seriousness. "Just as Rastakhan cares nothin' for his subjects."

"But Shadra has never hurt us!" Apari insisted. "Can't we trust her? You've been her priestess all these years—"

"We trust poison, my daughter. We trust information and cunning. Shadra may possess these things, but she is a loa. When given the opportunity, Shadra will always choose what serves her best. And I will do the same. Put your faith in your own hands, Apari. A god is nothing without believers—and we do not have to submit to them, just as we will not submit to a crown that enslaves us to a loa's whims."

The next day, Yazma had helped set into motion a coup that nearly toppled King Rastakhan's rule. She burned bright, bound by no gods or kings, and had fallen in battle. If only Apari had listened then, if only she had seen Talanji and her father for who they truly were, if only she had gone with her mother . . . would things have turned out differently? She could not say, but at least she would have died at her mother's side.

That regret festered as viciously as the wounds in her leg.

Apari sat on the cliffs of Zeb'ahari, Tayo standing beside her. The village below went on as it always did, placidly removed from the chaos of the city, its inhabitants unaware of the Widow's Bite followers hidden around them in the hills and trees.

"They . . . they disappeared."

"How?" Apari demanded, slapping the spyglass out of Tayo's hands. It dropped like a stone, smashed to pieces on the rocks below. "How!?"

Spotting the abandoned ship in the distance had been an accident. Each day, Apari commanded her followers to search the horizon and make certain no ships slipped the net of their storms. By chance, Tayo saw the wreck floating in safe waters, just beyond the edge of the squall, and there she had seen Jaina Proudmoore.

At first, Apari didn't believe her. Couldn't. Jaina Proudmoore? The human who had assaulted the Great Seal, killed Rastakhan, and left the palace in ruins? Left her life and her body in ruins? But Apari looked through the spyglass and saw with her own wide eyes the proof. With Tayo guiding her, Apari handed her back the glass and called out to the storm, commanding it. The sacrifice's spirit, the dead noble, found new life in her body, a soul snatched away from Bwonsamdi, its unnatural existence fuel for her magic.

"Guide me!" Apari had called to Tayo. "Take me to her. Let the storm be her end, the sea her grave! I command the skies, they bend to my will!"

What a fitting end to her, ambushed and overcome by a troll she had never known nor even seen, but whose life Jaina Proudmoore had destroyed.

Ya don't know me, human, she had thought, ready for the nourishing taste of revenge. *But I know you. Oh, by my ancestors do I know ya.*

All of a sudden, Apari was entrenched in memory, back in

Zuldazar, a younger, more naïve girl. Alliance cannons bearing Kul Tiran anchors fired in deafening sequence, rattling her teeth in her skull. The noise was so overwhelming that it concealed the cracking of stone all around her. Concealed it until a palace pillar collapsed on top of her. "Loa . . . !" She had wheezed, all breath forcefully thrown from her lungs. "Help me . . . ! Loa, please!" Who could tell how long she laid there, trapped and utterly alone? But she remembered the silence that followed her pleas as no gods or friends came to her aid.

"Apari." Tayo stood, approaching her with the tentative steps of a child anticipating a scolding. "More shrines remain. We told the pale rider they would all be burned by sundown. Ya will have another chance to kill the Proudmoore woman one day."

"No, Tayo. I won't." Daz flew in lazy loops up from the shore, gorged on some unlucky creature he had found below. The dreadtick landed on Apari's shoulder, and she winced. Her body was growing frail, the infection in her leg sapping more and more of her energy. Only her own spite and the power of the sacrifice she had drained kept her from collapsing on the spot. "I don't have much longer to live. Only enough time to see the traitor queen brought low."

"That vulpera, I know she still be willin' to take the leg and save you."

Apari glared at her, quelling the urge to lash out and give Tayo a slap. "No. And we won't speak of it again. One more word and I'll toss ya off this cliff."

A flicker of anger or resentment crossed the troll's face, her left nostril twitching, but Tayo said nothing, simply bowing her head and disappearing into the trees where the remaining Widow's Bite followers waited and watched.

However much Tayo had annoyed her, Apari did intend to finish the task the pale rider had set them. The blazes at Bwonsamdi's shrines had brought gawkers and some worshippers trying to put out the fires. It was too dangerous to linger near them, but now it was time to seek the last three shrines and weaken the loa, a few more blows before the fatal strike. The bitter disappointment of missing her chance to drown Proudmoore had to be swallowed. One more mouthful of sorrow; she knew its acrid taste well.

She wrapped her hand around the badge hanging from her neck, the old, tarnished gold trinket Nathanos Blightcaller had offered as his own sacrifice. It thrummed with a strange, cold power.

"Widow's Bite! Hear me now!" Apari turned to face the jungle, feeling the hidden eyes there find her, her secret audience. "The evenin' comes—our swiftest runners to the city, rouse our spies. Our fiercest warriors with me to the northern shrine. No rest and no hesitation—Bwonsamdi's pain will be ours tonight, better food than fish, stronger drink than wine. Take it in and let it sustain ya!"

CHAPTER TWENTY-ONE

Dazar'alor

Thrall caught his breath beneath the great arch framing the Port of Zandalar. The massive, curved pillars invited one into a crush of bodies, merchants shouting their wares, porters balancing impossibly heavy baskets on their heads, and urchins weaving in and out of the throng looking for an easy pocket to pick. The scent of salted sea air fell away, the senses overrun by a hundred warring odors drifting down from the marketplace—the sweat of hardworking laborers; roasting spices that stirred the imagination as easily as the statues and emblems that gave the city its grandeur; the perfume of meat on the spit; the lush vegetable tang of vines and flowers dripping from the terraces.

"It will be a long climb." Ji sighed and pushed his way into the crowd milling before the immense, troll-headed fountain central to the port. "We should get started."

Before them, the great city of the Zandalari trolls rose like a golden promise, the top of the pyramid so tall it was shrouded in thin tendrils of mist.

"She could have dropped us closer," Thrall groused. "But perhaps it is better to make a slow approach instead of falling out of the sky and into the throne room."

"Any competent queen would have spies littered all over her city," Ji added in an appropriately low voice. "She will know of our coming before we even reach the Terrace of the Speakers."

"Then she will be warned." Thrall spoke it with his voice but did not feel it with his heart. Why did Talanji refuse their help? Could she not see this was the most expedient path to victory? She may have been competent, but she was also proud. Too proud. Any leader must understand their limitations. Talanji had clearly reached hers; now it only remained to see if she would set aside her personal grievances for the safety and betterment of her people.

Personal grievances. It occurred to Thrall then that Jaina might have placed their portal to the city so far from the palace exactly because of those grievances. How would Talanji greet them if she watched them drop out of a portal unannounced into her throne room? Her suspicious mind might go immediately to the worst-case scenario and, in this instance, the correct one.

The last thing they needed was another reason for Talanji to mistrust them.

They began the long, long journey toward the palace, an untold number of stairs lying between them and their goal. The humidity and noise did nothing to ease Thrall's troubled mind and tight stomach. Fortunately, they stood out less than he expected, the popular port drawing a diverse crowd, from reptilian tortollans to towering vrykul from the Broken Isles. Even the odd enterprising pandaren merchant wandered by. Many of the sailors and purveyors stood in clumps, complaining bitterly about the storms raging around the island, preventing the flow of commerce. Each and every one of them seemed ready to blame the queen for their financial woes.

"When we reach the bazaar we can hire a beast to make our journey shorter," Thrall said, shouldering his way through the crowd.

"*If* we reach the bazaar."

Thrall glanced down at him, brow lifted with concern.

"We are being followed," Ji whispered. "They have kept us in their sights since we arrived at the port. Trolls. Six of them. White paint on their faces."

The orc took his time appraising the situation and their odds, picking out the trolls Ji described. They looked thin, underfed, but he noted an intensity in their eyes that he did not like. Sometimes, the starved and the desperate were the most difficult opponents.

"Draw them out," Thrall muttered back. "Follow me."

They climbed to a terrace that overlooked the port. The Grand Bazaar proved less busy, as the stall owners shooed away anyone who didn't seem ready to actually spend their coin. Thrall continued higher, leaving behind yet more of the concealing crowd. Only a handful of stragglers continued up the grand flight of stairs overseen by an immense, gilded pterrordax, whose white eyes seemed to see everything and nothing. She rustled her wings, then calmed and settled back down on her magnificent jeweled perch. Few dawdled in her shadow. If he and Ji managed to stay out in the open, he doubted the trolls would strike.

He was wrong.

Just before his foot landed on the final stair, a lanky, green-skinned troll darted toward him. Thrall anticipated the blow, aimed with a spear, and whirled, grabbing the weapon as it missed his right flank. Using the troll's own momentum against him, he spun, fast, sending the troll flying toward the base of the sky queen's perch. Ji faced the remainder of the ambushers head on, feet planted wide, furred hands curved like talons, his weight shifting from side to side.

"Death to the traitor queen and her Horde allies!"

A scream went up, and a young vulpera carrying a basket filled with bread on his head was shoved aside as a female troll in a simple black dress lifted a blow gun to her lips and blew. The boy toppled down the stairs, bread spilling in every direction. They were drawing an audience.

Thrall raised his right arm, his thick gauntlet protecting him from the dart. He knocked it away with a grunt, then unsheathed the axe strapped to his back. Swinging in a wide arc, he won them some space, the loud whoosh of the axe head frightening the ambushers back, putting them at a disadvantage and giving Thrall and Ji the high ground. The pandaren leapt into action, propelling himself with the fury of the wind down the stairs, leg outstretched, his foot slamming into the throat of a masked and hunched troll. It was more than enough to stagger him, and the troll slid back down with the boy and the bread, his dagger clattering to the stones.

Blow Gun wasn't finished. She charged Thrall, shrieking, trading her darts for a mean little hunting knife. She slashed like a whirlwind, like she was possessed, and managed to land a hit. A glancing blow. Thrall shrugged it off. He snatched up the troll by her neck and shook her, hard, then threw her with a rasping bellow against the stone pillar at the top of the stairs. Unconscious, the troll slid down to join her friend, slumped and still beneath the Sky Queen.

"Step aside! Step aside, I said!"

Thrall recognized the voice. Darkspear Chieftain Rokhan slammed a pair of tortollan gawkers out of the way. Two heavily armed and armored Rastari enforcers emerged to tamp back the masses, using their staves horizontally to nudge them away from the commotion.

"Thrall!" Rokhan half laughed, half shouted, drawing his daggers and standing shoulder to shoulder with the orc. "Didn't expect to see ya here, and certainly not startin' a fight in the Grand Bazaar!"

"Ambushers," Thrall told him in a snarl. "Rebels. We've come to speak with the queen. Urgently."

"Take the pterrordax! I'll deal with dis rabble! Enforcers, to me!"

The pterrordax presiding over the ambush flapped her wings, buffeting the crowd and Thrall with a sudden gust of wind. She let loose a primal, deafening cry, swooped down from her perch, and landed, shaking the tiles beneath Thrall's feet, sending dust into the air. Ji somersaulted away from the stairs, catapulting himself on the final bounce onto the creature's back. He ducked down, offering Thrall a hand.

"Go!" Rokhan assured them, delighting in the chance to let his daggers dance. "See to da queen!"

Thrall nodded and took Ji's hand, hoisting himself onto the beast's back, holding tightly to the harness decorated with gems and slivers of bone. At once, the beast pushed off, the force and speed of it drawing awed cries from the crowd.

They soared above the Terrace of the Speakers, spinning higher and higher, the Great Seal no longer just a distant, formless mountain. Now tower and waterfalls, manicured palms, balconies and windows came into view. The seat of Zandalari power and the queen's throne was spread beneath them, though with rebels openly challenging her allies in the streets, it was a throne she might not hold much longer.

"Who has come? Why was I not warned of visitors to my throne?"

Queen Talanji was ready for them. Little eyes, little spies, had carried word of the ambush and bloodshed in the Grand Bazaar to her on swift wings. Those spies, dismounting their pterrordaxes, had gone at once to Zolani, and Zolani had gone at once to the queen, and now Talanji stood before the Golden Throne, fists tight at her sides, eyes blazing. Just sitting upright was an ordeal now, her body growing weaker by the moment, but she refused to show her faltering health to those who depended upon her.

Even warned, their intrusion stung. Talanji had not extended an invitation to the Horde leadership, and they had already insisted on embedding Zekhan with her. That was more than enough. Between Rokhan and Zekhan, they should have been satisfied with her cooperation. But no, there they were, appearing in her port, causing trouble in her city, and now striding toward her as if they had every right to be there.

Zekhan hurried up from the council chambers below, huffing for breath, his cheeks stained pink from his haste. He bowed several times to Talanji before trying to meld into the wall beside the throne. She glared.

"Did you know of this?"

"N-no, majesty! No! I would have told ya!" Zekhan sputtered.

"I apologize for the intrusion." Thrall stomped his way to the throne, pausing to show her the expected courtesy. He was visibly sweaty, spattered with blood, boots as wet as if he had just walked out of the surf. The pandaren, Ji Firepaw, bowed gracefully. Behind them, framed by the purple glow of dusk hovering on the horizon, the Sky Queen waited to take flight.

"You will *explain* the intrusion," Talanji corrected. "Now."

"A new threat rises, Queen Talanji, and we have come to offer our guidance and our aid," Thrall replied.

Zekhan perked up, nodding his head vigorously. "The rebels, yes, it is as I said, ya majesty, the Horde is willin' to help!"

"I am the queen, and I speak for the Golden Throne; Zekhan, be silent. This is not my first brush with insurrection," Talanji fired back, directing herself first to the spy and then to Thrall. The

Rastari honor guards protecting the chamber inched closer to Thrall as if sensing her growing irritation. "Like the traitors Yazma and Zul, this rebellion will be crushed and order returned to Zuldazar. This is Zandalari business, and it will be handled the Zandalari way!"

The pandaren plucked a stray poisoned dart from Thrall's pauldron. "Indeed. It looks very handled."

Talanji took a single trembling step down from her throne. Even the bottoms of her feet ached. "How dare you—"

"There is no time for this. We work together or these rebels win the day and topple your rule, your majesty." Thrall's voice rose to the threatening timbre of thunder. "Listen, and listen well, your majesty. Our shaman sense terrible unrest in the spirit realm; these rebels attacking you grow stronger, bolstered by the dark rangers of Sylvanas Windrunner."

The chamber fell silent. Talanji's heart clenched in her chest. Could it be true? The Blade of the Queen fidgeted, nervous, now she too was sweating in her pauldrons decorated with sharpened tusks and helm bearing a plume of emerald and blue feathers. Talanji exchanged a glance with Zolani, who gave the tiniest shrug of confusion.

"Dark rangers? Here? That is not possible," Talanji felt her hands growing cold. "I . . . I would know of this."

"No, you might not." Thrall sighed and raked his hand through his dark, coarse hair. "Sylvanas works in the shadows. Her forces are minimal; they must use whatever resources they can. Whatever reinforcements they can."

The world spun a little. Reinforcements. Yes. That would explain how the Widow's Bite seemed to be everywhere and nowhere, how they could attack so many shrines and afford new weapons. They had borrowed the tactics and resources from an outside source. A blight had landed on her shores and begun to infect the most persuadable. *Sylvanas Windrunner.* A name synonymous with chaos and death. And what did the Widow's Bite attack? Shrines belonging to the loa of graves—the weak spot in her rule. Slowly it began to intertwine, making a sick sort of sense.

"Oh," she murmured. "There is proof of this?"

"Your reaction is proof enough," Thrall said solemnly. She noticed him flick his eyes toward Zekhan. "But there is more. My . . . sources tell me that you have taken an Alliance spy into custody. He was investigating these exact suspicions. The rebels are using dark ranger arrows, and communications in their language have been discovered among abandoned camps."

Talanji wished to grab the throne's arm for support, but instead forced herself to stand still. The news washed over her in a powerful wave. They had indeed come across an Alliance dog sniffing around their lands, and her jailers reported that he insisted on a meeting with her. The dire threat of the Widow's Bite had kept her from visiting his cell. In a certain light, it was a relief. This at least explained why they had been so unsuccessful in stopping the insurrection. Or . . . it partially explained it. Still, she wondered what "sources" had given him these tips. If it was Zekhan, then the ambassador had lied, holding back vital information. And yet her kingdom suffered, and had suffered for too long. It was time to be honest. It was time to admit the odds were becoming insurmountable. They no longer faced just one nest of vipers but two.

For a moment she simply observed Thrall, then bit her lip, making her choice.

"These are grave tidings indeed. These signs . . . I should have seen them."

"That is how Sylvanas works," Thrall said softly. "They would have infiltrated carefully. They will use all possible means to stay hidden." He came nearer to the throne, gazing up at her. "We are not blaming you for their presence, Queen Talanji, only demanding that you take it seriously."

"I will," Talanji breathed. "I do." She turned to Zolani, the

Blade of the Queen. "We can delay no longer. Dispatch our forces to the remaining shrines. The Widow's Bite are conspiring with a known war criminal and no friend to us. The people of Zandalar cannot accuse us of turning on our own, not when the rebels have chosen such vile traitors for friends."

"Right away, my queen." Zolani bowed and left to do the queen's bidding.

"I can go, too," Zekhan volunteered, placing his hand up just a little above his shoulder. "Lead some soldiers, I mean. I serve the Horde, my queen, but I serve you, too."

"You should wait for our forces to support your own," Thrall interrupted swiftly, addressing them both. "Dark rangers are formidable—"

"My soldiers are formidable, too," Talanji told him, holding her head high. Her gaze fell on Zekhan, and he straightened with pride. "Summon your Horde forces, Thrall, bring them to our aid, but Zandalar can wait no longer. Zandalar acts *now*."

CHAPTER TWENTY-TWO

Dazar'alor

The walls of the prison might have glittered with all the promises of a poor man's dreams, but a golden prison was still a prison. Shaw had to hand it to the Zandalari—even the dungeons in the city of gold lived up to the name. They really committed to the theme.

Relieved of his weapons, even the knife he thought he had pretty handily stashed in the false bottom of his boot, Shaw had nothing to do but lie back on the rock-hard bench they gave him for a bed and stare up at the cracks in the ceiling. For a while he counted them, desperate to employ his mind. Then, of course, his thoughts began to wander. One of the bricks was shaped sort of like a moon, or maybe a boat. Definitely the hull of a boat.

Fairwind and the crew had gotten away. That was his one and only hope, a notoriously unreliable pirate captaining a slapdash crew through an impassable, deadly storm. Great odds. He'd seen worse, of course, in his long, long career as spymaster, but these odds ranked pretty low . . . Maybe just above the time he had relied completely on a shoddy network of spies embedded in a cheese business. Not all of a man's schemes could be brilliant.

He sprang up off the bench. It would take a brilliant scheme indeed to get him out of this prison and make a dent in this mission. So far, the Zandalari had treated him well enough, affording him the usual prisoner of war amenities—a bench for rest, a bowl for slop, and a bucket for his business. They had wisely chosen a cell at the very end of the prison. Twenty-four cells total, a few occupied, but they shoved him away from everything. Two guards stood sentry just outside his tiny golden room, changing shifts at breakfast and dinner. He was never left unsupervised. The kids watching him looked green, probably new recruits. That was odd. He thought a spy would rate at least a few grizzled veterans.

"This your first stint guarding the prison?" He had tried, the second day, to make conversation. The guard on the left looked like he barely fit into his armor, the pauldrons forged for a much larger troll. He saw the kid shift from foot to foot, glancing at his mate for help.

"Don't look at him, look at me," Mathias said.

The second guard muttered something, but Mathias didn't catch it. His Zandali was all right, but the boy had said it fast.

"You two aren't even a little bit curious about me?" he asked a few hours later, letting them settle down after his first try. The kid swimming in armor actually glanced his way, pale blue eyes flashing, brows tight with alarm. "Hey. I don't bite."

"We are not to speak with you," he stammered, clutching his halberd for dear life.

"Says who?"

"Overseer. Everyone. Shut up!"

That was that. Mathias didn't get an answer the next time he prodded them, so he tried a different tactic. He had once talked his way out of a headlock during a bar brawl in Dalaran. That time it was a gnoll latched around his neck, and if he could reason with a gnoll, he could reason with anyone.

"Bit boring down here, don't you think?" Day three. Shaw leaned against the bars of his door, casually picking his nails. Usually he whittled bird statues to keep his hands busy, but he was down a few crucial items for that. "I was going to take a vacation soon. Guess this is it now. Not really what I had in mind . . . Guess Valeera was right."

The guards ignored him. A mosquito had found its way in, buzzing around Shaw's ear. Because he was locked up, he let it go on principle.

"I thought maybe I would just disappear into the highlands. Had a cabin out there once. Small. What you might call cozy. Get up whenever I happened to, go to bed just the same. Put a chair out in the tall grass and kick my boots off. Whittle some. Work on my birdcalls. They're pretty good, but they could always be better."

Mathias closed his eyes, thumbnail gliding over his palm. *Just keep your hands and mind busy. Pass the time. Don't go mad. Stay sharp.* "That whole thing sounds lonely, doesn't it?"

He saw, out of the corner of his eye, the little troll nod, forgetting himself.

"You're right. I shouldn't go alone. I'm good at that, being alone. Comes natural to me. I was never all that personable—liked watching people, sure, observing, but too many and I just felt . . . swallowed up, like everyone could see me just fine but I couldn't see them. I like to be above it all, perched. But I should find a friend."

Mathias stopped, realizing he had stumbled into a truth he hadn't meant to bungle into. "Well. I should make a friend. A partner."

He thought he had one, or the start of one or something more, but that remained to be seen. If—when—he got out of the prison, he would just ask the man directly. There were ways, of course, that he could gather information and circumvent the discussion part, but Mathias, just then, wanted desperately to talk.

After all, they had a lot to discuss. He was just warming up to Flynn when that damn storm tossed them into chaos, and the pirate had even told him about the death of his mother. That couldn't have been easy. There was so much Mathias now wanted to tell him—about himself, about his family, about the life he led for his country but not for himself.

They would have the talk eventually, of course, Mathias would get out somehow. This time it wouldn't be on a ship where they could be interrupted by storm or sailors. That cabin might be the perfect location, come to think of it. Just the two of them with their chairs in the tall grass. The mountains all around would be standing guard, enfolding them like an embrace, a flock of distant birds calling to each other as they grew smaller and then were swallowed by the dark orange sun hanging low on the horizon.

"I never got to finish telling you about my grandmother," Shaw would say. If he closed his eyes and concentrated, he could feel the stiff grass of the highlands poking into his calves.

Flynn would say something flippant like, "I thought you just wanted to enjoy the sunset."

And Mathias would sigh and wait for the inevitable prodding. Flynn Fairwind was, of course, incorrigibly curious. Then Mathias would snap off a piece of grass and play with it, not nervously, but to give himself a focus. "Pathonia Shaw, the Silver Cutpurse."

"Pathonia?" Flynn would cackle. "That's a dreadful name. Full apologies to your granny."

"She's long dead, and it would take more than a cheap insult to bring on her fury." Shaw would sigh and shake his head, and bend the grass into a moon shape. "No, she was made of iron. Caught three times for stealing and given the choice by the guard of Stormwind—work for them or hang."

"It's safe to assume she chose Stormwind?" he might ask.

"Oh, yes. She chose Stormwind. She chose to assassinate whomever they told her to and make it look like an accident, or a robbery gone wrong, or anything but what it was. She taught my mother the same trade, and when my mother died Pathonia taught me, too." The little piece of grass would make a perfect circle, and he would hold it up and catch the sunset inside it. "She chose Stormwind for me, too."

The bitterness broke the scene playing out in his head. He opened his eyes, and there was no tall grass and no cabin, and no Flynn there beside him to hear this tale. His grandmother Pathonia always wore a grotesque amount of rings, jewels glittering on every knuckle, but on her right ring finger she wore only a tied red string. As a boy, Shaw had asked what it meant once: Pathonia had cuffed him across the cheek and he never asked again.

He thought then of that small red thread, saw it unwind, growing longer, and longer, until he saw it connect from that scared boy to where he stood now, a line drawn in blood. How different his family's legacy could have been, how different *his life* could have been, had he been given the freedom to choose for himself. Did Flynn Fairwind feel the same? Doomed to a life of piracy, of theft, because his mother had put him on that path?

Shaw leaned against the cold gold wall, forehead instantly chilled, and wondered about freedom, about how much of it he had felt aboard the *Bold Arva*, and the man that had been there with him. A man that smelled like whiskey and salt and soap, whose coat had been warm in his hands, as warm as sun-baked stones. He pushed himself away from the wall and retreated to the stone slab, finding only fitful sleep.

On the fourth day, the skinny little troll in the too-big armor slipped something under the door with his gruel. A long, wide piece of grass, perfect in every way, firm enough to take a slice. Like from a fingernail. Mathias picked it up, confused, studying it from every angle. Not much of a digging implement, not much of a shiv. Then he remembered all the junk he had spilled to the guards at the door, and he smiled at the blade of grass.

It was for his vacation. For the birdcalls. He clasped his hands together over the piece of grass as if he were praying, and maybe he was. If he did have a friend in the world—a real friend and not just an ally or an acquaintance or a source—then he hoped that friend had gone for help. Flynn had it in him. They had made a good team on the *Arva,* good partners. He hoped that partner hadn't shipwrecked somewhere, that he wasn't drifting dead at the bottom of the sea.

He had a lot of things to say to that man, if and when he got out.

CHAPTER TWENTY-THREE

Nazmir

Shallow pools of orange light glistened on top of the tar pits. Just as they had feared and expected, the rebels had reached the shrine. Zekhan held up his hand, the lieutenant at his side doing the same, both of them calling for silence. Soldiers crouched in the brush that grew thinner and thinner as the sandy hillside gave way to the hardened earth before the pits. Juho, the lieutenant, grumbled wordlessly, shifting his spear to the ground for a moment.

The pterrordaxes had dropped them off a mile back up the hilly approach to Shoal'jai, diverting around the sharp peaks where more of the birdlike creatures nested. Speed and discretion demanded that they risk the dangerous maneuver. They had not been seen, but that didn't matter.

"Too many," Juho said. A square piercing hung from his lower lip, and he nudged it nervously with his tongue. "The fire . . . With those torches, they can control the pits. We can't go near them."

"We have to try," Zekhan told him. "The queen needs us, Juho. Zandalar needs us."

He scrunched his nose. "Dis is for Bwonsamdi."

"No, Juho, it's more than that," he insisted. They were running out of time, and this hesitation was not helping. "These rebels are stealing trolls from their beds, sacrificing them for dark magics. Do ya not want to stop that? Do ya not want to protect ya city?"

Juho drew back, staring ahead, the glow of the torches hovering near the pits reflecting in his eyes. "To the west, then, fewer rebels that way."

Zekhan grinned, and with another hand signal, the soldiers began their approach. He saw Juho lean down and gather sticky mud in his hand, then rub it over his golden armor, obscuring the shine. The others followed his lead, and Zekhan pressed forward ahead of them, already dressed in dark leathers.

The soldiers began to veer to the left, to skirt the nearest pit and try to strike with surprise along the far shore. Zekhan noticed the rebels clustered on the opposite side of the tar lakes, dark rangers among them, their eyes glowing faintly in the dark. A man stood among them with his own pair of pulsing red eyes, bright as the braziers lit at his feet. The loa's shrine rose out of the middle of the black, smooth tar pit before Nathanos Blightcaller, he, the rebels, and the dark rangers nocking lit arrows and firing at it.

Something squirmed on top of the shrine. Something *alive.*

"Ancestors have mercy," Zekhan whispered, rushing toward the nearest edge of the tar pit. "*Children.*"

"Zandalari! Now!" Juho had given the order, and the trolls rushed forward, spears raised.

Zekhan went his own way, watching the arrows sail over the shrine and over the children, landing on the far bank, mere feet from where he crept along the edge of the stinking black pit. The Zandalari soldiers cut through the rebels easily enough, but the dark rangers were already upon them, forcing a retreat. A perfectly aimed gust of wind might push the children to safety, or it might just shove them into the tar. He closed his eyes tightly, knowing he couldn't just let the little ones be shot to death, but also keenly aware that this was bait.

And it was working. He felt power surge from his toes to his hands—he had to try the spell. Had to try *something*. He could never live with himself if he just left them there.

Air rushed between his hands, gathering into a larger, louder vortex as he channeled all his energy into it. Another arrow landed, *thwip*ping into the dirt at his feet, disrupting the spell. He glanced up, just in time to see Nathanos Blightcaller lowering his bow. He was too far away to read any expression, but Zekhan already knew he was grinning.

The dark rangers emerged from the treeless shadows at his side, their drawn daggers slashing the air louder than their actual footsteps. He cried out, dodging backward, ducking, finding himself teetering on the edge of the tar pit, and then, as the closest ranger sliced at him again, *in* it.

They holstered their daggers and drew their bows, and Zekhan pushed farther into the tar and away from them. Where else could he go? The children were still there, behind him, wiggling helplessly on the shrine. The Zandalari regrouped, honing in on the two rangers that had knocked him into the pit.

The going became harder and slower. Slower. Zekhan couldn't move. Death hovered like a thin shroud over his head. Death. Not Bwonsamdi, not the loa of graves, but a cold and unfeeling end. The tar pulled him downward, froze his feet in place so that it hurt even to try to move. He saw, at the edge of the tar pits, the torches moving toward the very edge, the killing flame that would set the tar ablaze and burn them all to ash.

"Turn back!" Juho screamed.

Behind him on the southern bank of the tar pit, he heard Talanji's soldiers calling him back. But he pressed forward. There, straight ahead, huddled on the ruins of Bwonsamdi's shrine, sat the two troll children, shaking with fright, their bodies tied together. Target practice for the heartless.

While the dark rangers continued firing toward the children, Nathanos Blightcaller swiveled and walked toward the road leading east and deeper into Nazmir, going at the languid pace of a completely unbothered man.

"Leave the children!" he heard one of the soldiers scream. "They are lost!"

No. Zekhan wouldn't accept that. He had volunteered to lead this detachment of Talanji's forces, and he would be damned if he let her warriors see him turn away from innocent villagers. And he was close, so close now, he could see the terrified dance of their eyes as they caught sight of the torches, too. They squirmed to the edge of the shrine, a toppled pillar sapped of its magic, a skull carved into its face. The children's feet were tied, too, and if they fell into the pit they would drown in the sticky tar. Zekhan pushed through the sludge, forcing himself to look at the children, only the children.

Arrows began to fall from the far side of the pit, persuading Talanji's already sparse forces to fall back, abandoning Zekhan to his fate. They had managed to fell two dark rangers, but now they were the focus of a dozen more.

There. It would have to be enough. He stopped, chest-deep in the stinking tar, black ash falling like snow all around them. Vultures circled, perhaps sensing an available meal. Stained white ridges rose like sharp mountains from the tar, the long-dead remains of immense beasts.

Closing his eyes, Zekhan summoned the power of the wind again to his hands, hoping the gust he conjured would be strong enough to carry the children safely to him. The children shrieked, but Zekhan only heard the wind pouring from his hands. He warped it, giving it spin, lifting it at a careful angle until it scooped the captives up in a chill embrace and whisked them over the tar to his arms. The gust died down as he opened his eyes again and reached for the little trolls, hoisting them awkwardly across his shoulders.

"Stop ya squirmin'!" he grunted. "I'll get ya to safety now."

The torches had come. He heard the fire rip across the tar, a sound like a rockslide, the children slung over his back as he summoned the wind once more and let it speed his feet. Nothing happened. No sudden speed, no saving burst of wind to carry them to safety. Heat roared toward them, and the night sky was suddenly bright. Talanji's soldiers screamed. The Widow's Bite trolls screamed. They had too far to go. The fire would burn them up long before they ever reached the shore.

What now, ancestors, what now?

A voice answered, but not one of his kin.

You know.

Saurfang. Zekhan did know. He slowed and then stopped, the children beating his back black and blue with their fists, urging him forward. But he found the power of the winds once more, less careful this time, more desperate. The children soared above his head, carried on the last magic he could conjure. They hit the ground with a thump, but they were safe. Talanji's soldiers rushed in to grab the little ones, and two stayed behind, finding a long sliver of dinosaur bone to shove out into the tar, pushing it toward Zekhan while dodging the hail of arrows. A lifeline.

Every step felt harder, the tar an unforgiving impediment. The flames engulfed him as he reached the tip of the bone and he lunged for it, but he saw the fire reflected in the eyes of the trolls trying to help. He saw their mouths drop open in horror as Zekhan felt the first vicious kiss of the flames and smelled burning hair.

The pain made him spasm and then gasp, his hands trembling

and blistering up as he grabbed hold of the lifeline and the trolls pulled.

Go, he wanted to shout, but he couldn't form words around the agony. *There's no savin' me. There's no use helpin' a corpse.*

He expected death to be different. Slower perhaps, and kinder, more like turning away from a sunset and walking into the night. But death came on like one of his conjured whirlwinds. Zekhan watched the world fall away, ripped out of his body by some unseen hand flinging him toward a vortex that disappeared down and down. A down that never ended, a plunge over a waterfall of pale souls. Others fell with him, their images ghostly thin, and he wondered if he looked as shocked and afraid as they did. Chains snaked up from the pit below, ghostlike and silver, clamping over his shoulders, clanking over his wrists and dragging him down, down . . .

Time became meaningless. There was no telling how long he and the others fell. The void below him growled, shaking and rumbling like the belly of a hungry world. Whatever lay below him, Zekhan did not want to go. Every ounce of sense left in his soul cried out in protest. The spirits plunging toward the void began to cry and moan, wailing, a rising dirge of terror that drowned out all thoughts, all desires. There was only fear, and one truth that occurred to him as he hurtled toward a morass of black and purple that swirled at the end of their long drop. Whatever lurked behind the veil of that murky pit stirred, and it wanted him to break. Something was there watching him. Something noticed him, only him. An evil too terrible to name waited there for Zekhan, ready to consume. This was death. It was nothing like the sun-drenched reunion he had experienced through Saurfang's eyes, no joy, no paradise, just endless suffering, a darkness that obliterated all the life that had come before it.

"Summon the healers! We must attend to his burns at once!"

The voice rippled on the fringes of his consciousness. It wasn't like the mournful howls of the spirits, but clearer, almost sweet . . . Zekhan flailed, trying to move toward it.

"How did this happen?" the voice, a familiar voice, demanded.

"The . . . the dark rangers, my queen, they were waitin'. They set a trap for us at the pits. It was a bloodbath."

A queen . . . It was too hard to think of names; they were slipping away like water through his fingers.

She spoke again, louder, more forceful, traces of lightning streaked across the sides of the vortex, glittering in time with her words.

"Where are those healers!?"

"Ya can do nothin' for him, child. But there's somethin' I can do."

A new voice, stronger even than hers. The souls tumbling down around him grew quiet, as if they wanted to hear that voice in particular. Zekhan felt something reach around his ankle and pull, hard, speeding him toward the nameless evil seething in the swirling black and violet pit. He clawed at the air, but he couldn't fight it.

"Not yet, my boy. Not yet. I need ya services a little while longer . . ."

Now he was pulled in both directions at once. A more insistent hand wrapped around his right hand and guided him up. Neither force wanted to let go, and for a moment he was sure they would break him in two. But at last he was free, rocketing upward, flying with dizzying speed away from the lights below, a glimmer that grew fainter and fainter.

But the thing lurking in the shadows had seen him, and he didn't hear it speak so much as feel it, a sensation like a cruel idea unfurling inside, a shadow hatching in his mind: all-consuming, never-ending suffering.

Zekhan flew faster and faster, yanked back toward a pinprick of light that he hadn't noticed before. Had it always been there? It was approaching very quickly, and he didn't know if he could fit through it, but he wasn't slowing down . . . He closed his eyes and braced, and with the force of a slap inhaled breath on Azeroth once more.

Blinking erratically, he found himself on his side, curled up on a cot in a small house. His entire body ached, feverish and trembling, but a smooth, cold substance had been smoothed all over his many, many burns. Zekhan didn't want to look, but he did, shuddering at the sight of his charred and blackened hands, the skin peeling up in angry red blisters. Even shuddering was agony, and he winced. Wincing hurt, too.

"Ow."

"He's alive!" Talanji stared down at him, hands covering her mouth. "You really did it."

A blue-and-gray-masked figure hovered behind her, eyes seething with turquoise fire. Zekhan whimpered. He didn't want to think about, see, hear, or smell fire ever again.

"I . . . I saw something . . . But nothin' like I expected! It was . . . t-terrible. Ya lied, Bwonsamdi. Ya lied!"

"What did ya see?" Bwonsamdi demanded, tripping over his words, breathless with panic. "Tell me!"

"Save ya strength," Talanji gently chided. Next to her knees, six empty earthenware pots held the remnants of the herbal paste used to treat his burns. "The healers will return soon, but Bwonsamdi wanted them out."

The loa sagged, so transparent it was hard to make out the movements of his hands and feet, as if he was collapsing from the outside in. "It's an ugly business, shoving a troll's soul back into his body. Almost didn't reach ya."

"I . . . I saw a pit, or a portal, purple and black, a place I would never escape. Torment, suffering . . ."

Bwonsamdi sucked in a breath through his teeth. "What else did ya see, boy?"

It was too much. His head wouldn't stop spinning. "I . . . just saw spirits, chains, darkness, everything felt so . . . cold, cruel. Like I would never know peace again. A place where only evil belongs." Zekhan coughed. Even just clinging to life, the fleeing memory of that place broke his heart. He somehow felt simultaneously hot and freezing.

"Ya be right about the suffering. 'Tis the place for the 'unredeemable'."

"What did I do to deserve that abyss?"

Talanji shook her head, leaning over him. "Ya saved those little ones, Zekhan, they are already callin' ya the Light of Shoal'jai."

Bwonsamdi cackled. "Then they be old enough to know a good joke when they hear it, eh?"

But the queen didn't laugh, and neither did Zekhan. She glared up at him, pointing an accusatory finger. "Why *did* he go to this horrible place, oh wise loa of graves?"

The loa glanced down and to the side. Zekhan noticed then how weakly his vision appeared, almost as thin as a trail of old smoke. He heaved a weary sigh and spread his hands open, palms up, as if presenting them something.

"Ya saw the Maw, boy. A hopeless place that holds the darkest spirits. But now it be consumin' every soul, no matta their deeds in life. Good or evil, thief or prince, they all go to the Maw. Nothin' is as it should be. And *I* be keepin' as many trolls away from there as I can, and at no small cost. It's takin' all I have left just to keep them safe." He held up one of his translucent hands and grimaced. "Which is why ya must stop these rebels and Blightcaller. If they have their way, nothin' will stop all souls from enterin' the Maw. For good."

Both trolls fell silent, as if the word itself had stolen their ability to speak. The queen herself grew wide-eyed and pale.

Talanji stood, her skirt overturning one of the clay pots. "How long?" she asked when resolve finally found her. "How long has this been happening?"

"I saved your fa'da from this fate," Bwonsamdi growled. "If that is what ya askin'."

"The Spirit Realm . . ." Zekhan managed to choke. He wanted more than anything to just close his eyes and sleep, but he feared what dark dreams of the Maw might await him there. His teeth wouldn't stop chattering. The *pain*. He needed something for the pain . . . "Thrall knew. The shaman t-told him it was broken."

"Yes, he said as much in the throne room," Talanji agreed, still jabbing her finger at Bwonsamdi. "You are the loa of graves, you must know what has gone wrong. Sylvanas and the Forsaken are here for *you*, Bwonsamdi. You will tell me why."

The loa's gaze drifted past her, landing on Zekhan.

"They be workin' with forces I cannot see, but whoever be givin' the orders wants me gone—it wants *all* obstacles gone. I will tell ya more, Talanji, but not here, not like this. The boy needs rest and all the relief ya priests can muster. He has earned that much."

CHAPTER TWENTY-FOUR

Stormwind

Anduin's hair felt like old, wet ribbons, bootblacked and slicked into a tight braid, hanging greasy and limp over his right shoulder. The hood stayed high around his face, ragged and patchwork, something he had fished out of the rubbish left behind by fresh recruits joining the Alliance ranks. Many of them gave up their old civilian clothes, trading in everything for the bold gold and blues. *Rebirth,* he thought, *into a chosen family.*

What would those stalwart recruits think of him now, he wondered, dodging from shadow to shadow, swallowed up by an abandoned cloak that still smelled of its former owner? The clothes underneath were his own, just a plain, dark tunic, loose trousers, and a nondescript belt. His boots looked too expensive, and so he brushed them with mud, just like he had tried to conceal his memorable golden hair. Even if he smelled questionable and looked even worse, he felt exhilarated, leaving his chambers behind, and then the castle, and then the gated city altogether, soaking up the crisp night air as he followed the winding path down to the Goldshire Inn.

Sometimes he felt like a coin satchel, and every worry, every problem, every mistake, every crisis was another fat, heavy coin falling into that bag. It got heavier and heavier, but usually it was manageable. After a while, however, the fabric started to strain. Some of the coins had to go or the satchel would rip, the bottom falling out, the coins spilling everywhere. Every breath he drew in, every moment that passed, another coin came—Sylvanas evading them—*plink*—Alliance soldiers washing up on shore—*plink*—Alleria and Turalyon—*plink*—Jaina questioning him—*plink*—Tyrande—*plink*—Teldrassil—*plink*—the Forsaken in the Highlands—his spymaster taken prisoner—*plink, plink.*

Another coin had fallen right in before he returned to his chambers to don his disguise. Prisoners from Alleria and Turalyon's search arrived in Stormwind, and he had been summoned to watch their procession into the stockades. He commanded they be treated fairly, that once they were thoroughly questioned, they could be set free. An old Forsaken in a robe caught his attention, a tortured bend to the man's spine, a crazed and haunted glint to his eye.

When the coins spilled, Anduin found himself before the great carved fireplace in his bedroom on the floor, legs tucked up to chest, catatonic, eyes unable to close, mind unable to clear, the flames just inches before him searing into his vision until tears poured down his cheeks.

Now he sensed when the coins were piling up, and he took measures to alleviate the strain. This was acting out, and stupid, he knew it, but it was what he needed. To be a nameless face in a tavern, if only for a few hours, to escape the duties and the pressures that haunted him. A priest was never without his power, and he had brought a dagger, hidden it on the back of his belt, not wanting to provoke a fight but ready for one nonetheless.

Two girls rushed passed him, hurrying back to Stormwind and probably back to worried parents. They both had long, dark hair, coiled over their heads in intricate braids. One glanced up at him as he passed, her face delicate and soft. She almost recognized him, frowning and squinting, her interest so keen then that he was sure he had been made. It nearly made him trip and fall down the slope.

But the girls ignored him and carried on. He breathed a sigh of relief—the last thing he needed was the scandal of being found out, of having to drag himself into the keep looking like a mess and explain to his advisers and Jaina why he had been skulking around in a disguise. Anduin pulled his hood down lower and pressed on. Jaina. He didn't want to think about her scolding him, or how her questions lingered, just more coins for the satchel. Those weren't the kind he could pluck out with a stunt like this. Those stayed around forever.

She had every right to worry, of course, but the passion in her voice and the fear in her eyes had burrowed into him deep. Two men outside the inn were arguing, drawing a crowd. That was good. Anduin used the distraction to duck inside and take a table near the door, but put his back to it. When the barmaid came by, plump and beautiful, dark-skinned, with a ready, brilliant smile that would've made another boy blush, he slid her a normal sum of money and asked for an ale.

Then he remembered that he wasn't Anduin just then, so it was all right to glance at her, admire her smile and blush, so he did.

He let himself sink into the delirious joy of anonymity. When the barmaid stayed a little and flirted, asking his name, he winked, still swathed in the hood, and said, "Jerek. And what do I call you?"

"Amalia."

"That's a lovely name," the king of Stormwind said. Amalia curtseyed and went to see to another table. Anduin felt incredible.

Free. And then, of course, he felt guilty. One coin slid out the top of the satchel, and another dropped right in. He hovered over his ale, letting the foam gather on his upper lip, letting himself be gross and coarse, burping, drinking too fast, burping some more.

He wiped at the remnants of ale on his lips, finishing the one and only drink he would allow himself, and felt the guilt swell again. The door banged open near him, a trio of young soldiers rushing in, bringing with them a blast of fresh air. They had already hit some other pub, clearly, weaving into the tavern with their arms locked, all of them fresh-faced as Goldshire dairy maids, not a whisker or scar between them. The one closest to him had a thatch of shiny red hair and a lopsided nose, the middle one was tallest, a young woman with hooped blonde braids framing her ears. The third was another young man, the shortest of the trio, though he had the stocky frame of a seasoned farm boy. They were in the middle of a song, though their many ales had muddled the words.

Before Anduin could glance away, he saw all three of them whirl in his direction. He ducked down, but too late.

"Aha! Another stalwart recruit," the redhead hiccuped. "Join us in a song, brother."

"Plenty of room at your table," the young woman added, dropping into the seat across from him. Anduin went rigid with alarm, tugging nervously at the edge of his hood and keeping his eyes low.

"I . . . I prefer to drink alone," Anduin murmured.

"Nonsense, friend!" The stocky one clapped him hard on the shoulder and then fell down next to him, landing on the bench and making it sag. "Another round, Amalia, for the nervous one here! We'll have him singin' and dancin' in no time!"

"You're here to be a soldier, are you not?" the young woman asked. "To enlist? I can spot a fighter at twenty paces!"

"She can, she can," the redhead giggled.

"Chin up, brother," the boy beside him said with a nudge. "There's ale to be had and glory to savor. Glory in the name of our king! My father died fighting for us, died holding the line against N'Zoth's fiends in Orsis, in the shadow of a great . . . a great, um, temple. I think. Or oblerisk. And I vowed to take up his sword and carry it myself."

The words came out deeply slurred, but Anduin untangled them with a wince. "I'm sorry to hear that. I'm sure your father was a brave man."

Amalia returned, setting down four fresh tankards. The redhead gulped his in one. "The field of battle . . . That's . . ." He lost his train of thought briefly. "That's where I belong. Where we all belong. Shnampins all!"

"Champions, you drunk halfwit," the girl giggled. She noticed Anduin wasn't drinking. "Don't fret, stranger. You look healthy enough, I'm sure you'll have a long and storied career."

"Surely." Anduin sighed, taking up his tankard to evade further suspicion. They lapsed into song, forgetting all about their new "friend." But Anduin wouldn't soon forget them. He looked at each of their faces in turn, memorizing them, wondering how long it would take until they too turned up on a freezing slab beneath the Cathedral of Light, innocent lambs before the slaughter.

Soldiers. *His* soldiers. And he would command them, and tell them to fight, for that was a king's right and duty. They wanted glory, hungered for it, but did not know what it was or what it cost. Anduin opened his mouth to warn them, to tell them to be serious, to really think hard before they took the blue and gold, but a fiddler started up near the counter, and his new friends scattered, taking their drinks and leaving behind only puddles of ale.

The drink in his stomach began to sour. He needed to leave before he felt well and truly ill. And more, he felt eyes boring into him. Real ones, this time, not just the thousand pairs of dead and haunting eyes that seemed to follow him, accusingly, everywhere he went.

Anduin searched the bar, eyes rolling over a dozen unfamiliar faces, until at last he noticed the clean, white-robed woman in the corner near the stairs, her face in view of everyone, her white brows drawn down in confusion, her lips slightly parted around what he could only assume was a curse.

Jaina.

Her eyes flared wide. Anduin slapped another coin down on the table and shoved himself out of the chair, around the corner, and out the door, gasping as if struck when the warm, body-damp air shifted from hot to cold.

More cold was soon to follow. Anduin looped around to the back of the inn, forgetting it was soggy and marshy there and grunting as his boots were nearly sucked off his feet. The ground beneath him grew suddenly slick and hard, and his arms pinwheeled as he managed to catch himself just before the humiliating fall.

"Hello, *Jerek*."

"I can explain—"

"You're the king, you do not have to explain." Jaina's voice dropped to a steely whisper, and she took him by the arm, spinning him away from the ice she had shimmered across the ground. They stood together huddled under the narrow overhang of the roof, crickets and frogs blissfully unaware of who had just interrupted their song.

"What did you do to your hair?" She drew back, laughing.

"Boot polish," he muttered, pulling the hood down hard and avoiding her gaze. "And I suppose Jerek is a very stupid name."

"No, I think it's great. Really suits you." Jaina had the grace to cover her next guffaw with her fingertips. "It's all right, Anduin. Your secret is safe with me."

His eyes blew wide. "Jaina . . . Listen, I know we quarreled. I know we don't always see eye to eye but . . . but surely you can understand." Sighing, he leaned back against the inn. "Sometimes I need this. Sometimes I need to be a boy again. I think about all the soldiers giving their life to serve the Alliance, and I think: How? How can they be so young? Those three brave souls inside, they think they're ready to die. Ready to die *for me.* It isn't fair. It . . . it should make everything stop. The whole world should stop and point at that, but it doesn't. Everything just rolls on, the world forgets, and I have to pretend like their sacrifice isn't a cruel, heartbreaking joke."

Another coin dropped into his satchel of worries. The last one, the heaviest one. He covered his face with his hands, and felt Jaina touch his wrists lightly, pulling his arms down again. Her eyes were glossy, her mocking smile gone. She ducked her head a little, bringing them face-to-face.

"You're young, too, Anduin, and if you need Jerek to help you remember that, then yes, I understand." Jaina let go and took a small step back. "I was here tonight, too, right? Red-handed."

"At least you can show your face," Anduin said. "I just . . . can't. Part of why I need this is because it means I'm not me for a while. I'm dumb, sloppy, probably a shit-shoveler Jerek."

Jaina nodded and gestured to the end of the wall, where it gave way to the stables. "I'll find another doorstep to darken. Go back inside, Jerek. You've had a long day."

CHAPTER TWENTY-FIVE

Dazar'alor

They left Zekhan behind in the Zocalo with Talanji's personal physicians, the priests and shaman who tended to any member of her family or the Zanchuli Council. Bwonsamdi could make his own way to the palace, but Talanji urged her ravasaur, Tze'na, to her greatest speed. The beast took the stairs four at a time, carrying the queen to her chambers with Gonk's own swiftness.

Night would soon give way to dawn, but Talanji felt no closer to victory. In fact, she only felt closer to death, which meant closer to the Maw. Bwonsamdi had said it cost him dearly to keep troll souls from the Maw, and it cost her dearly just to walk now, every step a chore. Her heavy heart did nothing to ease the pain surging through her body—they had lost too many trying to protect the final shrines. Dark rangers had helped lay the traps that defeated her warriors. And her old, dear friend had been spotted among the Widow's Bite. No, not just among them, *leading* them.

"We saw a witch with the rebels," one of the surviving Rastari guards reported while the healers covered poor, burned Zekhan in salve. "She was misshapen with injury and wore strange garb, but I have seen her face in the palace countless times before, my queen. It was Apari, I would know the look of her anywhere."

Apari.

Talanji reached her chambers and decreed to the guards she would be taking no visitors. One would arrive, of course, but he did not need a door.

While she waited for Bwonsamdi to appear Talanji drifted to the bed, wishing she could simply sleep and dream and try to forget the horrors that seemed to multiply by the hour. Once, she considered Sylvanas an ally, and now the Banshee Queen's forces emboldened rebels trying to tear down Talanji's rule. That stung, but Apari's betrayal . . . Talanji sighed, sitting heavily on the mattress and removing her crown. She rubbed at her aching forehead with both hands.

As girls they had been a couple of pests, running wild in the halls of the Great Seal, causing trouble wherever and whenever they wanted. They had perfect immunity, Talanji's princess status granting them more power than any child should have. They played pranks in the gardens, splashed in the pools, stayed up late every night, and lay on their backs staring up at the stars, spinning prophecies for each other. When they were grown, Apari's loyalty never wavered, though she had every right to be jealous of Talanji's status and riches.

"Even Yazma," Talanji murmured. "Even after all of that . . ."

Apari's mother—high priestess of the loa Shadra, the crown's own spymistress—had fomented rebellion, too, conspiring with Zul to overthrow Rastakhan and end his line. But Apari stood by Talanji. She disowned her own mother and chose the crown's side. So what changed? What drove her to this?

Her last image of Apari was one of paralyzing pain. It was the day King Rastakhan died at the hands of the Alliance. Gnomish siege weapons assaulted the Great Seal, walls crumbling, ceilings caving in . . . Reports had come that her father was facing the Alliance himself, hopelessly outnumbered, and Talanji had raced to aid him, pelting through the halls, dodging debris and danger as she tried to save her father.

That was when she last saw Apari. Her friend had been pinned under a fallen pillar, blood trailing from her lips, her eyes bugging from her skull as she strained to push the stones off her lower body. Her mouth seemed to move on its own, as if in prayer. Her voice was hoarse as her weak gaze found Talanji.

"Help me, Tali! Help! I . . . I can't move!"

Talanji had only paused for a moment, weighing impossible scales. Her best friend or her father. *I am a princess*, she had thought. *My first duty is to my family and to our rule.*

She left Apari there, choosing Rastakhan.

"I will send someone for you, Apari!" Talanji had shouted as she ran. "Hold on!"

Then the memory collapsed, time distorted, the experience of finding her father's nearly lifeless body corrupting what came before and after. She remembered screaming and pointing at a royal guard at one point, but had it been for Apari? Had she forgotten, in all the chaos, to help her dying friend?

"I've failed so many," she whispered.

"Ah, but my queen, there is still time to protect me and ya kingdom."

Bwonsamdi. Talanji lifted her head slowly, finding him there by the door, all but a ghost, the golden columns behind him perfectly visible. Just raising her head took monumental strength, as if her skull were now made of lead. Her neck ached, her back splintered in agony in four places. His power was fading. Fading, because she had rashly sent her troops to defend the shrines without a plan.

And now her power faded, too, her life intertwined with his by no wish or action of her own. It would take too much energy to hate him.

"Please," she murmured. "I am . . . I feel so lost. Please let me see my father. He would know what to do. I promised to protect you, but I . . . I cannot do it alone. Summon his spirit, Bwonsamdi."

He floated closer, a grim frown etched across his face, and Talanji dreaded his refusal. Shuffling to the balcony, she beheld her crumbling kingdom. Would Thrall even return? Perhaps if word reached him that his ambassador had nearly been killed in the shrine assault, he would reconsider his offer to bring support. If that was so, they were truly lost. She gripped the railing, digging her nails into the soft gold. The nail on her middle finger cracked, blood oozing through the gap.

And of course, Bwonsamdi followed, lingering behind her, emitting his bleak aura of decay.

"Ya need to find ya own strength," he rasped, his voice as weak as his image. "Ya own way."

"The Zandalari way?" Talanji scoffed. "It failed. *I* failed."

Like I failed my father. Like I failed Apari and Zekhan . . .

"It might sound strange comin' from the loa of graves, but there is always hope, ya majesty." Bwonsamdi joined her, his eyes glowing faintly behind his bone mask. "Death brings life. The great wheel turns, slowly, yes, over eons, but it turns. Bodies decay and new life springs from it, all things that seem eternal end, then rise to find new purpose . . ."

Talanji gazed up at him, her heart beating faster. "Then my father—"

"Sh-hh. Ya not listening, child. Ya only hearin' what you want to. There is a harmony to things. A way and a flow. Ancient ones, spirits, loa . . . In time, we, too, must embrace the end, the long, deep slumber. And without us? Eh, our followers find strength in other things, in themselves, or new beliefs. They grieve, they grow—just like you. And when the veil of dreaming lifts, the eternal and great beings climb on the wheel once more, bound to it, and slowly, ever so slowly, the wheel spins." He paused, waiting until she locked eyes with him. "In that way, the ancient and powerful things of this world are eternal, ya majesty."

"Zandalar," she breathed. The fires burned in the jungle. Smoke rose above the trees. Out there, hidden in the shadows, the dark rangers and Apari with her Widow's Bite fanatics plotted their next move. "It is not lost."

It is never lost.

The loa nodded, his frown at last dissolving into a familiar smirk. "I am weak, but not gone. They will try to take the Necropolis now, my place of power. Stop them there, and I will help ya rebuild this land."

"But I cannot do it alone," Talanji whispered, frail. How she wished she could speak to her father, just for a moment. But Rastakhan himself had failed many times, his complacency and neglect bringing about the darkest times of their rule. It brought her no joy to think ill of her father, and so instead she chose to think better of something else.

The ancient and powerful things of this world are eternal.

And so was hope.

"The Horde will come," Talanji murmured, turning away from Bwonsamdi to survey her lands. They burned, they struggled, and she would worry every moment until they were safe, but they were hers. A queen's to protect. A queen's to honor.

"Once," she said softly, "I left my home, desperate to save this place. I risked my pride and my life, but I turned to the Horde and they answered my call. They did not let Zandalar stand alone. Tonight, the Horde ambassador did not let my people stand alone; he nearly gave his life to save our children. I have to risk my pride and my life once more, I have to believe the Horde will stand with us again, to fight this darkness, to raise a light together and banish the shadows from Zuldazar forever."

CHAPTER TWENTY-SIX

Nazmir

"Did you have your fun?"

Sira Moonwarden pushed off from the damp, crooked tree trunk and snorted. Fun? She had lost the meaning of the word when she rose anew in undeath. In the shallow clearing off the road, the Widow's Bite leader spoke in low tones to her followers. They were in a celebratory mood. The shrines had fallen. More had come to join the Widow's Bite in the wake of their campaign, their numbers swelling to more than forty trolls and twenty dark rangers. Apari did not have armaments for them all, but the dark rangers provided daggers and bows. Their blades were sharp, their spirit undeniable. All that remained was the final assault on the Necropolis, and then they could finally leave wretched Zandalar for Sylvanas Windrunner's side, their task complete.

Victory made her bold. She ignored Nathanos.

"Those theatrics with the children," Nathanos clarified, stepping deliberately in front of her, blocking her path. "I trust it sated your bloodlust for the moment?"

Behind him, a blood-red dawn broke, bathing the Necropolis in a crimson glow. Swarms of flies thick enough to eat a man whole gathered above the quaggy water separating them from the Zo'bal Ruins. The combined dark ranger and Widow's Bite contingencies avoided the direct road, wary of alerting any remaining Rastari enforcers of their whereabouts.

"I never took you for a man with a weak stomach, Blightcaller."

Nathanos rolled his eyes, one hand resting on a dagger tucked in his belt, the other fiddling with the feathers of an arrow sticking out from his hip quiver. "You risk galvanizing the Zandalari to greater purpose. Our plans have proceeded nicely because the queen is isolated. Grant her a few orc battalions and our odds change significantly."

"They have lost," she replied bluntly. "The storms will cut off any reinforcements by sea, and our traps will slow any soldiers arriving by land." To punctuate her point, she shrugged and removed her helmet, rotting fragrantly inside the clammy metal dome.

"Hmph." Nathanos took a few steps toward the dusty path leading to the Zo'bal Ruins. They had already sent scouts ahead; now they waited on a reply.

"Is this not the hell our queen seeks to correct? Is this not the hell she will save us from? Teldrassil burned. Darkshore burned. I assure you far more than two screaming brats were killed."

"Indeed, Sira, you have made your point. Ah. Here is Visrynn."

Their forward party returned, Visrynn and Lelyias emerging from the shadows with their hoods drawn up high over their heads. Visrynn's wrist was held together with a tight bandage. Removing her hood, she pointed back the way they had come. Mist hugged the ground, partially obscuring the mire and the fragments of stone littering the path to the Necropolis. There was only one safe approach—to secure the Zo'bal Ruins and use the passable bridge through the murky water to get at the temple itself.

Among the mist, Sira spied what looked like paler wisps, ghosts or spirits, echoes of Bwonsamdi's followers drawn to his seat of power.

"There is a small standing force; the queen must have sent them," Visrynn reported, her eyes shining brightly against the red flowers tattooed on her face. "But we outnumber them."

"They do not stand a chance, sir," Lelyias agreed. "The camp is largely pilgrims. We could take prisoners and forego bloodshed."

Sira fidgeted with her helmet, displeased.

"You have thoughts, Sira?" Nathanos drawled, clearly poking at her.

"They should suffer as we suffer," Sira replied. The round, red moon hanging above them drew her gaze, and she spat. "Unlife's only pleasure is to spill blood before Elune. The goddess did not save me. I wonder, will anyone come to save this loa?"

"A pity there are only a handful of soldiers and pilgrims to dispatch." Nathanos plucked the glove from his right hand and gave a short whistle. The celebrating in the clearing died down, and slowly the Widow's Bite rebels came to mingle with them near the road. Apari could hardly walk, but she held her head high, that loathsome little tick perched on her shoulder. A distinct odor of infection came with her, and Sira could see the other Zandalari trying not to hold their noses around her, and visibly keeping their distance.

"The ruins are ours to take," Nathanos announced. "Prepare yourselves, I shall tolerate a short rest once we secure the ruins and make camp before our final assault."

The trolls swarmed to the east, following Visrynn and Lelyias as they led the charge. Apari stood before him, her face and hair damp with sweat behind her unsettling mask. It made for a wretched sight, yet the troll smiled with beatific calm, watching her troops stalk toward the ruins under the blood moon.

"You do not look well," Sira remarked. "Lelyias is a skilled healer; she can ease the pain of your leg."

Apari trembled, her green skin patchy and pale. It looked as if even drawing breath gave her great discomfort. But the troll waved her off. "No. That will not be necessary."

Her bodyguard, Tayo, flinched.

"The Widow's Bite are loyal to you and you alone," Sira continued, impatient. The troll's pride astounded her. Such foolishness would lead her to an early grave. "We need you to survive until the loa is no more."

Behind her mask, Apari's eyes danced, bright. "That is all I live to see," Apari replied. "Bwonsamdi's end and the traitor queen powerless."

Startled shouts rose from the ruins, the ambush beginning as the rebels overran the small encampment, and the dark rangers circled the perimeter, drawing their bows and finishing any who tried to escape. There were more civilians pouring out of the ruins than Sira expected. A young male troll draped in furs appeared between a gap in the wall, wedged himself free and sprinted toward them, orange hair mussed from sleep, blood splattered across his face and tusks.

Sira donned her helm once more and drew her crescent glaives. The troll neared their hiding spot off the road, so close that Sira heard his frantic breathing as he hurled himself away from the carnage.

"Another one for you, Sira," Nathanos said, bending down to pick up his pack, preparing to join the others in the ruins. "Perhaps allow him one last piss in peace before you strike."

"One more soul for the Maw."

Sira's curved blades flashed with ruthless precision, and the troll's head fell to the ground, his look of terror frozen there, his body slumping into the bushes at their feet. While his head still rolled away, Sira stepped over his torso, matching Nathanos's easy stride. It was time to claim yet another small victory.

"Not much of a prize for your mistress," Sira murmured, inspecting the broken pillars and vine-covered walls of Zo'bal. There were no more screams from within the ruins. All had gone quiet, and then the Widow's Bite trolls began singing and a fire was lit, the smoke rising high above the fractured columns. "But everything in this accursed jungle is pathetic. Destroying it would feel like a favor."

Nathanos shook his head, pausing outside the entrance to the camp. Bodies littered the ground. They had suffered no casualties on their side, though several Widow's Bite members were being treated for wounds near the building fire. Apari and Tayo went ahead, joining their singing and dancing kin.

"Every victory we hand her matters," Nathanos told Sira bluntly. The flames reflected in his eyes, flickering and hot. "I claim this one with pride, just as I will claim the Necropolis and destroy Bwonsamdi. He will no longer be a threat to Sylvanas. Little stands in her way now, and soon nothing will. Nothing ever stands in her way for long."

Nathanos Blightcaller had no use for sleep. The fragile still-living bodies of the Widow's Bite trolls, however, required it. Even the witch Apari and her faithful bodyguard found a corner to claim and a wall to nestle against. The tarnished badge Nathanos had given Apari to fuel her magic against the shrines glinted around her neck. Many times, he considered taking it back from her, either stealthily or with force. But each time, he heard the silken whisper of his queen, urging him to let such things go.

Trinkets and trifles, her voice reminded him. *The impermanent, unimportant relics of life.*

His loyalty to Sylvanas did not hinge upon such things, even without a physical reminder of their bond. Nathanos considered it a tangible thing, as real as the stones beneath his feet and the sludgy water lapping at his boots and the cricket song filling the swamp. He patted his coat pocket, feeling again the vial there. Now that he had given his badge away, it was the only gift from Sylvanas that remained in his possession.

Dark rangers kept the watch, posted at the corners of the ruins, sinking into the shadows with their dark hoods pulled low over their faces. They too had no need to rest and stood as silent sentinels, as unmoving as the statues carved into the stone pillars of Zo'bal.

To the north, waiting upon its own small island, the Necropolis rose, its pronged central tower spearing up toward the blood moon as if its arms were raised in supplication. He wandered to the edge of the broken bridge that once joined the Zo'bal Ruins to the Necropolis and its large, open court. They could still pass unimpeded, the water no deeper than his ankles. Still, something kept him from venturing farther across the shattered bridge.

Always on the eve of battle he felt restless, but this was something else. He felt the hounds of memory biting at the heels of his mind, something invisible and dangerous pursuing him. It was good that he did not sleep, for he knew it would only invite tormenting nightmares.

The winds there howled as if in pain. He had a letter to write, a message for Sylvanas letting her know of their progress and their impending victory, but something in the stirring mist called to him. An archway yawned open at the center of the Necropolis temple, blue flames glowing at its corners like eyes. Eyes that saw him and knew him, eyes that sent a chill down his spine.

"Hello, Nathanos."

A coin splashed into the water near his feet. Nathanos hunched and then crouched, reaching down to fish the sliver of gold out of the muck. He traced his thumb across its face, revealing a familiar etching.

"You are not real," Nathanos said, both to the coin and to the voice. But when he stood and turned, he came face-to-face with his cousin, Stephon Marris. "You died a long time ago."

It was like looking into a forgiving mirror. Stephon had always been the more handsome of the two of them, with twinkling hazel eyes and a thick mop of dark hair that turned auburn at the edges. He had lips prone to smirking, dimples curved around his mouth, hiding in his beard. His skin still held the ruddy pink hue of a living man, further proof that this was only a hallucination of some kind.

Stephon Marris was long dead, ending as little but a greasy smear on a table, his body the raw materials that built Nathanos anew, and in Stephon's image.

My one regret.

"Why did you let her do it?" Stephon asked softly. "I was your cousin, Nathanos. I looked up to you, I wanted to be you, but not like that. Not like *this*."

The gold coin in his palm had the weight of the real thing. He sighed and closed his fist around it. When his cousin Stephon was just a young lad, Sylvanas had given him the coin, a gift to fund his first sword. Stephon always wanted to be a paladin and serve the Silver Hand, and had indeed achieved his dream, a dream that was soon ended when he became the clay to shape and rebuild Nathanos. His body had been ripped to shreds by an abomination, and then he had risen as a thrall of the Scourge, a mindless ghoul until Sylvanas freed him from that fate. The process had left him renewed in undeath, but in a mangled body that grew ever weaker. Sylvanas sought to repair that crumbling form.

And used Stephon to do so.

"I had no choice," Nathanos replied, unable to meet his cousin's eye. "My bones were falling from their sockets, my sinews torn and useless, I needed a new body . . ."

"When you stole my flesh."

Nathanos flinched. "Sylvanas made that decision. I could not be made whole without the sacrifice of a family member."

Stephon shook his head sadly, regarding Nathanos not with rage or disgust, but pity. "And yet still you serve her. After what she did to me. After what she did to our family. I am the only ghost that moves you, but how many ghosts have you given others? How many men now live, tormented by the loved ones you murdered in service to your vicious queen?"

Whatever guilt he felt over Stephon's end vanished. Nathanos stared back, suddenly emboldened.

"Did you know," Stephon taunted, his face changing slightly, no longer so friendly or handsome, an odd, blue light suffusing his skin, "Your queen has made some nasty friends on the Other Side. The power she has been granted can be taken away, the lords of death will never let her win. Her power is nothin' next to theirs. As she is chained to undeath, she is chained to the forces of the Shadowlands."

"You know nothing of it," Nathanos spat. "You do not know her as I do."

He squeezed his hand, obliterating the coin put there by trickery and magic. Bwonsamdi. Of course. Stephon's face dissolved into a hideous, grinning skull, a white bone mask hovering in the place where his cousin had been.

"You are in my world now, boy," Bwonsamdi jeered. "This be my game, and we be playin' it with my rules. Good luck to ya."

"You're finished," Nathanos replied, cold.

"We be seein' about that."

With that, the loa, or the vision he had sent, vanished into a twist of mocking laughter. Nathanos sneered, returning to the ruins with his hand still tightened into a fist. There was work to be done, a letter to write. He roused a dark ranger posted at the ruins entrance, her red eyes the only part visible in the darkness.

"Make yourself ready, I need you to deliver a message. In one hour you depart for the *Banshee's Wail*," Nathanos instructed her. *One more precaution*, he thought. *Like it or not, we are in Bwonsamdi's territory*. "Have our mounts at the ready. I refuse to meet my end in this swamp."

CHAPTER TWENTY-SEVEN

Dazar'alor

"They have taken Zo'bal, my queen. Blightcaller and his rangers have been sighted moving on the Necropolis. What are your orders?"

Perfectly still, Talanji's eyes fixed on the road ahead, the shaded avenue that led through the Zocalo to the Old Merchant Road, and then deep, deep into the green crush of the jungle, taking them over bridges and past waterfalls, down steep hills, to the Rivermarsh, to the Zul'jan ruins. At the end of that path, many miles of marching away, the destiny of her people awaited.

Zolani shifted. "My queen?"

"Then there is no more time," Talanji at last replied. *One last push*, she told herself. *Patch yourself up, find your last shred of strength. Hold your head high, let your people see it. March.* "We march on the Necropolis."

Alone.

It was difficult to find her voice. She had spent a sleepless night kneeling beside Zekhan on his cot, listening as Rastari enforcers, reserves, and what volunteer militia could be roused arrive to round out their forces. Zekhan twisted in his sleep, mumbling of spirits and shadows, his body covered in thick bandages applied by her priests. At some point in the night, she had drifted off, one arm resting on the bed, her head pillowed there, dreaming of the mighty Horde battalions that would be waiting outside come morning.

But her dream was just that, a dream. Thrall had not returned, and with much pain, Talanji washed and dressed, preparing for battle, schooling her face into an expressionless mask, knowing that when she beheld her forces in the Zocalo it would be an underwhelming sight.

"Is this all?" she had asked Rokhan and Zolani. Forty soldiers. Hardly enough to guarantee victory against the sly, skilled rangers of Sylvanas. "So few . . ."

"Many refused to come," Rokhan informed her grimly. "The Widow's Bite took hostages, made threats. Dazar'alor quakes, afraid of their wrath."

"That ends today," Talanji said. She meant it. Either they managed to chase the rangers from their shores and disbanded the Widow's Bite, or the rebels won, and they would bring their chaotic rule to the Great Seal until the Horde came to avenge her.

At least she hoped. Perhaps they would not even do that.

I waited too long. This is the cost of my pride.

"We should go now," Zolani advised. "Before it grows too hot for marching."

"Give the signal," Talanji agreed. It was time to decide their fate, even though she felt like a walking corpse, it was time. The others had noticed her state, of course, but nobody dared suggest she was too frail to lead.

Rokhan swung himself up onto his armored raptor, daggers glistening on his belt. He had wrapped leather straps studded with spikes around his great tusks for the occasion. Behind him, the pyramid sparkled in the morning sunlight, sleepy merchants and nobles beginning their day, oblivious to the gravity of the moment. Rokhan blew the war horn, her warriors shouted their response, and the Zandalari army followed her to war.

I will keep my promise to you, Bwonsamdi, though it may mean the end for us both.

They had passed beneath the magnificent golden arch of the Zocalo when a second, softer war horn blew in the distance.

"Did you hear that?" Zolani reined up her raptor, turning it back toward the city.

Talanji spurred her own mount, Tze'na, down the column of Zandalari soldiers, riding ahead of Zolani and Rokhan. She crossed the bridge back into the city, reaching the other side to hear another horn blast, this one closer. The tops of banners crowning the spikes appeared, the ground beneath her shaking rhythmically. From the zigzagging ramps of the Great Seal pyramid, Wardruid Loti, green hair flying behind her, raced toward Talanji. Breathless, she skidded to a stop beside Talanji's raptor just as the first banners cleared the tops of the stairs leading up from the bazaar and port below.

"The Horde! They just started appearing, your majesty!"

"I see them, Loti." Talanji didn't bother suppressing her joy.

"There's more." Wardruid Loti finally caught her breath. "People are going mad in the markets. They think it's an invasion."

Talanji had feared as much. With the storms raging around Zandalar, any travel into the continent would have to be by magical means. Thrall must have used portals to transfer the troops.

"Find Lashk, go with him to the bazaar. Quell whatever fears you find there and then join us at the Necropolis."

Loti fled without another word. There would be challenging times ahead, Talanji realized, for even if they succeeded in protecting the Necropolis, her city had suffered greatly from the Widow's Bite meddling, threatening, and spreading false rumors.

But first, Bwonsamdi must be protected and the efforts of Sylvanas and Apari halted.

Riding swiftly to meet the vanguard, Talanji encountered Thrall atop an armored gray wolf, red-and-black Horde banners hoisted behind him. First Arcanist Thalyssra could be seen riding among the soldiers, radiant in purple and blue, silver feathers shining on her pauldrons, a small host of nightborne elves marching in the wake of her manasaber. Her presence explained the portals, and the speed with which the Horde had arrived.

And last, but certainly welcome, the tauren chieftain Baine Bloodhoof joined them, accompanied by several shaman in elaborate headdresses, totems the size of tree trunks strapped to their backs.

It was, in all, a company of no more than what Talanji herself could muster, but that doubled their odds.

"You came!" she greeted Thrall, beaming. "I thought . . ."

"Forgive the lateness," he replied. He wore a war harness that crisscrossed his chest and his usual battered leather gauntlets and grieves, an axe held in his right hand. His wolf shook out its great head, whining a little, and Thrall ruffled the fur on its forehead. "Easy, Moonpaw. This is all that could be gathered without leaving Orgrimmar undefended. It put considerable strain on Thalyssra to teleport all of us here. Will it be enough?"

Talanji inclined her head respectfully. "It will have to be. It is far more than we had, thank you. Zandalar will not forget this."

Baine lifted the war horn he had brought to his lips and blew twice. The orc warriors, tauren shaman, and nightborne archers marched faster, and together, Talanji, Thrall, Baine, and Thalyssra gathered to lead the Horde forces toward the Zocalo, there to meld with the Zandalari army.

"How many cavalry?" Baine asked, immediately to business.

"Only us, Rokhan, and Zolani. Wardruid Loti will ride to the

Necropolis when my people have been reassured this is not an invasion," Talanji explained.

Thrall nodded, bobbing in the saddle of his wolf. "Perhaps with our forces divided, we can attack from two sides, send the cavalry up the center, and try to trap Blightcaller in the middle."

"That will be difficult," Talanji warned him. "The Necropolis is surrounded by swamp. The safest approach is from the Zo'bal Ruins, which Blightcaller holds."

"That will pose no challenge to our shaman," Baine interjected. "They can pass on top of the water."

"And with some recovery I can teleport a number of us wherever you desire," Thalyssra said in her soft yet direct way. "It will increase the element of surprise."

"No surprises here," Talanji told her. "If you reach the Necropolis, there is a clear view in every direction."

"Then speed will be our greatest asset," Thrall said. He twisted to regard Thalyssra, who looked weary, her shoulders slumped, her hands only loosely gripping the reins of her feline mount. "How long? Could you send some of our warriors ahead?"

Thalyssra straightened and quirked her lips to the side. "I shall endeavor to try."

They crossed the bridge beyond the great pyramid and west of the terraces, the Zandalari forces visible down the road. Rokhan had kept the trolls marching, the colored frills of their feathered helmets dancing with each step. A million thoughts and ideas assaulted Talanji's brain. Thrall's arrival had changed everything. She should have believed. She should have trusted.

That her eventual trust in him had brought this boon filled her with hope. Perhaps Bwonsamdi was right—all the broken hearts, spirits, and minds in her kingdom could be mended, if only the proper effort was put forward. Friends and allies made, bonds and promises honored and kept. They had come for her, come for her people, in the hour when she needed them most. They had come even after she refused their well-meaning aid and their ambassador—

Their ambassador.

"Zekhan was badly wounded," Talanji blurted. "He tried to lead my men and defend one of the loa's shrines. He was caught in a blaze at the tar pits. My healers have seen to him; they say he will live."

"He is a strong boy," Thrall replied simply. "And if he volunteered to lead, then he understood the risks."

Talanji nodded. Still. Her thoughts wouldn't quiet down. How would they ever reach the Necropolis in time? How could they organize a proper attack when every minute of hesitation might cost them? How could she so much as lift her staff when her body felt so broken?

"Thalyssra, how many of us can you safely bring to the Necropolis?" Baine asked. He rode atop a towering, furry beast, a kind of stag with pale horns as impressive as Baine's. They were a motley assortment of folk and animals, and Talanji wondered what they must look like, strange allies tied by a common cause.

"And how quickly?" he added with a huff.

"Why do I get the sense you are annoyed with me, Bloodhoof?" Thalyssra said with a lilting tease to her voice.

"Those pretty feathers of yours will droop in the jungle heat; it is not a short march," he snorted.

"Fair point." The First Arcanist uncorked a flask tucked into a pocket of her elaborate runed saddle, taking a long swig. Her eyes brightened as if she had taken a drink of pure light. "Give me a moment, and I can teleport the entire host."

Thrall banged his fist on the pommel of his saddle, and the gray wolf beneath him gave a long, chilling howl. "Then it is settled. We divide into three forces and give them no chance to retreat."

"The sea . . ." Talanji frowned. "The Necropolis lies along our northern border. They could escape by sea. The storms surrounding these lands are under their control."

"That is why we target their mages first," Thalyssra said.

"And why Lor'themar and Gazlowe are sailing with all speed," Thrall added, eyes fixed on the road to the north. "Once the storms break, they will cut off any retreat by sea."

Talanji couldn't help but gaze in admiration at each of them. Apparently, they had thought of everything. Perhaps that accounted for their delay in coming. Thrall leaned down in his saddle, sending a warrior running ahead to speak with Rokhan and stall the Zandalari armies, preparing them for Thalyssra's magic to whisk them away.

"Then it is settled," Talanji echoed Thrall's words. "They will soon know the strength of the Horde."

"For Zandalar," Thrall agreed, raising his axe. "And for Zekhan."

"For the safety of my people," Talanji agreed. "And for the Horde."

CHAPTER TWENTY-EIGHT

The Necropolis

"Where is he?" Sira Moonwarden demanded, stalking in tight circles around the altar facing the Necropolis temple. Her temper flared as high and red as the blood moon only then fading into the dawn light. "Why does he not appear?"

Nathanos allowed a cooler mood to prevail, studying the scattered carvings and drums on the altar. Perhaps they had missed something. Every shrine of Bwonsamdi's had been desecrated; surely that would be enough to enrage the loa and inspire him to retaliate. Yet an eerie silence persisted in the Necropolis, that whispering, taunting wind still swirling in unnatural configurations, the suggestion of spirits hiding at the corner of his vision.

He would not be denied victory—the Banshee Queen's victory—when it seemed so tantalizingly close.

"Ya must know Bwonsamdi is a trickster." Apari slumped toward them, her tick pet pulsating like a boil on her shoulder. She drew her greasy white braid of hair over one shoulder and gestured toward the pit on the other side of the altar. It formed a kind of amphitheater, or court, and it seethed with dark promise. Even Nathanos found its presence unnerving.

"Where is he, witch?" Sira demanded, impatient.

"I honor our friendship," Apari assured her, smiling. "I honor our bargain."

"Ha! We are not friends. Do not waste our time with flattery! We desire only the loa. How do we summon him?" Sira crowded the witch, looming, her crimson eyes flashing behind her strange horned helm.

Apari did not shrink away, but her bodyguard, Tayo, bared her teeth. They were filed into hideous points. "Like this."

Nathanos had assumed Apari sending her rebels into the temple had been only to scavenge for offerings and treasure. Instead, he found them returning in groups, bringing with them bound and squirming hostages.

"Supplicants," Nathanos murmured. "Yes. This will do nicely."

"These are Bwonsamdi's faithful worshippers," Apari explained. The Widow's Bite fanatics had rounded up six: two old troll females, three elderly troll males, and a young troll girl no older than nine.

The child would go last, and only if Bwonsamdi had a mind to resist.

"That one first." Nathanos pointed to an older troll male, his hair stark white, his ears drooping from time and the heavy bone jewelry adorning them. He was the strongest of them, aged but still with all his teeth and both eyes. The other elders appeared one footstep from the grave.

Two rebels dressed in the white-and-black tunic of the Widow's Bite shouldered the old troll forward. He didn't fight. "Good morning, sir."

"Darkness take you," the troll spat.

Nathanos sighed and wiped the spittle from his chin. "I see. In that case, I too shall dispense with pleasantries. There is no need to torture you and kill the child. You are Bwonsamdi's faithful, are you not? Prove your belief sufficient, summon the loa here, and all of you will live."

Over the troll's shoulder, Sira scoffed. Nathanos gave her the tiniest shake of his head. *Don't be stupid; of course they will not live.*

"What is your name?" Nathanos asked. The witch, Apari, circled closer, reaching into the medicine satchel around her waist and producing a small pouch.

"Tezi."

"Very well, Tezi. Let us be reasonable. Help us reach Bwonsamdi and you will all be spared."

Tezi sighed and heaved his shoulders, eye to eye with Nathanos. "We worship the loa of death, strange one. We come each day to this place. You don't frighten us. Nothin' frightens us."

"Do not break, Tezi! They are scum! Bwonsamdi will protect us," the little girl shouted. One of the rangers slapped her silent.

Apari chose that moment to intervene. "Make ya offerin', old man, or this goes in the girl's mouth." She reached inside the pouch and held up a pinch of black powder. Captive, the troll girl gave a yelp. "Retchweed and riverbud root. Her insides will be comin' out her eyeballs. Is that what ya want?"

Tezi drew back. Out of the corner of his eye, Nathanos noticed someone diving toward the witch.

"She's just a child!" Tayo clamped her hand around Apari's wrist, the one holding the powder. She twisted and pulled, and the weak, septic Apari had no choice but to let go. Tayo threw the pouch in an arc, sending it splashing into the swamp, lost.

At once, Apari struck her across the face. She didn't have much strength left, but the slap left Tayo stunned. "I am on the very precipice of death, *zagota*. I will live. I will live just to see Bwonsamdi and Talanji fall. Nothing, not this girl, nor you, will stop me."

Whatever "zagota" meant, Nathanos didn't fancy it was anything friendly. Tayo marched away, back toward the Zo'bal Ruins. Dark ranger Visrynn moved to follow.

"Let her go," Apari muttered. "She will come crawlin' back. She always does."

"We have no need of her now," Nathanos drawled. "Now, where were we? Ah, of course. Tezi, my new friend, you will cooperate or the troll girl will be harmed. We have many resources beyond the witch's powders and potions."

"Do it!" the girl screamed, unafraid. Nathanos almost admired her spirit.

He drew a dagger from his belt. "For example, I will take her brash little tongue."

"I will do what ya ask," Tezi growled. "But I've no more power over a loa than a mouse over a snake."

"Scamper over to the altar, then, mouse, and be quick about it."

Nathanos grabbed the troll by the bone talisman around his neck and shoved him roughly toward the drums and relics strewn about the dais. Below, the mist of fog and spirits swirled, and either it was his imagination, or the silvery muck had grown thicker. Was this Bwonsamdi's wrath? Even a loa must find it difficult to stomach the mistreatment of "mice" such as Tezi.

The old troll dropped to his knees. The girl cried out for him, and Apari cuffed her, subduing her to silent tears. Tezi picked up one of the ancient drums and began to thump it with the heels of his hands, chanting in a low, haunting rasp, his song rising and falling above the constant buzz of insects filling the marsh.

It went on for some time, until Tezi's voice grew hoarse.

Sira paced faster. Nathanos couldn't help but concur.

"We know you are watching, Bwonsamdi," Nathanos called. Nothing. "Appear to us, loa, or your followers will soon be walking your spirit realm!"

Nothing.

"The girl," Nathanos sneered. "Start with her fingers. Flay them first, remove them slowly. After that, the ears."

The other captured worshippers fell to their knees, joining Tezi in his chant, but the girl simply trembled, tossing her head from side to side as she sobbed once more.

Nathanos took no delight in it; this was simply what was required. The Banshee Queen wanted Bwonsamdi gone, and they could not destroy him if he remained forever in hiding.

"Wait." Sira had come to a halt, peering over the edge of the altar and down into the court. The soup of mist and spirits began to spin, creating a vortex that shot up into the air and dispersed with a ripple, sending the columns of the Necropolis shaking, unseen tombs deep in the ground rattling; the skeletons dotting the ruin shook themselves to slivers. Dust rose from the ancient stones under their feet. The blast knocked Nathanos back a few steps, his ears ringing from the force of it.

"Old Bwonsamdi is here, friends. What be all this racket now?"

The loa floated high above the court, ankles crossed casually, head cocked to the side. The tall bone harness he wore on his back swayed lightly, the ribs etched into his chest glimmered like stars, streaming blue vapor rising from the slits in his bone mask. His followers gasped, falling flat onto the ground.

"Dark rangers at the ready!" Sira screamed.

"At last." Nathanos sauntered to the edge of the altar, staring up at the larger-than-life loa.

It might have been an intimidating sight, but they had him surrounded, and the loss of his shrines would weaken him considerably. The recessed court simmered with glittering white fog again, spirits of trolls drifting out from their graves to gather around their master.

"I have my own army, little dead thing." Bwonsamdi chuckled.

"And soon my queen will be here. Ya been sneaky so far, can't deny it, but ya won't stand a chance against her armies."

"Armies?" Sira whispered, her eyes flying to Nathanos.

"He's bluffing," Nathanos replied calmly. "By the time she arrives, you will be destroyed. Sira, give the command."

"Fire!"

"Widow's Bite! My followers! My friends! No loa of death will rule us and corrupt our crown!" Apari's words were met with two dozen war cries. The arrows began to fall, screaming toward Bwonsamdi from dark rangers circling the court.

"Ya be in my world now! My house!" Bwonsamdi thundered, lifting his skeletal hands high. His arms shook, his image flickering like a dying candle about to sputter out. The spirits massing around him charged at terrifying speed, rolling out from him like a grisly tide. They swarmed the narrow stairs leading up from the pit, more resistance than Nathanos had anticipated.

On the east side of the court, he watched Visrynn and Lelyias spring back on agile feet, firing into the mob of spirits while the Widow's Bite rebels joined in with slings, bows, and blow guns. Apari let her head drop back on her weak neck, raising shaking arms to the clouds, calling down a surge of lightning that struck the stones between the rangers and the mass of spirits.

"Destroy him!" Nathanos roared, reaching for his own longbow. "For Sylvanas!"

CHAPTER TWENTY-NINE

Nazmir

The Horde leadership arrived first, landing outside the Zo'bal Ruins on animals agitated from the unusual journey.

"Whoa there," Talanji soothed Tze'na, stroking the raptor's coarse scales. A single fall from the saddle and Talanji might be done for. "Find ya feet. There is war to be waged."

At that, the raptor let loose a shrill bellow. Thrall's wolf joined in the call.

The First Arcanist dismounted from her manasaber, batting away a bothersome cloud of gnats with an elegant hand. "Go to the ruins. Our armies will follow."

"Will you be all right alone?" Baine asked from atop his painted and beaded thunderhoof.

"Oh yes, I am quite capable." Thalyssra nodded. "Go!"

As if to punctuate her haste, a crack of lightning rippled down from the sky, hitting somewhere inside the Necropolis.

"They are already attacking him!" Talanji cried, urging Tze'na to carry her toward Zo'bal. "There is no more time!"

Thrall and Baine raced toward the Necropolis with her. The ground shook, not from the lightning this time, but from the combined weight of twenty orc warriors, armed and thirsty for a fight, landing in the road. Talanji glanced over her shoulder as they rode, Rokhan and her vanguard of Rastari enforcers and civilian militia arriving next. They immediately broke into a run, following the cavalry through the central approach to Zo'bal, through the ruins and across the shattered bridge leading to the Necropolis.

Baine's shaman and the orc troops would continue east down the road, then swing north and cross the swampy barrier with their power to walk across the water. Lastly, Thalyssra's nightborne archers would head immediately north toward the Necropolis, taking the western approach, teleported into the battle once the first wave of screaming orcs and magic-wielding shaman had ambushed the enemy.

"Stop! Ya must stop!"

Thrall had almost trampled the troll that popped out from behind a fall of rocks in the open courtyard of Zo'bal. The orc drew his axe, and Talanji summoned a crackling bolt of death magic to her hands, recognizing the ugly black-and-white spider design on the troll's tunic.

The Widow's Bite.

She was thin but muscular, tall, with leather straps hanging from her shoulders holstering dozens of poison darts. Her long hair had been slicked up into a tail and streaked with black mud or paint. She put up both hands in surrender and dropped to her knees.

"Give me a good reason not to take your head," Thrall muttered.

"My name is Tayo," the troll spoke quickly and clearly, without a hint of fear. "I served the witch Apari."

"Served?" Talanji pressed.

"I can serve her no longer." The troll, Tayo, sighed. "She is not the leader I knew. The leader I admired. This—this cruelty is not her, and I cannot follow this Apari. Her hate for you, ya majesty, is all she has."

"Then fight with us," Baine encouraged. "Help us stop her."

Tayo stood, slowly, wary of Thrall's sharpened axe. "I will. All I ask is that ya give her a merciful end. Death is already about to claim her, just make it swift."

"Done," Thrall said, and Talanji bit her tongue.

"The bridge is riddled with traps and mines." Tayo turned and swept her arm back toward the Necropolis. "Too many to count. They knew ya might come. Do not go that way."

"That sounds like Blightcaller, all right." Sheathing his axe, Thrall leaped down from his wolf and produced a few silver orbs from his pack. "A little gift from our clever trade prince."

"What are those?" Talanji asked, observing from Tze'na's back while Thrall set the orbs down on the ground and twisted each of them. They began to click and whir, then shot out toward the bridge, rolling so fast they became three little blurs.

"Goblin seeker bots," Thrall replied. "Be ready to charge."

The orbs cracked open halfway across the bridge, each producing six tiny contraptions, shaped almost like men, that bounced their way this way and that. A red light on top of each of the bots blinked, frantic, then the first trap blew.

Smoke and chunks of stone exploded, and then another mine was triggered, and another, until they could see nothing but a haze of debris and fire. Thrall stepped back into his stirrup and, without another moment's hesitation, rode toward the chaos. Talanji followed, squinting, Baine ahead of her and to the left. Tayo joined them on foot, bringing up the rear.

Talanji had no idea what to expect when they soared through the cover provided by the smoke. On the other side, Bwonsamdi towered above the Necropolis, gritting his teeth as he raised spirit after spirit and flung them toward his attackers. The rebels were easier to spot, the white flashes on their tunics standing out against the commotion. They had already suffered several losses, troll bodies littering the ground.

Nathanos, an armored dark ranger, and Apari stood at the altar before the Court of Spirits, Nathanos firing on Bwonsamdi, Sira fending off any spirit that came near them with her twin glaives, the witch bringing down the wrath of the storm on the waves of spirits conjured by the loa.

The traps and mines triggering drew their attention, of course, and Nathanos spun to discover Talanji, Thrall, Baine, and Tayo approaching from the Dreadmire.

"Nathanos Blightcaller and Sira Moonwarden," she heard Baine rumble. "I do not recognize the troll."

"That is an old friend," Talanji told him. "But she must fall with the rest."

"Ha!" the ranger, Sira Moonwarden, shouted toward them. "Is this all that you can muster? Pathetic."

"Do not let them reach the loa," Nathanos commanded. He left them behind, disappearing behind the band of white-and-black-clad rebels that rushed them. Sira put her head down, weapons flared to her sides as she led the defense.

"Do not underestimate her," Thrall warned. "Wardens are formidable."

Thrall swung his axe in wide arcs, sweeping aside the trolls that threatened to overwhelm them. It was good, Talanji decided, that the enemy assumed it was just the four coming to protect Bwonsamdi. It was not good, however, that they might be overrun and killed before the reinforcements ever showed.

Where are they?

She looked in desperation to the east, expecting to see the shaman and orcs sweeping toward them at any moment. Was the swamp booby-trapped, too? What delayed them?

While they had not yet shown, her army had. The Zandalari came pelting out of the lingering smoke on the bridge, spears raised, feathers and golden armor a bolstering sight.

The Zandalari, Thrall, and Baine took on the brunt of the rebels, Talanji supporting them with her death magic and glistening barriers that warded off any incoming arrows from the dark rangers. The glittering streams firing from Talanji's staff left behind trails of shadow, the power of Bwonsamdi's Necropolis imbuing her magic with darkness. Half of the red-eyed Forsaken elves had turned their sights on them, while the others continued to assault Bwonsamdi.

The loa. *Her* loa. Though the Necropolis empowered him, the spirits he summoned to his side came with less and less frequency. Could he hold just a little longer? And where were those damn orcs . . .

A blinding spear of lightning struck the barrier she had conjured around Baine, shattering her train of thought. The shield faltered, but she quickly refocused, finding a reserve of energy she had not anticipated, and then she saw the very source of the storm.

Apari.

She waded slowly through the throng of rebels trying and failing to knock Thrall and Baine from their mounts. Sira danced in and out, parrying thrusts from Thrall's axe but never landing a blow herself. The chaos worked against her, bodies blocking a direct line to the orc. When fighting Thrall and Baine proved fruitless, she turned her attention to the Zandalari soldiers, picking them off.

Talanji did not flinch away from Apari's searing gaze. It was as the troll Tayo described. Apari looked more corpse than living being, her skin grayish, her hair soaked in sweat. Talanji couldn't help but sympathize, every inch of her was similarly aching and weak. They had once been like sisters, but now Apari limped toward her with a discolored leg, bloated with infection. She reached up and removed the gruesome bone mask covering her face, tossing it aside.

This was a distraction, Talanji knew it, but she could not let Apari continue to call down lightning while they fought, not when Bwonsamdi was already so vulnerable. A small, white shape zipped toward them, flying from somewhere over Apari's shoulder. It smacked into Talanji's face, but didn't move, suctioned to her skin.

She tried to scream, but the creature attached to her muffled the sound. Talanji flailed, her barriers sputtering out. Tze'na tossed, and Talanji lost her balance, tumbling to the ground. Blood slicked the stones. She slipped trying to right herself, but the fall had dislodged the creature from her face. It bounced away, a disgusting dreadtick.

Baine had noticed her fall, and smashed his totem down on the tick, splattering it. There was no time to thank him. Talanji crawled to her knees and stood, pushed this way and that by the dizzying throng of rebels all trying to bring down Baine. The Widow's Bite fell like a tide against Baine and Thrall, but each time they were driven back with a few left alive and standing.

The sky opened up once more, and Talanji saw the flicker of lightning there in the clouds, just a suggestion, before it came at her fully formed, snaking and hot. She heard Apari's cry of triumph, saw her old friend laughing as she brought down the storm on the queen's head.

"No!"

Talanji threw her arms wide, the glossy magic barrier deflecting the lightning strike just as the hair on her head began to bend toward it. Her spell did more than just protect her; the ricochet arced across the battlefield, punching Apari in the chest. Her screams ended, the blow shooting her back against a column decorated with skulls.

"Go!" Baine thundered. "End it!"

"Here," Tayo held out her hand and Talanji did not hesitate to take it. "We can give her mercy together."

Did she deserve it? They forced their way through the rebels, Tayo knocking them aside with her gauntlet. Apari had tried to poison her, assaulted the palace, kidnapped innocents, sacrificed Zandalari citizens, all in the name of revenge.

I should have helped her when the Alliance attacked. I didn't help her then, but I can now.

Apari sat with her legs splayed out in front of her, a drip of blood speeding down her cheek. The impact of her skull had fractured the stone column. What was left of her childhood friend was unpleasant to look at, but Talanji knelt beside her, cradled her neck, and tried to smile.

"I'm sorry, Apari," Talanji murmured. "The siege . . . My father was dying. I wanted to help him but I should have stayed to help you, too."

"Ya can rest now, it's all over," Tayo added, producing a small dagger.

"It's not over," Apari whispered, her words mingled with bubbles of blood. "Not over . . . You should die for what ya did to me, to my mother. You should die, and Bwonsamdi, and P-Proudmoore."

Talanji flinched. Of course Apari would hate her, too. Jaina Proudmoore had been the face of the assault on Dazar'alor, the Alliance leader that had sacked the palace and murdered the king.

"Vengeance will only take you so far," Talanji told her gently, wiping the matted hair from her face. "You need more than that to survive. I did not help you then, my friend, but I will help you now."

Talanji held Apari's hands and looked into her sad, terrified eyes. Though she trembled, though her spirit felt threadbare, she conjured a soothing spell for Apari, hoping it might ease a little of her fear and pain. Life had not been kind to the girl, to either of them, but when Apari was gone, her body would nourish the earth, and Bwonsamdi would keep her spirit from the Maw. Ironic that she wanted the loa dead, when he was the one who would now save her from everlasting darkness. Talanji squeezed her old friend's hands, Tayo drew the blade.

Tayo did not stay to mourn after it was done. She hurled herself back into the fray and Talanji followed, her heart a little heavier than it had been before.

Thrall and Baine stood victorious, the rebel line broken and scattered. Those who survived fled, most simply tossing themselves into the swamp to swim away.

Sira Moonwarden, however, did not retreat.

She whirled at them like a hurricane, flashing her blades, almost impossibly swift, dancing in and out of range, slashing at Thrall and then leaping back, twirling, avoiding the heavy, slow swing of Baine's totem.

"Nathanos!" Talanji heard the dark warden call. "The rangers! Send them to me!"

He did not hear her; in fact, he had pushed deeper into the Necropolis, vanishing into the swirling mists at Bwonsamdi's feet.

Some of the rangers, however, heard her, and Talanji hurried to protect her allies while a hail of deadly arrows fell. A war horn echoed through the haze rising off the Dreadmire. Talanji was beginning to love that sound.

The ground quaked to the east, orc raiders and tauren shaman colliding with the small detachment of dark rangers firing on Bwonsamdi from the far side of the Court of Spirits. The rangers spun, trying too late to repel the onslaught of axes and cascades of lightning. They fell, swift, but not swift enough.

Sira Moonwarden fought harder, enraged at the passing of her kin. She slid to her knees, gliding across the thin lake of rebel blood, a nearly invisible strike opening a gash on Baine's right forearm. The tauren tossed his great mane and horns, whirling, his pain or his fury granting him the necessary speed. At last, Sira took a hit, as the flat end of Baine's totem, still covered in mashed bits of Apari's dreadtick, caught her in the stomach.

At the sight of their lieutenant spinning to the ground, the dark rangers gathered near the altar dispersed, retreating to the concealing fog of spirits in the court. They liked their odds there better, firing indiscriminately into the silvery morass.

What little remained of the Zandalari forces circled Sira, trapping her. Miraculously, the dark warden climbed to her feet, battered but unwilling to surrender. She readied her blades, just in time for First Arcanist Thalyssra to arrive with her nightborne archers. Sira paused, red eyes aglow with the outrage of defeat.

"Put down your weapons," Thalyssra warned, brandishing her crystal staff. "Or my archers will pin you where you stand."

"Never!" Sira bellowed. While she twirled her glaives and glared at Thalyssra, Thrall slowly made his way around the Zandalari troops to encircle her. He gave the First Arcanist a subtle flick of the head and Thalyssra whistled, her archers forming ranks and marching quickly toward the Court of Spirits.

"Do not look at me with those gloating eyes!" Sira shouted, poking her glaive toward the nightborne. "Nathanos! Nathanos? No . . . No, I will not be abandoned again, not now. My goddess . . . No! I will not submit! You have accomplished nothing! Do you hear me? Nothi—"

The blunt end of Thrall's axe cracked into her helmet, silencing her. Sira crumpled to the ground, her glaives clattering to the stones, her helmet slipping off her head and rolling away. Thrall broke through the crowd of Zandalari and stopped the helm with the toe of his boot.

"Bind her tightly," he told the trolls. "I know exactly what to do with her."

An unnatural cackle rippled out from the center of the Necropolis. *Bwonsamdi.* Talanji raced to the edge of the court, the loa beside himself with amusement as Blightcaller's rangers fell, one by one, overrun by the orcs or fried by shaman lightning, some slumped against a wall, prickly with nightborne arrows.

At the center of it all, still stubbornly brandishing his bow, Nathanos Blightcaller raged against Bwonsamdi.

"I told ya, dead man, ya no match for my queen."

Talanji nodded, grabbing her left shoulder as she circled the stone court and took the stairs down, going to join her loa. It felt like her heart had gone numb as she clutched it, her last reserve of strength long gone. She dragged herself along, unwilling to let Bwonsamdi face Blightcaller alone. They were connected, blood and fate twining them together, and if this was to be their victory or their end, she would spend it in the thick of battle.

He was utterly outnumbered, alone, the bodies of his defeated comrades surrounding him like a grim barricade of cold flesh. Talanji could get no closer to him, but that did not matter. She sank to her knees, closing her eyes, raising her hands and breathing in the cool, prickling mist that swirled at the bottom of the court. A loa's power came from his believers, and though Talanji had no strength left to give, she had her words. She had her belief.

"Mighty Bwonsamdi, loa of graves, your strength is mine, my strength is yours." Her voice grew louder, unnaturally so, echoing across the Necropolis with the thunder of a god's. Bwonsamdi spoke through her, and she felt ice swirl around her, bracing her against the weakness that threatened to make her crumble. "Your enemies have fallen before you, their reward for doubting you is *death*."

Either she laughed or Bwonsamdi did, a sound like chattering teeth, like knuckle bones clattering.

Nathanos was not foolish enough to fight on. He simply glared up at the loa, his hands and coat splattered with blood, his hair uncharacteristically mussed. His plans had failed.

"I will swing the axe." Talanji's voice boomed across the Necropolis again, emerging as if from the massive loa hovering above her. "For what he has done to my people."

"Many will wish to see his demise," Baine called down to her from the edge of the court, a hand clamped over his bleeding arm.

The combined forces of the Horde inched toward Blightcaller, hemming him in, his last free moments spent in speechless fury. Unlike Sira, he gave them nothing, no taunt, no mockery; he simply shouldered his bow, pulled a vial from his coat, uncorked it, and bowed his head.

At last he spoke, strange coils of black smoke seeping out from between his fingers where he clasped the vial.

"My queen," he said, clearly enough for all to hear. "My lady!"

It was no blast of lightning that struck him, but a liquid tendril of purple and black that emerged from the sky, enveloping him and twisting around him, swallowing him whole . . .

"No!" she heard Thrall shout. "NO!"

The orc chieftain raced for the steps, axe at the ready, but it was too late. The tendril recoiled back into the sky, leaving behind nothing but a few wisps of shadow where Blightcaller had been.

"That magic . . ." Baine growled. Talanji had covered her mouth with both hands, frozen, still on her knees in the mist. Nathanos was *gone*. But how? She stood, feeling, at last, like some of her vigor was returning. "Sylvanas used something similar at the mak'gora. Ancestors watch over us, her power is growing . . ."

"Ah, the dead one slipped away . . ." Bwonsamdi seemed unconcerned, shrugging. "He be tricksy indeed, just like ya old friend Bwonsamdi. I, however, plan to live a lot longer than him."

Talanji watched as the Horde warriors, shaman, and archers realized, gradually, that they had won. The skies had cleared over the horizon, the storm abated. Sira Moonwarden squirmed on the ground, captured. The wounded were gathered, the dead having found their end in a place already thick with graves. Talanji drifted away from the worst of the carnage, climbing the stairs to her left and joining her allies again.

"Don't look so sad," Bwonsamdi chided, wagging his finger at Thrall. "Ya came for me, and here I am. Whatever the Banshee Queen had planned here today, ya stopped her."

"He's right." First Arcanist Thalyssra strode down the stairs to join the crowd forming in the Court of Spirits. "The Horde stood together as one behind our ally."

Talanji took Baine's offered arm, the uninjured one, and went to gather with Thrall and the others. "Not just an ally," she said as they amassed, friends finding each other and clasping hands, warriors standing with mingled disbelief and pride.

"I wish to take my place on the Horde Council, it is where I belong—speaking for my people, and listening for them," Talanji stated, to a resounding war cry. "Our armies must be rebuilt, our city secured, and the trust of the people won, but we will emerge stronger than ever."

"It would be our honor." Baine Bloodhood bowed his head. Thrall had recovered from the disappointment of losing Nathanos and added his solemn nod to the chorus.

"Very touchin'." Bwonsamdi pretended to wipe a tear from his eye. But Talanji saw the undeniable gleam of mischief in his bright blue eyes. Not just mischief, but relief.

"Now,"—Talanji turned back toward the south, where beyond the swamps, jungles, and mountains of Nazmir, the golden city, Dazar'alor, waited—"I believe I owe you a feast. No assassins this time." She smiled. "You have my word."

CHAPTER THIRTY

Stormwind

Mathias Shaw had never sailed a Zandalari ship, but he learned damn quick. He had never been so happy to be back on the sea, and that was saying something. But what he had learned, and what he brought, was needed urgently in Stormwind.

He watched with a full stomach and fuller heart as Stormwind City rose up from the horizon, a white beacon, a more than welcome sight. The Horde leadership had let him go, no strings attached, introducing him to a crew of merchants willing to smuggle him quickly to familiar soil. His initial reaction was one of suspicion. A spymaster never accepted anything at face value. He searched the ship, the hold, and his bags for traps, explosives, and anything strange. To his everlasting surprise, they had kept their word.

As something of an apology, or perhaps thanks, Queen Talanji had filled the ship with food fresh from their celebratory feast. Mathias was hungry enough to eagerly get a taste for the spiced meat heaped as tall as a man in the hold. Prisoners didn't exactly get the finest cuts. In fact, he didn't want to know what parts of what animals he had been eating. Maybe that was the real punishment.

"Do you have papers?" Mathias asked the captain, Halfkan, a sour-faced vrykul with shockingly red hair.

"Papers?" Halfkan snorted. "I have *you*."

The spymaster grinned. Fair enough.

Speaking of fair, the seas proved mercilessly smooth, no trace of the magical storms darkening the way home. They sailed into Stormwind Harbor four days later, with the feast food dwindling as steadily as Shaw's patience. He kept dawdling in the brig, checking every hour or so to make sure their prize was still there.

It was.

Another unexpected and generous gift from the Horde. The only catch, outlined to him by the tremendously tall orc warrior Thrall, was this: The prize must be delivered exactly as he instructed, to exactly whom he instructed, with the note he had entrusted to Shaw unopened.

Thrall was not the sort one quarreled with in person. Shaw agreed to all stipulations—he could hardly refuse, given his circumstances—and boarded the craft sailing east.

A bevvy of fluffy white seagulls saw them home, gliding on the winds alongside the ship. Mathias propped one foot on the railing, hand looped through a sail rope, a welcome party standing at the end of the dock flanked by six keep guards.

Jaina Proudmoore, Flynn Fairwind, looking a bit worse for wear, and King Anduin Wrynn were there to greet his return.

The ship bumped gently into the dock, rocking, and Mathias gave his king a long, grateful bow. It was good to be home.

"Did they mistreat you?" Anduin asked, brow drawn down with worry.

"They had bigger problems." Mathias did not disembark, but

instead gestured for the others to board. "I can tell you about that later. There is something you need to see."

Anduin smirked, then Flynn Fairwind all but shoved the king out of the way, throwing himself at Mathias and wrapping him in a tight, warm hug. Mathias returned it, a greeting he had not expected, but welcomed all the same. He smelled like whiskey and salt and soap. Familiar. Like a dream remembered long after it occurred, like a word that was on the tip of the tongue for an age, and now captured.

"I sailed like a madman." Flynn pushed his sunburnt cheeks deeper into Shaw's shoulder. He felt slight in Shaw's arms, as if he had lost weight. The crazy pirate had nearly killed himself sailing for help, and all for him. While Shaw had been rotting in that Zandalari cell, mourning his lost chance at peace and rest, Fairwind had gone and rescued that shining little chance. Shaw didn't forget things like that, didn't take them lightly. "Never . . . never sailed like that before. But I had to get you back."

"And here I am," Mathias murmured.

"Here you are."

"Flynn . . ." Shaw started, clearing his throat. "There's something I'd like to talk to you about. Meet me at the Guilded Rose tonight, will you?" Slowly releasing Flynn from their embrace, Shaw pressed the perfect blade of grass into the pirate's hand. "Don't be late."

Flynn's expression didn't seem to register what to do with the grass, but the flush in his cheeks said all that Shaw needed to know.

"What is so urgent?" Anduin interjected, striding onto the boat.

"It is better if I simply show you. Come."

Mathias led them below, shooing the crew out of the hold, making certain they were all of them alone before opening the brig. The small, low-ceilinged cabin holding the brig was lit only by two meager candles, hardly enough light to see by. The door banged open. A figure slumped in the shadows, bound.

Jaina Proudmoore squinted, leaning forward and opening a gout of flame with her hand, the glow of the fire landing on the battered, gagged face of Sira Moonwarden.

"Sira," Jaina whispered. Her eyes flew to his. "The Horde gave her to you?"

"No strings attached," Mathias told her.

Anduin gently moved Jaina aside, squaring himself before the prisoner. She could have burned him alive with the hatred in her eyes.

"There are always strings," Anduin said. "Even if you cannot see them."

"Thrall wanted her delivered to Tyrande Whisperwind and Malfurion Stormrage, along with this letter." Mathias drew the sealed missive from his coat and handed it to the king.

Anduin blinked with confusion. "That is . . . oddly generous of him."

"I agree," Mathias replied.

"It will be done." Anduin tucked the message under one arm, returning his attention to Sira. "But first, I will have a word with the prisoner. Remove her gag."

Something had changed in her at the mention of Tyrande and Malfurion. The rage in her eyes did not ebb, but there was something more there. Fear, perhaps. Or anticipation.

"Where is she?" Anduin wasted no time. "Where is Sylvanas Windrunner?"

Sira Moonwarden rolled her eyes and glanced away. "Nowhere you will find her. Even if you did, it is far, far too late. You have lost."

"My spies tell me the opposite is true," the king told her. "They say you were not successful in destroying Bwonsamdi, that your dark ranger forces were annihilated and Nathanos Blightcaller escaped only because your mistress intervened."

She said nothing, but her lip curled at the mention of his name.

"Do you know how many deaths you have caused? How much misery you have brought upon my kingdom?" Anduin crouched, crowding her. "Do you know? Do you care?"

Sira smiled.

"Smile all you like, creature, there is little hope for you now. Your people will want to speak with you, want to understand how you could serve Sylvanas. You realize this, yes?"

The dark warden considered that for a moment, Jaina's magicked flame dancing across her pale, pale face. "I know it, yes, and I feel nothing. I will give them nothing. Once more you waste the little time you have left."

Anduin made a soft sound of disgust and stood, hovering over her, considering her for a long and tense spell. A wisp of purple energy traveled down his arm, gathering in his palm. It happened in a blink, coming and going, dissipating before Mathias could see for certain what the king had done.

It startled Anduin enough to make him stumble backward. Shaw felt Jaina's eyes upon him, and he glanced her way. If he was rattled before, the fear etched upon Jaina's brow shook him to the core. Anduin winced, breathing hard, shaking out his hand before leaning back against the wall. Shaw knew better than to be staring when the king's eyes began to roam their faces for a reaction.

Sira threw back her head and laughed herself hoarse. "Tell me," she mocked in a singsong voice. "How does it feel to know you have lost? For time will prove it so. Ah well, take heart, Falling Lion, you will serve well. You will serve well."

CHAPTER THIRTY-ONE

Stormwind

"She is through there. Nobody will disturb you."

Tyrande Whisperwind alighted the portal on silent feet, plunged at once into the damp, unforgiving cold of the Stormwind Stockades. She glanced to her left at the kaldorei mage who had offered to give her a portal from Nordrassil to the Eastern Kingdoms. Anduin's message of invitation had arrived, along with the sealed note from Thrall.

Come with all haste to Stormwind, Anduin wrote. *I have in my possession a gift from the Horde. It is meant only for you and awaits you in the Stockades.*

Intrigued, Tyrande came that same day, whisked magically from the World Tree and all its quiet beauty to the dank *drip-drip-drip* of Stormwind's dungeons, home to the very dross and dregs of Azeroth. Tyrande did not pinch her nose shut, but breathed in the stench. To her left, Shandris Feathermoon appeared, and to her right, Maiev Shadowsong. They had insisted on coming along, perhaps sensing that Tyrande should not be left alone.

The mage departed, leaving them completely alone in the outer corridor of the western wing of the stockades. It was a place rich in painful memories, redolent with sorrow, as if the years of wasted life locked in those cages had glazed the stones, hope turning to despair, despair leaking from every crack and crevice in the walls. One could contemplate it later.

Tyrande ducked through the short, human-sized arch and into the inner room of the cell, opening the iron-barred door, its lock mysteriously malfunctioning.

My thanks at least for that, lion son.

Maiev and Shandris followed wordlessly. She couldn't decide yet if their presence rankled or soothed her. The winding, hollow halls of the prison seemed engineered to send the cries of lonely prisoners from one wing to the other. Tyrande shivered, reminded of a different sort of howl and fury, the screams of the burning carried on hot, ashen winds.

The prisoner raised her head at the squeak of the iron door.

Sira Moonwarden's crimson eyes flared fire-bright in the gloom. No such brightness came from Tyrande's eyes, though if the blackened pits there could twinkle and dance, they would. Her prize. Thrall's gift.

This is not what was owed, he wrote. *But I hope it is a start.*

"A start," Tyrande murmured.

"You."

"Sira."

"Security measures in Stormwind seem somewhat lax of late." Sira glanced toward the wide-open cell door, then back to the three night elves who had come. Her armor had been stripped from her, leaving her in a threadbare linen shift and rough-spun trousers. Her cheeks were sunken, the undead pallor of her skin uglier than Tyrande remembered.

"I am the Night Warrior," Tyrande told her. "No way is shut to me."

"No?" Sira balled her hands into fists. "No way . . . Is that so? What about the way of compassion? Of loyalty."

Tyrande observed as her terror transformed into anger, then boiled into a rage. "Are you finished?"

"No!" Sira snapped. "Wait . . . I am. I suppose I am finished. You have come here to kill me, is that it?" She snorted, laughed, mad, perhaps, beside herself, snot running freely down her lips and chin. "Elune abandoned me. *You* abandoned me. My sister-warriors, and you did nothing to save me . . ." That seemed to stir a more raw, more recent memory. She pressed her knuckles into her eyes. "I have nothing left to fear."

Tyrande took a single step toward her. "You have me."

"Fear *you*?" Sira's hands dropped away, bluish marks blossoming over her eyes where her knuckles had dug in. "Do not be ridiculous. You, with all the rage of the dark moon, you have done nothing to avenge your people. You are wind, Tyrande. Impotent, worthless, cowardly *wind*!"

"I wish I could have done more to protect you," Tyrande said, cold. "But some natures prove too evil to curb. Too ambitious to abide. Sylvanas has such a nature, and I will not forget that. You are her servant now, Sira, I have not forgotten that, either."

She drew the long, curved sword at her side, letting Sira see it plainly.

"Tyrande." Shandris's voice was gentle as silk, as if Tyrande might startle and do something they would all regret. "Think. *Look*."

"I see a sad and defeated thing that has chosen a path," Tyrande replied. "Nothing more."

"I chose nothing!" Sira shrieked, and Maiev stepped forward, so close her shoulder brushed Tyrande's. "I did not choose to return. I would *never* choose to return. Everything inside me is ugliness and rage, and the only thing that quiets the scream is death. For what was done to me, I will see a hundredfold done upon this cursed realm!"

Maiev's hand fell on Tyrande's forearm, but the Night Warrior shrugged it off. Her wrist twitched, the blade shimmered.

"I knew you once to find a fawn with two snapped legs," Maiev whispered. "A fawn everyone, even I, claimed was beyond healing, beyond help. Many offered to end its suffering, but you saw inside of it a spark of life. A hidden light."

"It died," Tyrande murmured, squinting down at Sira. "I could not save it."

"How long did you try?" Maiev asked. "And would you try again? If you continue down this path, Tyrande, you will find yourself no better than Sira. She is in pain, can you not see it? She is in agony. The only relief comes from spilling blood. Is this what you want? To find your only comfort in the suffering of others?"

"And so I should do nothing?" Tyrande seethed.

"That is not what I suggest and you know it. Listen, Tyrande." Maiev went to stand beside Sira, a warden she had considered more than a friend. A sister. "I have lived as one consumed, and though there is no great love between us, Tyrande, I would not see you become what I was. What Sira is now. You are more than just rage and vengeance, you are more than simply the Night Warrior: you are a priestess and a leader. Can you not, as a priestess, take pity on this creature?"

Tyrande raised the blade again, considering it.

The corrupted, undead warden flattened herself against the wall, then hissed. "You will not," Sira spat. "You lack the—"

A single strike, swift and true, cut an opening in Sira's neck, but shallow, no deeper than the width of a fingernail. There would be no blood, for she had none to shed. Sira grabbed for her neck, sure it was the blow of death.

Tyrande raised the weapon again, a shudder passing through

her body. She had thought to feel nothing, to know nothing but perfect rage. She was the Night Warrior, revenge made flesh, but now with that one shallow cut, she felt suddenly, horribly alive again.

"Mercy," Shandris murmured, taking the blade easily from Tyrande's hand. "Mercy for that little hidden light."

"Mercy," Maiev added, "for a sad, defeated thing."

Tyrande simply nodded, no longer armed. Shandris and Maiev had more things to ask, but the Night Warrior was finished. She had seen what she needed to see. Turning to go, she paused at the door, opening and closing her fist around the blade that was no longer there. "Alas, Sira, I do possess the courage," she said. "And that is what frightens me. That is what should frighten us all."

CHAPTER THIRTY-TWO

Dazar'alor

"After that meal I am tempted to linger and see what golden delights your city holds," Thalyssra preened, spreading her arms wide and ripping a tear in the world before their eyes, magic crackling from its center in hypnotic blue torrents. The First Arcanist summoned her portal and stepped aside, ushering her archers through.

The port of Zandalar was busier than ever, with the skies cleared, the lanes for commerce by sea safe once more. Bwonsamdi's shrines were already being rebuilt, and word of his heroic stand in the Necropolis had spread, bringing more supplicants and pilgrims to his places of power and worship. He was not yet at his full strength, but Talanji knew it would only be a matter of time. For her part, she felt whole once more. Nearly. The wounds left behind by Jaina's assault on the city still throbbed, and one day Talanji knew the Proudmoore witch would have to answer for her crimes. But patience would win that war, she thought, and any wars that came before that would be fought in the company of her new allies.

"Thank you for your hospitality, my dear." Thalyssra took Talanji's hand just by the tippy tips of her fingers and gave it a shake. "Do vow to visit us in Orgrimmar soon. There is much the council will wish to discuss with you and much I wish to show you, all that can endear a woman of your taste to a . . . Well, an acquired taste of a city. You may trust that I know all the best places."

Talanji bowed her head respectfully. "You saved my city, First Arcanist. I will never forget your feats of magic, and I promise to visit soon."

"Excellent."

She stepped aside, waiting for the others to say their goodbyes. A bandaged but very much alive Zekhan hobbled toward her, supported on one side by Thrall. While the orc had spoken in glowing terms of their victory at the feast, Talanji sensed within him a private sorrow. Losing Nathanos Blightcaller clearly angered him, but he was doing his best to conceal it.

"Brave, honorable ambassador." Talanji beamed at Zekhan. "How do I thank you for your sacrifice?"

"With a kiss?" He chuckled and winced. "On second thought, no. I'm crispy all over. Was my pleasure to serve, ya majesty. I hope we meet again soon."

"You packed your salves, yes? And your special poultices. Say you have, do not make a queen fuss so in public." She sighed and frowned at his many, many bandages. "I must see to my people here. We must heal and learn to trust one another again. When Zandalar is strong, you will see me in Orgrimmar, Zekhan, and I will be bringing my royal physicians, just in case you try any more heroics!"

Thrall clasped her around the wrist, a sign of a warrior's approval. "The Horde is united and our purpose is clear. When you feel ready, join us in the hunt."

The hunt. Sylvanas Windrunner remained at large. It seemed like an impossible task, to search the entirety of Azeroth, and Talanji already felt weary with the scope of it. She felt weary, too, of fighting so hard for the soul and safety of her people. But she had made a promise. She had joined the Horde. They would need her now, just as she had needed them.

"Oh! And I hope you do not mind taking one more with you." Talanji spun, searching the endless crowd behind her for a specific face. She saw her there, Tayo, her hair shining long and ebony, no longer caked in mud. The glittering, enameled garb of the Zandalari fit her well, though she insisted on wearing her same old bone jewelry and bandoliers of poisoned darts.

"Tayo wishes to act as my ambassador," Talanji told them. "She will be my eyes and ears, serving me as Zekhan served you."

The troll smiled boldly, endearingly unafraid.

"Without her, we would have been torn to pieces by Blightcaller's traps." Thrall chuckled. "She is welcome among us."

"I'm Zekhan." The troll tried to hold himself up under all the stiff bandages. "I promise I'm pretty handsome under here. Or I will be, when all me hair grows back."

They joined the long line of warriors leaving Zandalar through the nightborne's portal. Talanji was surprised to find herself sad. The city would be much emptier without them.

But a queen's work was never done. With two Rastari enforcers to protect her, Talanji began the lengthy journey back to the Great Seal. She would take it on foot, among her people once more. As they approached the stairs leading out of the port, a young troll girl skipped toward her, angling past her guards. The enforcers made to stop her, but Talanji shook her head.

"Let her pass," she said, kneeling.

The girl pressed a squashed purple flower into her hand. "For you."

"That is a great kindness, thank you," Talanji said. "I do not know if I am worthy of your gift, but I will endeavor to be so."

"Ma'da says you not worthy, that you will make us worship

Bwonsamdi." The girl frowned, clasping her hands behind her back and swinging them. "Please do not make us worship him! I like Gonk!"

"Of course you do." Talanji touched the girl lightly on the chin. "He is the Lord of the Pack, what is not to love? You should give him many offerings and sing chants to him every day! We need all of our loa, small one, for our soldiers to grow big and strong, for our fields and seas to flourish, for the health of the Zandalari people. And Bwonsamdi is not so bad! He helped us fight off the rebels, and he protects our souls, keeps us safe when it is time for us to depart this place."

"Then . . . Then ma'da is wrong?" The girl scrunched up her nose.

"She is right to worry, but tell her that all loa will be whispering in my ear, that all will advise me," Talanji told her seriously. "That is my promise to her and to you."

"Okay!" The child squealed with delight and disappeared back into the crowd.

By the time Talanji had taken all the questions brought to her in the port and then the bazaar and found her way back to the palace, the sky had darkened, turning indigo and teal, the sun as lovely and lush as an orange. She watched a servant hum to herself as she pulled down a garland of flowers in the corridor outside the council chambers. Songs and the low thump of drums echoed through the halls.

Talanji removed her crown upon reaching her chambers, setting it gently in the velvet-lined case in her wardrobe. When she turned around to find her basin and splash her face with water, Bwonsamdi startled her, hovering in the purple dusk glow bathing her balcony.

"Big words ya said to that little girl in the market today."

"Words you do not agree with?" Talanji crossed her arms.

The loa shrugged and tapped his cheek thoughtfully. "We had

a deal. You protect me, our bond is broken, the pact undone. I keep my promises, girl."

With that, Bwonsamdi drifted back from her, scooping up handfuls of air that gradually became tinged blue and then black. Wisps of energy curled around his forearms, then gathered before him a vortex that gradually took shape, the ghostly image of a knife. The room grew unbearably cold, whispers circling the knife, unknowable and foreboding.

"Come forward," he told her. "The knife will sever our bond."

Something almost tempted her to take the knife, but then she shied away, retreating to her bed, staring at him from there, a smile building on her lips.

"I've thought about it," Talanji said, removing her sandals and rubbing her aching feet. "What I said to that girl is true—you must relinquish some of your say in matters, Bwonsamdi. There will be no crown for you to protect if things continue this way. You are still the loa of kings, but Gonk, Pa'ku, Akunda, all of the loa, they are crucial to our survival."

At that, his smile widened. "Hm. Might be I'm not the foremost expert on crops and the like. 'Tis a fair deal, unless there's a trick here I not be seein' . . ."

Talanji blew out a labored breath. "No. No more tricks, Bwonsamdi. I've had my fill."

"Then?" He gestured to the ghostly knife.

"We can make each other stronger, Bwonsamdi. I am not foolish enough to think this will be the last of my troubles, or the last time our kingdom is threatened. I want power. I want it on my terms this time."

"I still be the loa of kings?" He flashed her a ridiculous smile, the knife obliterated, the room suddenly warm again.

"You still be the loa of kings, Bwonsamdi."

"Then I suppose our bargain is . . . amended, eh?" The loa

bowed, and when he lifted his head again his blue flame eyes had darkened. "But I warn ya, Talanji: Do not gloat. This battle is won, but not the war. A time will come when ya will be tested, and that time is comin' soon."

She shuddered, hugging herself again. "I do not like it when you talk that way. It frightens me."

"Good." Bwonsamdi passed a shaking hand over his mask. "It should. I have one more thing to say before I go."

Talanji groaned. "I am exhausted, Bwonsamdi, little more than walking bones."

"Ya will like this. Trust me." The loa winked, stepping aside to reveal a familiar silhouette standing behind him on the balcony.

He glittered like silver in the falling light, his eyes glossy with tears even appearing as he did then, as a spirit.

"Talanji, my girl."

King Rastakhan opened his arms to her, and Talanji gasped. Warrior or queen, she felt no shame in rushing to her father, in letting him see just how much his presence meant to her. She wrapped her arms around nothing, his spirit chilling her skin as she tried to pull him into an embrace.

"Dry your eyes, my daughter," he chided, wiping a ghostly finger across her cheek.

"You first!"

"You have grown wiser and stronger, just as I knew you would," Rastakhan told her, craning back to look her up and down. "I am proud of the queen you have become."

"I . . . I made so many mistakes, Father. I do not know if the people of this nation will ever trust me again." Talanji shook her head, but her father laughed gently and hushed her.

His spirit wavered, as if the thought of being away from her was too much to bear. The light in him nearly went out, a darkness like a passing cloud casting him in shadow.

"What is happening?" Talanji demanded. "Bwonsamdi . . ."

Rastakhan's image strengthened again, and he clutched his chest. "Something unnatural . . . I feel oblivion is near."

"Say what ya must and quickly," the loa warned. "The Other Side be too unpredictable these days."

Rastakhan nodded, his hand hovering comfortingly above her shoulder. "Show me the perfect queen, Talanji, and I will show you a monument of stone. Perfect rulers live only in memory. Your mistakes will be forgotten when your victories and triumphs come. You have already faced so much, too much; if only I could be there to guide you."

"You do," Talanji murmured. "You guide me every day."

"Time to go."

Bwonsamdi watched them quietly from the corner of the balcony, but now he pointed to the setting sun. "The queen needs her rest, and 'tis time I returned ya to my care, Rastakhan."

The king nodded, taking one long, last look at his daughter. "Remember, Talanji, you are more than just my daughter, more than blood: You are the queen Zandalar deserves. You will make your ancestors proud, as you have already made me proud."

Talanji nodded, bracing for the moment when he left her. "Goodbye, Father."

"Goodbye, sweet little saurid. Be brave, daughter."

"I will." His spirit dissipated, dissolving into the cool dusk breeze like a soft puff of pollen, carried away and spread across the jungle on the wind. Bwonsamdi had already gone, leaving her alone with her thoughts and her kingdom. The fires had gone out. Tomorrow she would address her people. The Zanchuli Council must meet. Petitions must be heard.

The work of a queen never ended.

I will be brave, father, Talanji thought. *I already am.*

Epilogue

"That power will be your prison," the Lich King warned. But he was a broken thing, and no longer her concern.

"This world is a prison."

At last. *At last.* Sylvanas Windrunner's hands tightened around the helmet, finding the weak spots, digging in, savoring the deep breath in before the plunge. It had all led to this moment. All the power she had accumulated, all the bargains she had struck, all the promises she had made. Wraithlike wisps of ice gathered around her, the glacial exhalation of the mountains pouring down around her, Icecrown Citadel breached, its lord defeated.

Power surged through her. *Power.* Power unmatched. Ecstasy's twin. The Helm of Domination brittle in her grasp, the prison of Ner'zhul, the crown of Arthas Menethil, splitting down the middle, snapped like a bone. The barrier between the mortal realm and the Shadowlands, indeed the very Maw itself, was so perilously thin there, she could feel the other world vibrating just on the other side, as if eagerly awaiting her arrival. The helm seared her hands, resisting her, but Sylvanas had come ready. It could not resist the irresistible, the power of death and unmaking itself. She felt a scream well in her gut before it poured out of her, the Helm of Domination sundered, ripped in two, the blast from its breaking roaring up toward the sky, mingling with her cry.

And then it was done, and the helm useless, dropped at her feet, just rubbish for the pile. Bolvar Fordragon, the Lich King, a hulk of armor and cracked skin, riddled with arrows, stared up at her, and then at the sky, silent, in dumb wonderment at what she had done. At all that she had accomplished. *Let him stare,* she thought. *Let him wonder.* He was nothing now, alive but as broken and useless as Menethil's crown, to be forgotten and left behind.

"And I . . ." She finished her thought. "Will set us all free."

A new world was opening itself up to them, unfurling, the sky as torn and broken as the helm on the ground. The winds howled. Her cloak whipped at her knees. The heat of the helm still pulsed in her palms. Sylvanas gazed upon the tower that reached toward her from above, slender and dark, beckoning her like a finger.

She obliged. She took a step forward, closer to the realm of death. She could already hear a chorus of wails as high and sharp as the gales screaming down off the mountains of Icecrown. Here the wind tore at her just as steadily, but her gaze lay fixed on the way ahead. The Maw gathered, churning out its endless dark dirge, waiting and hungry.

She felt the ground suddenly tremble and ceased her advance. Black swirls gathered, then funneled toward the snow-covered peak. When the darkness abated, Nathanos was there, kneeling, his hands still clutching the empty vial.

"My champion," Sylvanas purred. "Your timing could not be better. Tell me of your victory as we take these first steps together."

Nathanos stood, slowly, and she noticed a tremble in his hands. Before he could even get his bearings, she felt simmering anger in her soul begin to boil. The story was etched in sorrow across his face.

"I . . . I failed you, my queen. Bwonsamdi lives. Sira Moonwarden has been captured. I could not carry out your command. The Horde . . . They came in force. They resisted us. I fear that Bwonsamdi will only grow more defiant now."

Sylvanas slid her gaze from his blubbering lips to the tower looming above. His failure would complicate things considerably, and soured the triumph that had a moment ago felt so complete. She raised her head higher, closing her eyes briefly. In the back of her mind, Saurfang's baritone mocked her: *You just keep failing!* With a snarl, she silenced the long-dead voice and dug her nails into her gloved palms. Nathanos stared at her, and his lips quivering with rage, his veneer cracking as he struggled, no doubt, to contain all the excuses and justifications he had prepared and that she would not hear. Sylvanas could strike him, scream and hollow out his soul, but it would not correct the failing. Only forward momentum would do that. This was a blow, but one she felt sure they could overcome. It would not be easy, but then, her mission required great sacrifice.

"Must I tell you to go?"

Nathanos swallowed hard, crushing the vial in his hand, a crunch like bone. The shimmering dust slid between his fingers like sand. "I will return to the Marris Stead, my lady, and await your orders."

She heard the note of hope in his voice, fragile as a fledgling dropped from the nest.

"Go where you will, Nathanos, but do not be idle. The loa knows the Shadowlands well, I expect you will return to me with means to prevent his meddling." Sylvanas flicked her fingers, as if ridding herself of a speck of muck. "My path lies ahead."

And so it did. And so she continued, for power sought power, and she would have more of it, not for its own sake, but to wield it. The unjust ladder of their lives must be dismantled, not rung by rung, but all at once. All of it. She had been the plaything of a self-righteous cosmos long enough. The Jailer, too, understood what must be done. She did not know if or when Nathanos left, it mattered not—she had merged entirely with the shadows there already, part of the darkness at last.

ACKNOWLEDGMENTS

A story of this scope involves a lot of eyes, and hearts, and hands, and there are many people who deserve praise for all that they contributed. First, I want to thank the entire team at Blizzard for creating this incredible world, a second home for me and many others. I would also like to sincerely thank Allison Irons, Chloe Fraboni, Cate Gary, Paul Morrissey, and all the editors that had a hand in helping me craft this narrative. At Del Rey, I need to acknowledge the hard work, humor, and patience of Tom Hoeler, and Elizabeth Schaefer for stepping in to help, along with Julie Leung and Lauren Kretzschmar. Thank you for sharing so many glorious memes in the margins with me and letting me take risks.

The Blizzard lore team was obviously invaluable during this project, and I want to thank them all for their insight and attention to detail, and I would like to specifically thank Steve Danuser and narrative designer Raphael Ahad. I want to acknowledge the hard work and creativity that came before me—Christie Golden and Richard A. Knaak have written some truly phenomenal books for Warcraft, and I found their work incredibly inspiring. It's a remarkable thing for a fan to have this opportunity, and I feel fortunate to be here at the acknowledgments after taking this journey with the Blizzard and Del Rey teams.

On a personal note, I would like to thank my agent, Kate McKean, for her continued support and hard work. My family and friends supported me through this project and were extremely understanding over the holidays, so thank you to Lynn, Yves, Nick, Tristan, my niece Gwen, and nephew Dom. Thanks also to Taylor Bennett for keeping my spirits up and always being my cheerleader. I want to also acknowledge my two silent writing partners, Smidgen and Bingley, who put up with late nights and long hours, and never complain when we miss a walk or two.

Finally, I want to thank the *World of Warcraft* players who have been so sweet and supportive—thank you for giving me a chance.

ABOUT THE AUTHOR

MADELEINE ROUX is the *New York Times* bestselling author of the Asylum series, which has sold in eleven countries around the world. She is also the author of the House of Furies series, *Salvaged*, *Traveler: The Shining Blade*, and the Allison Hewitt Is Trapped series, and she has contributed to anthologies such as *Resist*, *Scary Out There*, and *Star Wars: From a Certain Point of View*.

Twitter: @Authoroux

ABOUT THE TYPE

This book was set in Caslon, a typeface first designed in 1722 by William Caslon (1692–1766). Its widespread use by most English printers in the early eighteenth century soon supplanted the Dutch typefaces that had formerly prevailed. The roman is considered a "workhorse" typeface due to its pleasant, open appearance, while the italic is exceedingly decorative.